A Heart's Memory

Janice R. Johnson

FpS

Greenville, S.C.

A Heart's Memory
Janice R. Johnson

Copyright © 2021 Janice R. Johnson

Published by:

FpS

1175 Woods Crossing Rd., #2
Greenville, S.C. 29607
864-675-0540
www.fiction-addiction.com

ISBN: 978-1-952248-90-0

Cover & Book Design by Vally Sharpe

Cover art by the author's granddaughter,
Leira Trudy Johnson

Printed in the United States of America.

A dedication to my inspirations:

To my husband, John,
who has encouraged me at every step of the way
to follow my dream.

To my children, Jeff and Julie
for all the joy and laughter you bring.

To my daughter-in-law, Michele and son-in-law, Brooks
for all the love you share.

To my grandchildren, Jay, Reeves, Leira, Edie, Witt and Hayes
for the happiness you give.

And in memory of my parents
You will always be in my heart.

Prologue
October 1966

Jack reached to touch her hand. "We'll be home soon, Jess." They passed house after house, storefront after storefront, as they rode down Highway 29 toward Atlanta.

Jessie Reynolds listened to the sound of the wipers across the windshield. The afternoon rain added to her already heavy spirit.

She stared out the passenger window unable to speak. Denial had made its way into Jessie's every thought. *How will I ever face tomorrow,* she thought.

Chapter One
June 1965

Jessie and Robin grabbed their suitcases and pillows and headed to the church bus. Their much-anticipated summer choir tour through North Georgia and Tennessee was about to begin.

The girls took their seats and Robin glanced over her shoulder. "Jessie, they're sitting behind us," she whispered. Jessie turned to see William take his seat next to Mark. She knew Mark and Robin had been trying to get each other's attention for a long time.

In the past, boys and dating had not dominated Jessie's thoughts like those of some of her friends. But September would be the beginning of her junior year at Northwest and dating had become the main topic of her friends in every conversation.

Church friends like Robin had their eyes on the boys in their youth group. Jessie did have to admit there were a few boys at school and at church that she thought would be nice to date. In particular, William Douglas.

Outside of school, church was the place where Jessie spent much of her time. She loved singing in the choir. Like her two older sisters, she started singing early in their downtown Atlanta church. When she was born, her parents, Madeline and Leland Reynolds, placed her name on the waiting list for the impressive Cherub Choir program, and Jessie had sung her first solo at age two.

She'd spent every year since in the widely-known music program directed by Dr. Ray Sellers. Once she joined the Junior Choir, she'd performed during church services and sung at the Thanksgiving Rich's Department store annual Christmas Tree Lighting event. Youth choir now meant the addition of overnight choir trip opportunities. Families from across Atlanta attended the church with its many ministries and some of Jessie's closest friendships, like Robin, were there.

This choir trip was different because Dr. Sellers had retired. Mr. James, the new choir director, had recruited young people like William, who was known for his guitar playing, to build a larger youth group. Jessie was excited to be a part of the new youth council. Mr. James formed it to work with the music ministry and plan its tours and activities.

Robin was excited too, but she joined in with hopes of spending time with Mark. Like Jessie, Robin was the youngest of her sisters and knew the challenges or "privileges," as their sisters would say, of being the youngest in a line of sister siblings. They traded clothes for fun while on their trips, and it was Robin who initiated the plans on the ways they would couple with Mark and William. Robin was ahead of Jessie in developing her "list" of desired attributes for the perfect boyfriend. Although it did give Jessie hints for her own "list."

Robin looked at the rooming schedule when they boarded the bus. "Yay! They put us together. This is going to be great. I just know it!" Always fun, Robin radiated happiness. Her sun-bleached hair complimented her personality and her athletic abilities brought energy to the group activities. Together with Jessie's musical talent and friendliness, both were a natural draw to their choir mates.

William had been elusive to the girls in their church circle of friends. His tall, athletic frame and natural good looks had made him attractive to all of them, but their attempts to even engage him in conversation had failed so far.

The choir reached its first stop and after the performance the host church had dinner prepared for their guests. Mark and William stepped into the line next to Jessie and Robin. Mark led the way to find just the right table to accommodate the four. William stepped up to hold the chair for Jessie. "Looks like this table was waiting just for us."

Jessie took her seat aware of the other choir girls whispering across the room. "You played great tonight," she said. More than ever, she was glad Mr. James had recruited him. It was obvious they shared a love of music.

William blushed from Jessie's compliment. "Mr. James just wanted something light and fun. You know, to get the crowd to not be so serious after our anthems in the service."

Jessie and Robin stayed up late talking in their sponsors' guest room that night. "He likes you for sure," said Robin. "Can't you tell the way he looks at you? How he made sure he was in line next to you? When he played his guitar and sang at the after-concert party, he looked at you the whole time. What else do you need?"

In no time, the four were sitting together at every opportunity. Mark and Robin took the lead, but it wasn't long before William was reaching for Jessie's hand as they walked together to board the bus.

As the tour came to a close, they made plans for dating back home. The Douglas and Reynolds families were already close friends so their approval of William and Jessie's relationship came easily. They were inseparable with nightly dates to the movies and other youth activities.

She couldn't wait to share the news of him with her friends at school, but it occurred to Jessie that the fact she and William attended different high schools might be a challenge. Even so, she was optimistic that the future of their relationship would remain strong. Robin's daily calls boosted her optimism and they shared plans for double dating. "It's a perfect plan. This year will be the greatest!"

As she dressed for a date with William, Jessie practiced bringing up her questions about their relationship in front of her bedroom mirror. "Will we be seeing each other a lot less now that school is starting?" She made a face and attempted the wording again. "I'm looking forward to our dates now that school is starting back."

She heard a car door and looked out her window. William climbed out of a new maroon Oldsmobile Cutlass convertible. He wiped the fender as he passed it and walked to the door. She hurried down the stairs to meet him. Her parents were sitting in the living room.

"William's here!" she called.

"You two have a good time," said her father, his tone a clear indication of William's favored status.

As they walked toward the new convertible, Jessie grinned at William. "I love it!" she exclaimed. He opened the door for her and then climbed into the driver's seat. The top was down for their drive toward Peachtree.

"You okay with the top down?" he asked.

"Of course!" *Life couldn't get any better than this,* she thought.

They were deep in conversation about school and the car when William turned left into the Shoney's parking lot. He began to put up the top and Jessie pulled down the passenger mirror to check her hair.

"You don't need to do that. You look great," William said.

Jessie smiled. Despite all the time they had spent together during those summer months, it was the first real compliment he had given her. The comment brought her hope about the future of their relationship.

William glanced in his rear-view mirror. A patrol car had entered the parking lot behind them, and an officer was walking toward the car. He reached the convertible and stood looking down at William. "Driver's license."

The expression on William's face was one of true innocence. "License, sir?"

"No left turns over a median, young man." Jessie and William both looked back at the street. A low concrete median separated the lanes of traffic. "That median is there for a reason," said the officer. "Not to cross it."

William reached in his wallet and handed the officer his license. "Yes, sir. Sorry, sir." The officer went back to his patrol car and sat inside for a moment before pulling away. William looked over the ticket. "I should have been more careful."

"I'm so sorry," said Jessie.

"It's not your fault." He took a deep breath. "Dad won't be pleased about this. Just after getting my car and all. We had a pretty big talk about responsibility when he bought it for me."

Jessie placed her hand on his. "You are the most responsible person I know. It's one of the reasons that I like you so much.

William squeezed her hand. "Let's go inside." He climbed out of his seat and walked around to open her door. *Always the gentleman. There's another one for the "list,"* thought Jessie.

The host seated them in a booth near the windows facing Piedmont. Jessie hoped the distraction of the ticket wouldn't interfere with her desire to talk about their relationship going forward, and it seemed that it hadn't when William mentioned that summer was almost over.

"It's hard to believe, isn't it?" he said.

"I know," said Jessie. "With school and all, I wasn't sure how to bring it up. But what happens now?"

William seemed unprepared for her question. "I don't know. Maybe we just take things a day at a time?"

Jessie did her best to hide her disappointment. She had little experience with dating to guide her, so she chose the agreeable route. "Sure. One day at a time."

He reached for his wallet and nodded to the server. "School starts in a couple of weeks. We can take things slow and see what happens."

She tried again. "We'll have different football games on Fridays. Which ones will we go to?"

Again, William looked puzzled. He reached for the server's ticket. "I haven't thought about that, but we'll figure it out."

On the way back to Jessie's house, there was little conversation. William obeyed all the speed limits and traffic rules as they drove down LaVista to Peachtree Street and onto Northside Drive. He stopped the car at the top of Longwood before reaching the Reynold's driveway and turned to smile at her. "Hey, the Southeastern Fair is in town next week. Why don't we go and see if Robin and Mark want to go with us?"

All Jessie's doubts and concerns seemed to melt away when he pulled her in for a long goodnight kiss. "Sounds perfect," she said.

Jessie made her way upstairs to bed. She sighed as she turned off the lamp on her nightstand. Robin was right. *What else did she need?* William liked her—they would find a way to stay strong.

Chapter Two

That Sunday morning, Jessie met Robin at church. She told her about the ticket William had gotten in the Shoney's parking lot. "I feel so bad for him," she said.

"Don't worry. Mark said William's dad worked out a way for him to pay for the ticket."

"Okay," said Jessie. Robin always knew what to say to make her feel better.

Robin took Jessie's arm and headed down the church hallway. "I'm so excited! Mark and William want us to double-date to the fair on Saturday! Mark will pick me up and then we'll meet William at your house and all ride together."

Jessie began to laugh. "Maybe *Mark* can do the driving this time."

Being with Robin and Mark would be just like the times on choir tour when the two couples had been together nonstop. Jessie was glad they were planning double dates for another reason too—conversations with William had always seemed easier when the four of them were together.

The Saturday date would help them further seal their relationship before school started.

ON MONDAY MORNING THE PHONE RANG early. "Hey, Jessie! Want to go riding this afternoon?"

Jessie pulled the long cord of her telephone over to the window to look outside. The sun was shining, and the early fall temperatures were calling her to the outdoors. She and Sandy Patterson had spent many an afternoon riding her horse on the trails around the Chastain Park stables.

"Sandy, it has been way too long since we rode Josey. This afternoon would be perfect!"

The two girls had been friends since first grade. It was when they started eighth grade that Sandy's parents had bought her a horse and boarded the mare at the Chastain Park stables. Knowing that Jessie loved the outdoors, Sandy had invited her then to come to the park and ride with her. Over time, their rides on Josey had become a routine on many afternoons. Having a horse had taught Sandy responsibility, something Jessie appreciated about her friend. Taking care of Josey took discipline and commitment—a virtue not always seen in some of their other friends.

Jessie loved riding with Sandy, too, because it reminded her of summer visits to Grandmother Danby's in Alabama and riding Molly in Mr. Joe's pasture. Josey was a special horse—she had always been gentle when the girls rode together bareback. Unlike Molly, who had disliked saddling up for the young cousins at the Alabama farm.

"Great!" said Sandy. "I'll pick you up at two." Like William's father, Sandy's parents had surprised her with a new car for her 16th birthday—a yellow convertible Mustang. Jessie considered Sandy her most humble and unselfish friend. Like the rides on Josey, she shared her new car rides with all her friends.

The Chastain stables had recently been replenished with fresh hay and the sound of sneezing could be heard throughout the barn as riders groomed their horses. When the girls arrived and opened the padlock, Josey's whinny signaled her delight. Once the horse was saddled, the girls climbed on and they started toward the hills of the park.

The mare needed no coaxing along their regular route. Josey could sense their balance and would slow down if they needed to adjust and continue the trail path. They passed the Witches Cave and amphitheater as they bounced on Josey in the afternoon breezes. The girls' caught up on their summer activities as they rode and Jessie told Sandy about William, the choir tour and her upcoming date to the fair. She valued Sandy's friendship and perspective and in particular, thoughts of beginning a new school year with a new boyfriend.

Sandy grinned. "I met a new guy too. At the Zesto—with some of the girls—while you were on choir tour. His name is Rick and he's coming to Northwest this year. He might go with some of us to the fair."

Jessie noticed that Sandy blushed as she talked about Rick. This made Jessie even more excited about the beginning of the school year. She wanted Sandy to have a relationship like her own with William. "That's great! Where did he come from?"

Sandy shrugged. "I haven't learned much about that yet. But he's very friendly and fits right in with the group."

"TURN ONE MORE TIME," said Jessie's mother. "I need to finish pinning the hem in the back."

Madeline Reynolds was an excellent seamstress. With three daughters, her skills had been a plus for the family. She bought fabric for her daughters and made skirts and blouses to complement the sweaters and jackets they purchased at one of the department stores downtown.

Madeline pulled the last pin from her mouth and inserted it into the cloth. "Do you want to wear this tomorrow night to the fair?"

Jessie grinned at her mother in the dresser mirror. "That would be great. I'll wear it with the new sweater we found at...at..." Jessie turned her head to sneeze and then coughed. "...the sweater we found at Rich's."

Madeline raised her head to look at her daughter. "That doesn't sound good."

"It's nothing." Jessie remembered the new hay at the stables but decided not to mention it. She didn't want anything to stop her from going on the date to the fair with William, but she coughed again as she stood waiting for her mother to finish.

"You know how important it is to have a good first week of classes," said Madeline. "I'll see what we have in the medicine cabinet to help that cough."

When her mom left the room, Jessie glanced at herself in the mirror. Her thoughts drifted to holding William's hand as they walked the fairgrounds and of a cozy ride on the Ferris wheel. Then she thought of the reality that her mother was not one to allow any activity that might interfere with her health or school performance.

Madeline returned. "There's nothing for a cough in the cabinet. I'll have to call Springlake Pharmacy and talk to Dr. Ellis. You know I cannot let you go out in the night air if your cough doesn't improve."

By Saturday morning, the cough had only gotten worse. Jessie finally picked up the phone to dial Robin. "I'm not going to be able to go tonight," she said. "Spending tonight together could have helped our relationship before school started. I don't know *how* William and I can get more serious if we don't have more time together."

"Don't worry, Jess. He is more serious about you than he shows. I don't think he knows how to express it. Mark gives him a hard time about it all the time."

"Maybe. If you say so," said Jessie to her trusted friend. "Have fun and tell me all about it tomorrow."

It was only minutes after hanging up with Robin that William called. She could sense his disappointment about their date. "Feel better, Jessie. I'll see you soon." She nestled down in her bed and tried not to think about the fun she was going to miss.

Jessie woke the next morning to the sound of her father's voice from downstairs. "Well, well, well. What in the world is this?"

"What is it, Ladd?" Jessie heard her mother say. Although his legal name was Leland Reynolds, Jr., Jessie's father had been called Ladd since childhood. Protective of his daughters, he could seem intimidating to some of their dates. He never let his guard down for their welfare.

Jessie heard the sound of footsteps on the stairs. Her bedroom door slowly opened, and her mother peered around it. "Morning, honey. You feeling any better?" Jessie raised up from her pillow. "We had a surprise visitor during the night on our front porch!"

Her mother came into the room holding in her arms a large stuffed pink dog with floppy ears and a rhinestone collar. Jessie smiled and took the dog from her mother. "William. How sweet."

"I would say he was thinking about you last night, wouldn't you?" Jessie could tell from the statement that her mother knew how disappointed Jessie had been that she hadn't let her go to the fair. "Dad and I are going on to church this morning. I left you some breakfast in the kitchen." She closed the door behind her.

Jessie stroked the dog's pink fur. *Maybe there is hope for us.* She thought.

After church, Robin called to report on their night at the fair. "All William wanted to do was play the booths to win you that prize! I told Mark he should take lessons from him. It became a competition on which one of them would make the best shots and earn the most tickets to choose a prize." She giggled. "I guess you see who won!"

Jessie took a deep breath and tried not to cough. "I wish I could have gone last night. I know you had fun."

"It was your typical fair. There was really nothing special. It obviously would have been better if you had been with us. Maybe we can plan another double date soon."

It wasn't long after Robin's call that the phone rang again. This time it was William. "Are you feeling better?"

Jessie could tell he wanted to know what she thought about his surprise. "Yes. Especially now that I am holding this sweet dog. I love it!"

"It took some work, but I knew when I saw it that it was leaving with me. I wasn't sure how to get it to you, but I wanted you to have it this morning when you woke up."

"My dad found it on the front porch this morning." She paused for moment. Since school was starting soon, Jessie hoped the conversation would shift to their talking about the future, but William remained silent.

"I need to think of a good name for her," said Jessie. "Any ideas?"

"You decide. I hope it makes you feel better."

Chapter Three

J essie woke Monday morning and pulled her bed coverlet up to her chin. Despite her excitement, the hum of the air conditioner window unit had lulled her to sleep and she looked around the bedroom with renewed energy. She had inherited the favored upstairs bedroom and bath when her sister Meredith left for college. The first day of classes was finally only a week away and she couldn't wait to tell all her school friends about William. She stepped from her bed to her dresser and walk-in closet to survey the folded items and new dresses hanging in view for her careful selection of what to wear once school started.

Her cough had improved and Claire Clayton was first on Jessie's list to call. Claire lived two doors up the street and they had grown up together—meeting at neighborhood backyard sandboxes, pretending at dress up parties, and making clothes for their paper dolls. Jessie's older sisters had even taught them how to make clover and dandelion necklaces and later introduced them to pop beads. Together they would form their own "big girl" jewelry box collections of necklaces and bracelets.

Claire's mom made the best cookies and her dad had been the coolest when he'd driven the morning carpools to Brandon Elementary. He entertained the riders as Superman by bragging how he would fly them over the cars in the line ahead.

But when they had all entered high school, Claire's parents divorced. It was a time when Jessie remembered her mother's words in understanding the pain of life's realities and a respect for privacy. "Let trust, hope and love for your friends guide your heart, Jessie."

"Can you believe it?" she said to Claire. "We are actually going to be juniors!"

"I know! And guess what? Mom says I can drive the car to school next week," said Claire. "Missy and I can trade off weeks." The girls had entered an age of "ultimate freedom"—Monday's orientation would provide their cherished parking passes with all their rights and privileges.

Jessie thought for a moment. "I'll need to go home with Sandy some afternoons—we've already scheduled some rides at Chastain."

"I'm sure that won't be a problem," said Claire. "I'll drive next week. Missy can drive the next week. I can't believe Missy will be a senior. By the way, she told me that she has us down for some major help with Pep Club."

The third member of their neighborhood trio was Missy Davis. She was the incoming president of the Northwest High Pep Club, and vice-president of the new senior class. Although she was a year older than Claire and Jessie, that fact had never been an issue for any of them. They had shared many a birthday party at the Rollerdrome and at picnic tables in their back yards.

It was hard for Jessie to believe how quickly the years had passed for her neighborhood friends. Now they were making plans for their college futures. She thought of two of the boys who had always been around. "Don't forget Robby and Michael. They may want to ride some mornings, too,"

"Don't worry," said Claire. "I'll work the driving schedule out. And speaking of the boys, I heard they both made the varsity football team. Coach O'Connor said we have a great team this year. I can't wait for our first game against Fulton!"

"Oooh," said Jessie. "I wonder if I'll get Coach O'Connor for algebra. Missy said he can be tough."

When they hung up, Jessie sat back in her bedroom window seat alcove. The cushioned dormer adjacent to the telephone encouraged her to linger. As she looked over the street ourside, memories floated in. She thought of all the times she, Claire, Missy and the boys had ridden their bikes up the street's rolling hills and coasted down hands-free with a "look Mom, no hands" trick.

Growing up on Longwood Drive had been wonderful. Parents in the neighborhood knew to be on the lookout for bikes racing in and out of driveways, flying kickballs, and an occasional baseball flying from Robby's yard. Michael had always been assigned as the lookout to yell, "Car!"

Jessie smiled to herself. Then there was the trips to the Garden Hills pool. The downside had always been the required spring visits to the Howell Mill Medical Clinic, but the trips were worth it. No one was allowed in the pool unless they had had their annual typhoid shot.

The older kids often gathered at Memorial Park. In their younger days, Jessie and her friends hadn't been allowed to go as far as Peachtree Creek. But they had had Slippery Rock, a small waterfall on the creek closer to home. The woods surrounding it were a perfect spot for natural playhouses. In her mind's eye, she could see Michael corralling tadpoles from the stream in mason jars on hot summer days.

Although she had no brothers, Jessie had learned early on how to relate to the boys in the neighborhood. It hadn't hurt that she could run faster than most of the kids on the block and could steal bases with the best. She had always been proud to be chosen first when Robby yelled, "*I choose Jessie!*" and Michael protested, "*Aw, I wanted Jess.*"

Michael, who lived across the street, had always provided the ball, but Robby's house, with its flagstone home plate and the city water meter for second base, had the best yard for kickball and baseball. They had all come a long way—now she would see them play for the high school team.

The conversation with Claire had reminded her of the football dilemma. Northwest would play Fulton in their first game, but Dykes High would be playing O'Keefe and she and William still hadn't discussed whose football game they would attend together.

She stepped back from the window to look in her dresser mirror and shook off her concerns—as Robin reminded her regularly, it would all work out somehow.

Chapter Four

On the first day of school, Jessie stepped inside the front door at Northwest High School to a roar of hallway conversations and welcomes. Excitement was in the air. Jack Mason's ever-present smile greeted her. "Welcome back, Jessie!" he said. He glanced at her carpool friends. "You, too, Claire and Missy."

One never had to look far to find Jack. His laughter could usually be heard above his classmates and it always brought a smile to Jessie's face. He was the first person at school most days and known by his schoolmates for his class spirit and friendliness. But it was as if his job as the unofficial greeter was done when he saw Jessie.

"Jack! You look great. I missed you!" It seemed to Jessie that his chest was broader and his arms larger and he even stood taller. It was evident how much work he had put in during summer training with Coach O'Connor. Jessie saw, too, that she wasn't the only one who noticed her friend's enhanced physique—the eyes and whispers of the girls passing them in the hallway made that obvious.

Jack stopped in front of her and smiled. "I missed you too."

Jack's friendship had been special to Jessie over the years. Although he had a reputation of joking and never being too serious, there had always been a special bond between them. She had seen him during the summer at the Buckhead Zesto, but somehow he seemed different now.

"I hope you have a good class schedule, Jess," he said. "I think Mr. Baker will have us both down for his art class again."

The first bell rang, and lockers slammed as everyone scurried to their homerooms. Jessie looked down to check her schedule and started down the hall. She turned back to him. "Let's catch up soon," she said.

Jessie passed the doorway to Mrs. Laney's classroom and waved to her. The junior class adviser, Mrs. Laura Laney was a favorite teacher of Jessie's. She made students feel she was genuinely interested in them. When she had learned it was Jessie's goal to be a teacher, she spent extra time reviewing her assignments to be sure all was on track. Her close counsel in preparing Jessie for going to college had been invaluable.

Once settled into her desk, Jessie thought of William and wondered what he was doing on his first day back at school at Dykes. She couldn't wait to talk to him when she got home that afternoon. With him now in her plans, everything about her junior year was falling into place.

Homeroom was buzzing. Mrs. Horton called the class to order and the loudspeaker crackled. Mr. Kelley, the school principal, welcomed the students back and challenged all to have a great school year. Miss Clay, the school counselor, and Mrs. Morton, the school secretary, made announcements reminding students to turn in all their parent-signed forms for the new year.

Jessie glanced around the room and saw Jack who had slipped into the room two rows over. Fran arrived just as the announcements ended and grabbed a seat on the row between them. She reached for Jessie's schedule sheet and read. "Oh, wow. You got Coach O'Connor for algebra. Too bad."

Jessie winced. "Yeah, I'm a little nervous about his class. I hear he's tough, but Mrs. Laney told me he's a great teacher."

"You know his wife died last year. Some say he came back too quickly."

Coach Paul O'Connor had lost his wife Ann a little over a year before. Those who had known her had talked about her inner beauty and her quiet, soft spoken ways. Jessie supposed they had balanced each other given what she'd heard about Coach O'Connor's classroom demeanor. She had seen some of Mrs. O'Connor's knitted items at the annual fundraiser for Egleston Children's Hospital. Mrs. Laney told her that Ann O'Connor had recruited teachers to make knitted caps for infants at Egleston and newborns in the preemie unit at Piedmont Hospital nearby.

A BELL SIGNALED THE END OF homeroom and Jack followed Jessie through the door. He had heard the conversation between Jessie and Fran. "Don't worry about Coach," he said. "Just wait till you see our team." He stood in the hall watching as she walked away.

Terry, Jack's best friend, stopped beside him and followed his gaze. "Jessie looks good," he said. "This could be your year."

"I wish," said Jack, "but she still doesn't have a clue to how I feel about her."

With his eyes on Jessie, Jack hadn't noticed the tall frame of his coach standing in the classroom door across the hall. The coach's broad shoulders and trim physique conveyed the fitness he demanded of his athletes. "You two best be getting to your first classes or you'll be late," said the coach. "And remember, Jack, practice starts immediately after sixth period."

Jack came to attention. "Yes, sir, Coach. I'll be there."

Chapter Five

Jessie had survived her earlier high school years with little drama among her classmates. To this point, her world had been insulated and simple—with little complexity. Getting approval from her parents for dating William had been easy given the two families' connections at their church.

As the youngest of three daughters, Jessie had been the beneficiary of her parents' "learning curve" and they were somewhat more relaxed with her—according to her older sisters, of course. Madeline and Ladd had worked hard to instill the traits of dependability and responsibility in their daughters. Their neighbor, Mrs. Bryant, frequently called on Jessie to babysit. Ladd had introduced her to his bank officer, and she had opened her own bank account and deposited most of her earnings and allowance, with thoughts of college. Jessie took nothing for granted—and her goal was to have a successful junior year as part of her plans for the future.

Jessie had met with Mrs. Laney at the beginning of her junior year to make sure that all was on course for the year. Her favorite classes so far were business and math, although she still had some doubts about Coach O'Connor's algebra class. This year no longer included piano lessons, but she still sang in the school chorus and the church choir. Things were shaping up well. Nothing was standing in her way, except that William still hadn't called. She was grateful for her afternoon riding routine with Sandy because it offered a diversion from her disappointment.

On Wednesday, Jessie waited on the sidewalk for Claire to pull up to the curb. She was about to open the car door when she turned to see Fran Barnett running toward her.

"Jessie! I'm glad I caught you!" she said. "I have someone who wants to meet you!" Fran panted to catch her breath. "His name is Carter Powell and he asked me about you."

In addition to her surprise, Jessie was puzzled. Although they had a couple of classes together this year, she had not known Fran that well over the years—they had run in a different circle of friends.

Fran didn't skip a beat. "He saw you in the cafeteria today and wants to know who you are. He described your hair and the dress you are wearing to be sure I knew exactly who you were. He even said you were eating an apple!" Jessie squinted, trying to remember where she was sitting. "Funny," added Fran. "He asked if you ever wore your hair in a ponytail."

Jessie thought the comment about the ponytail to be strange. Although she never wore a ponytail to school, she almost always did when riding Josey with Sandy. But whoever this Carter person was, he was right about what she had eaten for lunch. Her mother had started sending her with a simple sandwich and some fruit to encourage some nutrition during what had turned out to be typically more a social time with her friends.

Fran was insistent. "Jessie, did you hear me? He wants to *call* you."

Jessie glanced toward Claire still waiting in the car. "I don't know, Fran. I'm…dating someone."

"You have to let him call you! Everyone likes him. He's a great guy."

"Is he in the yearbook?"

"Yeah! Look him up. I'm sure you've seen him at the senior lunch table."

Jessie climbed into Claire's car and rolled down the window. "He's a *senior?*"

Fran waved at her boyfriend Mike across the parking lot. "Gotta go. Yes, he's a senior. Look him up. And, by the way, I gave him your number."

Jessie looked back at Claire, who was now shaking her head. "What was that all about?" she asked. All Jessie could do was shrug her shoulders.

WHEN CLAIRE DROPPED HER OFF IN front of her house, Jessie went straight upstairs to her room and saw the stuffed pink dog in her vanity chair. *Why hadn't William called?* The conversation with Fran piqued her curiosity and she pulled her 1964 yearbook from the shelf. She flipped through the pages to the photographs of the last year's junior class.

There he was. James Carter Powell. The index listed him under other pages—varsity football, Key Club, ROTC and track.

The phone rang and she slammed the yearbook shut as if she'd been caught partaking of forbidden fruit. Picking up the receiver, she heard an unfamiliar male voice. "May I speak to Jessica?"

"This is Jessie," she said, with the invitation to use her nickname.

"This is Carter Powell. Fran gave me your number. She said she told you about me."

Jessie took a deep breath. "She did. She said you saw me at lunch and asked about me."

"Our classes must have had lunch at different times last year. I was sitting at lunch with Mike and Terry today and told them I had never seen you before. Terry knew who you were and Mike said that Fran knew you. So I asked Fran to tell you I wanted to meet you."

Carter's mention of Terry reminded Jessie of the talk at her own table that day...

Sandy leaned in and whispered, "Did anyone hear any more about Natalie and Terry?"

"What do you mean?" asked Jessie. The girls around the table stared at her with a "Where have you been?" look in their eyes.

Another friend, Christy, supplied the answer. "The word is Natalie has been seeing Terry in secret! He's not Jewish and if her parents find out, they will be furious!" Northwest High was one of two Atlanta area high schools—the other Grady High—that were in the vicinity of the two local synagogues. Up till now, Jessie's awareness of other religions had been limited to the high absentee rate of Jewish students during the holidays of Rosh Hashanah and Yom Kippur. She knew there were differences in their religious observances, but more than anything she appreciated their joyfulness and the openness of their personalities.

Jessie looked at a table of Jewish girls next to them. Today they were leaned in and whispering too. The joyfulness was clearly different for the girls next to them.

Sandy gestured in their direction. "Dating outside their faith is a big deal. And now, Natalie's secret is out. No one has seen Natalie today." The rumor about Natalie had caused a tightening of the Jewish girls' inner circle. The situation was one only friends of their faith could understand—Natalie had stepped into treacherous waters.

This was unlike any drama at Northwest in the past. "What will happen if her parents find out that she's seeing Terry?" Christy asked.

Sandy raised her eyebrows. "*If is not the question anymore. Who knows, but who could blame her? Terry's quarterback of the football team, popular and good looking.*" She leaned in again. "*He's known for taking risks on the football field—and now, in dating, too!*"

Jessie refocused on what Carter was saying. "Everyone was talking about Terry today at lunch. Is he really secretly seeing Natalie?"

"He really doesn't talk about that," said Carter. "From the sounds of it, I think it is better if the rest of us stay out of it."

It was clear to Jessie that Carter was not a gossip and was not one to become involved in the private matters of others. As their conversation continued, Jessie gained an insight into his maturity. There was no question about where he stood.

She couldn't help but notice, also, how easy it was to talk to him, especially in comparison to William. It was one conversation and yet, she had an insight into Carter's character like no one she had known.

Carter was silent for a moment. "I understand you have Coach O'Connor for algebra. Do you like it?"

Jessie followed his lead in changing the subject. "Math is one of my favorite subjects, but I'm not sure about this one."

"Give him a chance. He's a great coach. I think he misses his wife."

It was Jessie's turn to be silent and when she spoke, there was a softness in her voice. "Yes, I heard that she died last year. That must have been awful for him. Did they have any children?"

"No. School and the team are really his whole life now."

Mrs. Reynolds called from downstairs. "Jessie, Sandy's here!" She looked at her watch and couldn't believe how much time had passed.

"I'm sorry, Carter," she said. "I have to go. I promised Sandy I'd go riding with her today."

"Will I see you tomorrow? Lunch maybe?"

"Maybe so," said Jessie.

On their way home from riding Josey, Sandy asked Jessie to come with her to the Zesto. "I want you to get to know Rick. Christy and Diane are coming too. I have homework, so we won't be out late."

Jessie had not seen Sandy so happy as she was since she had started dating Rick, but none of Sandy's friends knew much about him either. Even so, given Sandy's reputation, Rick had easily been accepted into the group without question.

"I think he likes being the only boy at our lunch table," continued Sandy. "Come on. It will be fun!"

"I guess I will," said Jessie finally, but she was having a hard time not thinking about meeting Carter the next day at lunch. One thing was sure—she *did* want to know him better.

Chapter Six

Carter's hand rested on the phone. He was surprised that his attraction to Jessie was even greater after their conversation. He wondered if the call was too good to be true, given his doubts about some girls at school being out of his league.

At breakfast, his older brother Bobby had given him the confidence he needed to take the risk. Bobby had always been there for him—he'd even suggested that he call Jessie from the security and privacy of their basement. And it had worked.

He looked around the downstairs area of the house on Moores Mill. It was filled with reminders of his years growing up. The basement had been a retreat for him in good times and bad with all the memories accompanying them.

Bobby, four years older than he, was associated with much of what he had experienced. He had been a strong and positive influence on Carter. Theirs had been a simple childhood in some ways—and, in other ways, difficult, at least where their parents were concerned.

Carter walked over and touched the curtains hanging over the window. His mother Amanda had made them out of canvas so the brothers' getaway would simulate army tents. He pulled back the curtain to see the wooded back yard and pictured himself running to meet Bobby to play among the trees with the three Barfield brothers, who lived down the road.

The neighborhood gang enjoyed every kind of sport and outdoor activity, but nothing more than playing army. Carter could still hear Bobby calling out to the others. "Pack your gear and meet at the fort." They planned training drills required to become a part of their pretend infantry.

The hilly slope and woods were perfect for the creation of their maneuvers. The remains of the "keep out" fort they had built years ago sat empty in his view. He grinned, remembering his pride the day he was given the authority to approve the entry to the fort for those in their platoon.

Carter's eyes wandered to another corner of the basement. It had always been off limits. A stir of resentment tugged at his gut when his eyes passed the spot where his father Ross kept the cases he took with him on his business travels. Bobby had once taken the blame when Carter had accidentally disturbed a box in the "forbidden area."

He glanced back through the window at the storage shed. He and Bobby still kept the yard equipment in it, but it reminded him of a time when his father had shoved a rake in his young hands, commanding him to help Bobby with the yard chores. The whole episode had started an argument between his parents about his being old enough to pick up responsibilities at home. It might have erupted into an even uglier scene had James Crawford, their mother's father, not appeared from what seemed like nowhere. He had gently calmed Carter's fears and taken him aside to begin the first of what would be many lessons in gardening and an appreciation for its joys. Carter smiled, remembering planting roses and vegetables with his grandfather in those early days. Unable to say

"Crawford," Carter had given him the nickname "Papa Ford," a name both boys would continue to call him until his death several years before.

After the yard incident, Papa Ford had become more than a regular visitor to their home. The Barfield kids and other neighborhood boys were equally drawn to Papa Ford—he entertained them with stories of his military service during World War II. They learned from him about leadership and respect, and to say "Yes, ma'am," and "Yes, sir" in demonstration of their military manners.

Carter heard a knock and the basement door opened. Bobby flipped on the light in the darkened room. "Hey, Bud. Did you call her?"

Carter squinted from the light in his eyes. "Yes. Thanks for the encouragement."

"Well, how did it go?"

"I'm going to see her at lunch tomorrow."

"That's great!" Bobby scanned the room. "Then why are you standing here in the dark?"

"Just thinking. I don't know. Memories, I guess."

Bobby knew that look from Carter too well. He glanced over at the tables and shelves lining the basement wall. The memorabilia displayed told many things about their family and lives. He pointed to the shelves. "Hey. I bet we're going to see some great additions to all that with football season starting up."

Carter shook his head. "Maybe. I hope so."

Bobby shoved him playfully. "Come on. Let's make dinner. You made the call to Jessie. Let's celebrate!"

Carter stood to join him but headed toward their wall of memories. "I'll be up in a minute."

Photographs, church basketball trophies, Boy Scout badges, a box of green plastic soldiers, and homemade army emblems of honor printed with his name lined the shelves. He stopped to touch a picture of his mother near a tray of his grandfather's Army medals.

Carter looked at the picture and thought of what Bobby had told him about their grandmother, Elizabeth. He compared his mother Amanda's picture with one of Papa and the woman he had called the "love of his life."

Bobby had said that Papa had found his wife on the kitchen floor, with their mother at her side. Bobby didn't know why their grandmother had died, but there had always been a connection to that memory. When times were tough with their dad, Papa would tell them not to blame their mother when she seemed depressed. When they'd grown older, the brothers understood that Papa was there to protect and love them, especially when they were ultimately placed in his care and he moved in with them.

Carter felt tears well up in his eyes. How he wished for just one more chance to sit next to Papa's old leather chair and hear of his World War II escapades. But more so, to feel his grandfather's life-changing love and care. He turned to head upstairs for dinner and saw the flag hanging next to his grandfather's chair. He had heard Papa say it a hundred times in respect for soldiers. *"It's a high calling, Carter."*

Bobby stood at the refrigerator and pulled out a large piece of cubed steak. A skillet sat ready on the stove. "You hungry?" he said, as Carter stepped into the kitchen. He had chopped some potatoes for mashing and green beans were already simmering on the stove top.

"Wish we had some of those beans Papa used to plant every year," said Bobby.

"Yeah, Papa made sure we ate right." Carter gestured toward the stove. "You didn't save much for me to do."

"You got the dishes tonight," said Bobby, pounding the steak. "By the way, I got a letter from the church. It has a reminder about the Veterans

Day service and picnic in November. The Crawford Scout Troop will have a part on the program."

"Can't miss that one," said Carter. He reached for the soap to wash his hands. "Remember, Rev. Hamilton wants us to come speak to the boys in the troop sometime. Papa starting it was a big deal."

Papa Ford had made church attendance a priority in the boy's lives. He had already been the rock of their family but had filled the void even more after that fateful night. James Crawford had relied on the counsel of Stephen Hamilton, then the new young minister of the Sandy Springs Methodist Church. Starting a scout troop was one of the suggestions the reverend had made to support his journey to parent his grandsons. The troop would benefit from James' character-building words, he had said, and lessons through his military experiences and his commitment to God and country.

Carter laughed at the mention of Papa and church. "Remember Papa telling us not to let those ladies sit next to him in church? I wonder what he would be saying now about my calling Jessie?"

"He'd be standing here cooking us one of his well-balanced meals like always, asking me about my day at work and your day at school and putting those ladies' casseroles for 'Big Jim' in the freezer." Bobby joked and pointed to the refrigerator. "When it came to you calling Jessie, he would probably be advising you by telling you stories about Grandmother Elizabeth. You could bet he would say how none of those women from the church could ever measure up to her!"

Carter shook his head and began to set the table for dinner. The phone call with Jessie had raised his awareness of many things in his life—most of all, the kind of love and bond of family he wanted.

Chapter Seven

Jessie watched as a black Chevrolet pulled into the driveway. Sandy was sitting in the passenger seat and Christy and Diane in the back. She could see that Rick was driving.

Jessie joined the girls in the back seat and Rick pulled away slowly. Once they were out of sight and sound of Jessie's house, he revved the motor and gunned the engine down Northside. As they headed toward Peachtree Battle, Christy leaned up in the space between Rick and Sandy. "Didn't want the parents thinking you're a wild and crazy driver, right?"

Rick glanced in the rear-view mirror at Jessie. "Well, you know. Why get them all riled up? I got it under control."

Jessie noticed a piece of paper near her foot. It was a server's number card from the Varsity. She knew then that Rick had *also* discovered the larger downtown North Avenue hangout since moving to town.

The Zesto had a good reputation for fun with no trouble. It was the place where lots of "checking out" the connections, school conversation, and notice of "who drove up with whom" took place. There was always a police presence inside and out of the Varsity, given the hangout's location close to Georgia Tech. As tempting as the Varsity was, Jessie's friends preferred the safe and secure home of the Buckhead Zesto. There had been no publicly known trouble at the Varsity, but the word among the Northwest girls was if you ventured to the Varsity, it would be smart to be cautious about anyone you met there.

Christy glanced over at Diane and Jessie. "Anyone seen Fran lately?"

Diane began to giggle. "Aw. She's probably at the river somewhere with Mike." There were numerous non-public places for private teen rendezvous meetings, and in that part of town, privacy was found along the banks of the Chattahoochee River. Some of the older Northwest boys were known to have explored its banks and forests to find abandoned dirt driveways leading to old home foundations with only a brick chimney remaining for their smaller gatherings.

Since Fran had been the one to tell her about Carter, Jessie wanted to better show her friendship but Fran's number one priority seemed to be keeping an eye on her boyfriend Mike. The gossip was that she did everything she could to make sure Mike wasn't around other girls who could compete for his attention. They rarely frequented the Zesto and the rumors were that Fran and Mike were spending time alone at their "special place," wherever that was.

The group continued down West Wesley to Peachtree and found a parking spot near the Zesto's back entrance close to the radio station tower. They ordered a quick snack to keep the staff's approval for their space.

Jack was standing in front of the Zesto and waved at the girls. He watched as Rick hopped out of the car and began making rounds to all the cars as if he were running for class president. Every time Jack started toward the car of girls, however, Rick would return. It quickly became apparent to Jessie that Rick was trying to create a barrier between his car and anyone else—especially Jack. Jack played Rick's game well—when Rick was otherwise distracted, he would work his way back to the car to talk to her.

Later, as the evening went on, there was a tense moment between the two boys. Jack caught Jessie's eye as Rick walked away. He shook his head and raised his hands to her in a questioning manner, as if to say, *"Who is this guy and why are you with him?"*

Rick's behavior seemed to become more and more difficult to contain as the night went on and Sandy tried to settle him down. When he disappeared again, Christy asked, "Where did he go this time?"

"I don't know," said Diane. "But it's getting late and I have homework. My parents will be mad if I'm not home soon."

"Sandy! Sandy!" A voice could be heard from high above them. Someone outside the car pointed up to the radio tower. They all got out of the car and looked up. It was Rick, waving now at the crowd below. Jessie gasped and grabbed Sandy's arm, but Sandy froze in disbelief, unable to respond.

Jessie ran to the base of the tower. "Rick!" she yelled. "Come down!" The rest of the girls tried to wave others away and not call attention to him. They knew he could likely get in trouble with the management and, if he did, so would his friends.

Slowly he made his way down the ladder. When he reached the final step, Jessie met him. "What were you thinking?"

Rick's foolish escapade seemed to crumple. "No one ever showed me they care like you do, Jessie. Do you love me?"

Jessie was caught off-guard by his question and responded without a thought. "Of course I love you, Rick."

Rick looked to Sandy, who had stepped up to join them. "Come on. I'll take everyone home."

The girls began to head back to Rick's car, when Jack stepped up and pulled Jessie to the side. "There's no way you should be riding with that guy. He's crazy and unpredictable. He even accused me earlier with trying to take up with 'his' girls!"

She was concerned for her friends, but Jessie didn't question Jack. "I need to get my purse."

As they approached the car, Rick opened the door for Jessie. "You're with me," he said, keeping his eye on Jack.

"Not now," said Jack. When Jessie had retrieved her purse, he turned her toward his car on the other side of the parking lot.

The ride home was a quiet one for the two friends. Thoughts raced through Jack's head. He so wanted to tell Jessie about his care for her, but decided against it. "You gotta be careful about that guy," he said, as he pulled in front of the Reynolds' house.

Jessie climbed out and closed the door. "*I'm* worried about Sandy."

Jack nodded. "I'll check on her. There's something about Rick that doesn't add up."

"Thanks, Jack. I'm glad you were there tonight."

When Jessie came through the front door, she found her mother with her sewing box in the living room.

"Did William call?"

"No calls tonight, dear. How was the Zesto?"

"It was okay. Jack was there. He brought me home."

As with William, the mention of Jack to her parents always brought an easy sense of acceptance. Jessie knew that it wouldn't take long before word would get out about Rick to them and other parents from school. Although Jessie had always been able to share her thoughts with her mother, something about what had happened was different. She needed to talk to Sandy first.

Jessie woke early with meeting Carter on her mind. She spent extra time getting dressed.

The events at the Zesto just seemed like a bad dream. When Jessie opened Claire's car door for their trip to school, Claire stared at her dress and makeup.

"What's going on with you?"

"Nothing." Jessie wasn't ready to talk about Carter with anyone yet, and she quickly changed the subject. "Are Robby and Michael riding this morning?"

"Nope. We're on our own." Before Jessie had a chance to ask her if she'd heard about what had happened at the Zesto, Claire asked, "Have you heard the latest about Natalie? She's gone! At school one day and then gone the next."

They arrived at school and learned that Natalie had "decided" to enroll in one of the private schools nearby—someone had said they thought it was Lovett. There was much discussion about how her parents found out about her dating Terry and what they had done. But one thing was for sure—everyone knew without question that there would be no more dating between Jewish and Protestant classmates at Northwest.

On the way to her locker, Jessie thought about all the complexities to life that were opening up in front of her. When she turned the corner, Fran was waiting for her.

"Did Carter call?"

Jessie looked around to see if anyone was listening. "Yes, he did."

"Well? How did it go?"

"It went fine. We talked about Coach O'Connor."

"That's it? You talked about Coach?"

Jessie was fairly sure Fran had an ulterior motive in asking and sidestepped the question. "Sandy came to get me to go horseback riding, so we didn't have very long to talk."

"But you will see him today, right?"

"Yes, at lunch."

"Great! He is terrific and a great guy. Give him a chance. I'm sure you'll like him." With a wave, Fran walked down the hall to her locker. She opened it to the large mirror inside the door and checked her makeup. Jessie saw Mike walk up and peek over her shoulder. Fran's reaction clearly confirmed that he was "her everything."

That was when Rick walked by and did a double take when he saw Jessie. The next thing she knew, Rick had his arms wrapped around her in a tight lock. "Jessie!" he said.

Jessie's surprise was noticeable. "Rick! Hey." Sandy, along with Diane and Christy, was not far behind and she could see the expression on their faces. She looked from side to side for a faculty member. Fran and Mike turned and began to stare. Fran made a face as if asking her "What are you doing?" and gestured down the hall. Jessie looked in the direction she'd indicated and saw Carter. He was standing with Terry and both were looking her way. Her heart stopped. Should she give Rick her attention? Would Carter think she had more than a friendship with Rick?

The bell rang and everyone scrambled in different directions to reach their first period classrooms. Except Rick. He had tightened his squeeze. Jessie tried to get him to let her go. "Rick. I'll be late for class."

Jack came up from nowhere on the way to art class. "Hey, man. You heard her. Let her go."

Rick released her and took a step toward Jack and then suddenly stopped. Coach O'Connor appeared behind them and stood with his arms folded. "Hey! Time for class."

Jessie backed away from Rick's embrace, mortified.

Jack stepped between them and walked her to Mr. Baker's class. He took his seat across from her and then spoke. "You all right?" Jessie, who was still shaking, nodded and gave him a grateful smile.

Mr. Baker's art classes were always fascinating and this one was a nice distraction from the hallway incident with Rick. His style of teaching was different in so many ways. His stop and "smell the roses" approach to life in the midst of all the world's craziness was a breath of fresh air for all his students.

The art room was filled with student creations and many of Mr. Baker's own paintings. The worktables and shelves were covered with supplies and each student had a section where they could store their work in progress. The classroom was one of the largest in the school and underscored Northwest High's commitment to art, as well as that of the whole city. Near the doorway were framed newspaper articles and pictures from the 1962 Paris plane crash when over 100 influential, cultural and civic leaders in Atlanta had traveled to Europe to visit famous museums. It had been a devastating event to Atlanta and the entire art community and Mr. Baker had lost many friends—he was determined to carry on their legacy for a new tomorrow for the art, theater and music scene in Atlanta. His optimism infected everyone. "Life is short," he seemed to say in everything he did. "Make the most of it." Jessie never knew what to expect, which always got and kept her attention.

Today, he entered the room and leaned against the front of his desk. He looked around quietly then gazed out the window as everyone watched and waited for him to speak. He glanced at the ceiling and with a sense of awe in his voice said, "Listen. Do you hear it?"

The class looked at him curiously.

"Listen to the quiet. What is it saying to you?"

He was silent and then he spoke again. "Now, paint."

All Jessie could think about was what had happened with Rick. She took out her brushes and began to paint an abstract creation. The result clearly pointed to the confusion in her head. Before she knew it, the bell had rung and art class was over.

Christy, who was also in the class, took Jessie's arm. "Save me a seat at lunch. We'll talk then." She was out the door before Jessie could even react. She had hoped that the talk at lunch would all be about Carter, but now she needed to talk with Sandy. She was worried that she might be upset with her, that she might think she'd been flirting with Rick. They were scheduled to go riding later but she couldn't wait until then.

Jessie's English and biology classes quickly passed, and the lunch bell rang for her A-Session lunch period. She headed to her locker with anticipation to retrieve her own bagged lunch. Others passed by her with less enthusiasm as they headed toward the not-so-enticing hot lunch line. She grabbed her Pep Club spirit ribbons with hopes of selling her allotment during the lunch break. The ribbon fund raiser roasting the week's high school rival brought money for the club's support of the school's sports programs.

Because Atlanta's northwest area had become a popular place to live, the school's population had grown as well, necessitating three lunch sessions to accommodate seating in the undersized cafeteria. For the smokers, this was the only time they could slip out to the only approved spot behind the ROTC building. The stand-alone brick fortress would be surrounded by boys lighting up and a few girls known for wanting to be part of their gang.

On the other side of the cafeteria were the "blue jean boys" who sat at their own lunch table. It was an unspoken rule that most of Jessie's friends thought twice about forming a serious relationship with one of them. The football team members were the center of attention and claimed the center row of tables. Conversations for the girls were all about clothes and boys. For the boys, it was sports and cars. They would have to admit that girls ranked high, too, and everyone loved music. Few steady couples sat together at lunch. Lunch was a time to connect with other girls. "Couples time" was standing in the hall before or after class or, if either had a car, on the way to and from school.

When Jessie entered the cafeteria, she saw Sandy and Christy at the long beige Formica lunch table in the back. She weaved through the crowded room in their direction but was stopped cold by someone stepping in front of her. "Heading to lunch with Fran?"

She was face to face with Carter. The gleam in his eyes gave her a feeling that no one else in the room mattered to him and she couldn't think of what to say next.

"Actually, I was going to have lunch with Sandy and Christy." She glanced toward their table and could see their heads together in serious conversation.

Carter guided her over to the windows where textbooks were stacked while their owners had lunch and found a couple of seats. "I bet the girls can wait," he said. "Don't you?" He gestured at the brown bag in her hand. "What's for lunch?"

She opened the bag to show her meal. "My mom put a sandwich in my bag this morning, an apple and some of her cookies. You hungry?"

"Nope. Already eaten. But those cookies look good."

The trend for the popular boys were outfits of Bass Weejun loafers, oxford cloth button-down shirts, gold cup socks to match their shirts, and clean khaki slacks with alligator belts. The girls had a bit more variety with a fair share of Villager blouses and alpaca sweaters with Pappagallo shoes. Jessie had picked a special dress and sweater to wear that morning. And, after several attempts at styling her hair, she had chosen to let it fall below her shoulders, pulling it away from her face with a tortoise shell clasp. She hoped it measured up to his neat appearance.

Carter's light green shirt, with the initials "JCP" on the pocket, was perfectly starched and ironed, and his shiny loafers were polished to military perfection. Jessie remembered that ROTC had been on the list of Carter's activities in the yearbook—cadets were judged on good behavior and the importance of being dressed properly in uniform.

At one point Fran passed by and quickly pinched Jessie's arm. Several friends of Carter's passed by too. "Looking forward to the big game!"

"Thanks. Me, too." Carter never took his eyes off Jessie when he answered them and he could see that Jessie was equally captivated by his attention. "This is a tough place to talk," he said.

Jessie juggled the spirit ribbons in her hand knowing she should be looking for the next buyer. "I should be selling these."

"How is Pep Club roasting Fulton this week?"

Jessie showed him the purple and white silken ribbons with the Northwest tiger clawing at the heels of the Fulton bulldog.

Carter smiled. "You need to make your quota, don't you? I'll buy one. A dollar?" Robin's "list" from choir tour flashed before her eyes. Carter's show of support initiated a "list" for him in her mind.

Jessie shook her head. "You don't have to. You're on the team."

Carter handed her a dollar from his pocket. "It's great to know you are in the Pep Club. They're front and center in the stands at the game."

The game? Jessie still didn't know if she and William had a date on

Friday or which game they would attend. Now, here was Carter suggesting he would look for her at the Northwest game. Carter interrupted her thought.

"You have Coach next for algebra?"

"What? Oh yes, on D Hall. It's kind of loud in here and I need to see Sandy."

"Mike wants everyone at the team table to talk before practice. See you later?"

"Okay."

She watched Carter join the rest of the guys on the team at their table. Their making room for him at the table with high fives showed his acceptance by everyone. She was overcome with self-consciousness when all the other boys turned to look at her and grinned at Carter. Her discomfort was lightened when she saw Jack on the junior end of the team table and acknowledged his smile.

She headed toward Sandy and Christy.

"Where have you been?" said Christy. "It is almost time for the bell to ring for B session!"

"But..."

"No buts!" Christy glanced toward Sandy and lowered her voice. "Meet us at the car after school. I'm going with you two to groom Josey at Chastain this afternoon. We have to talk about Rick!"

Fran appeared beside them and looked down at Jessie. "Looks like you and Carter made a connection. Mike gives the two of you a thumbs up. He and Carter are good friends from way back." Christy looked at Sandy when she heard Fran's comment.

The bell rang. There was no time to waste, so Jessie took a quick bite of her sandwich. She passed the team table and glanced around, pretending to look for customers for her spirit ribbons.

Carter had disappeared and she needed to hurry toward D Hall, which was on the other side of the building from the cafeteria. There was just enough time to reach class before Coach closed the door on late arrivals.

Carter was standing in the hall waiting for her. In her surprise to see him, she juggled the books in her arms. He reached for her books. "Hey. Looks like you need some help."

Jessie smiled as others rushed by her into the room, pleased they had made the cut before the late bell too. "I have football practice today after school," said Carter. Jessie looked at him with a questioning eye and he explained. "Maybe you could come out to watch?"

A loud voice announced, "Miss Reynolds! You are now officially late to my class!" It was Coach. Jessie had been so focused on Carter she had not heard the late bell ring.

Carter stepped up. "It's my fault, Coach. I stopped her and made her late."

Coach furrowed his brow and folded his arms. "Well, then! That will be extra time for you at practice today, Mr. Powell."

A shiver ran down Jessie's spine. She knew somehow at the very moment that Carter took up for her that he was special. She ducked by Coach and made her way quickly to her desk near the windows.

She had never felt such a protective, secure feeling with any boy she had dated. Not even the two months over the summer dating William had brought out such feelings. The day's events were not what she had expected when she'd dressed that morning. But in less than 24 hours, her expectations and excitement had surpassed her hesitation of yesterday's news of an unknown caller.

Jessie felt Coach watching her during class. She trained her eyes forward and sat at attention, her heart beating fast in her chest. Was he determining which difficult problem he would ask her to compute at the chalkboard? She anxiously awaited her doom, but it thankfully never came.

When class was dismissed, she headed to the door to make a quick exit but Coach O'Connor caught her eye and gave her a look she interpreted to mean, "Mind your step." She wondered which *step* she would face with Coach in the future.

As she headed to her locker the whole Carter, Sandy, Rick, Jack, Fran, William and Christy day was swirling through her mind. Mrs. Laney walked by. "That is an interesting look, Jessie."

Jessie grimaced in relief at the sight of her mentor. "Confused, for sure. What is with Coach O'Connor? Help me understand him."

Mrs. Laney stopped. "You have him for algebra?"

"Yes, ma'am, and I think he doesn't like me."

"My dear, I wish I could help you there. I would say many of Coach O'Connor's students feel the same way. Try not to take his way personally. As you probably know, he lost his wife last year and he's hurting. I feel sure that it's not about you."

Chapter Eight

S andy was waiting at her Mustang. "Hurry! I need to get to Chastain before the manager leaves. Josey needs her exercise and I have homework." Jessie noticed that Christy was already in the car and it was rare that she joined the two of them on their workouts with Josey. She knew from the lunchroom conversation earlier that they wanted to talk about Rick and what had happened at the Zesto and at school that morning.

Jessie was torn between her loyalty to Sandy and wanting to see Carter at football practice. In particular appearing at practice was important since he would be paying a price for defending her to Coach.

Before she could explain to Sandy and Christy, she felt Fran's hand on her arm. "Come on," she said. "I'm going to watch Mike at football practice. We can sit together! The south end will have a great view and we can get some sun."

Jessie turned to Sandy. "Carter Powell invited me to come and watch football practice this afternoon. I've been wanting to tell you about his call to me yesterday. I don't know what was going on with Rick at the Zesto or this morning at my locker, but you have to know as my friend, I'm not interested in him."

Sandy recognized the conflict in Jessie's eyes. She knew that Jessie wanted to go with her for Josey's ride, but she also knew Jessie was her friend and wanted to see Carter, not Rick. She gestured for Jessie to go on. "Go with Fran. And be sure to call me and tell me all about it!"

Jessie gave her an "Are you sure?" look. "Why don't y'all come with us. It'll be fun!"

Sandy smiled and waved goodbye. "No. You go ahead. Josey is waiting. Have fun!"

Jessie and Fran hurried toward the practice field and made it with time to spare. They climbed onto the bleachers at the end of the field and sat down. "So," said Jessie, "what else can you tell me about Carter?"

Fran thought for a moment. "Well, I told you how much everyone likes him, right? I don't really know why, but he lives with his brother Bobby, who is older than he is. Their grandfather raised them both and he died not long ago."

"His grandfather raised him?"

Fran nodded. "Yes. Their parents died in a car accident when Carter was in first grade. Carter and his brother have really handled it all amazingly. I think it is one reason he is so well liked. I cannot imagine being able to deal with it all." She stopped. "He never talks about it though."

Other friends began joining them, waving to their boyfriends on the track doing their warm-up laps. Mike made a "he man" gesture at Fran as he passed. She waved and smiled but kept talking to Jessie. "Maybe let Carter tell you about all that. I think he has stayed pretty private about it."

Jessie was stunned by the news of the car accident and Carter's childhood and tried to regain her composure to look for him. She finally saw him at the opposite end running "banks," as the boys referred to it—up and down the steep hillside at the back of the field. Coach O'Connor was standing with his hands on his hips watching him.

Another player ran over to the girls and jumped up and down to show his strength. Jessie laughed at the antics when she realized who it was. "He man Jack! Looking good!" she said, clapping. Jack ran backwards on the track, smiling at her all the way.

Jessie returned her attention to the other end of the field. Carter was swift in picking up his knees as he made his way up and down the bank, never showing any sign of fatigue. Jack reached the coach, and Jessie could tell he said something to him. Then, Mike came by and looked up the bank at Carter. He said something to Coach too. Coach waved them both on their way. Would Carter ever want to speak to her again?

Fran was oblivious to Carter's obvious punishment. "Mike will surely get a scholarship to a major college. You know he is team captain?"

Jessie nodded. Mike was definitely a star and everyone knew he would go on to play college football after his senior year.

She'd heard some of the gossip about Fran and Mike, like why they never came to the Zesto. She wondered if it weren't for Mike if Fran would be part of the school "inner circle." She appreciated that Fran had been the catalyst for her introduction to Carter, but she hoped Fran was being smart about her relationship with Mike.

Carter came down the bank for the final time. Jessie sat up to see better, and Fran turned to her and lowered her voice. "I think Carter's smitten. I wish Mike was."

"I'm sure he is."

Fran stared into space. "Jessie. You and Carter have just met! Mike has never looked at me the way Carter already looks at you."

"We barely know each other, Fran." Jessie's grin gave away the fact that she was smitten with Carter too.

The team jogged by the stands at the end of practice, and all the observers stood to leave. When Carter passed by, he caught Jessie's eye and winked. Jessie smiled and waved.

"See?" said Fran. "I told you. He's smitten all right!"

The girls walked back toward the school on the walkway near the boys locker room entrance. As they got close, Mike walked out with his letterman jacket and practice bag. He glanced toward Jessie. "Your guy is our secret weapon. We call him "Weap." He is the best running back on the team...no, in the city! He's why we will make it to city championships this year."

Fran dutifully followed Mike toward the parking lot. She turned and mouthed the word "Smitten!" They disappeared around the corner of the building. Jessie shifted her purse and her stack of books from one arm to the other, and looked up right into the face of Coach O'Connor. He stopped to speak to her.

"You know, Carter has great potential. He needs to keep his head in the game. You hear?"

Jessie gulped, trying to find some words to explain that she really didn't know Carter that well, but stopped short. "Yes, sir." She had known Carter barely two days, but the comments from Fran and Coach implied something else.

When she looked up at him again, she saw the glimmer of a smile. "Mrs. Laney told me you were concerned about me." The coach walked on toward the parking lot and turned back. "I'll see you in class tomorrow." He lowered his head, and Jessie saw the sadness that both Carter and Mrs. Laney had described.

"Hey!" Carter was standing behind Jessie. His hair was still wet from showering and the fresh smell of soap caused Jessie to breathe deeper.

She looked at him with new eyes. "Hey."

Carter switched his gym bag to his other hand and grabbed the stack of books from her arm. "You need a ride home, don't you? How about a soda from Springlake? Those banks made me thirsty."

As the two walked toward the parking lot, Jessie realized that she had no idea what car to look for. Carter finally stopped at a large green Buick.

"It's not much, but it gets me where I need to be." He quickly reached for the passenger side door. "Here. The door is little tricky." He opened the door and tossed his practice bag in the back seat. He closed the door slowly once Jessie was safely inside. Yet another check for Jessie's 'list.' Jessie glanced around the car's interior. Despite it's obvious age, it was clean and well cared for.

Jessie watched Carter as he walked around the car to join her. It felt like all was right and secure with him next to her.

Springlake Drugstore was on Howell Mill not far from Jessie's house. Once she had gotten her driver's license, she had gladly run errands for her mother and had gone there many times. The store was where the family prescriptions were filled and Jessie often browsed their beauty products and magazines. Most of all, though, Springlake was known for its great soda fountain.

Carter took the route down West Wesley then turned on Howell Mill near Morris Brandon. Crossing over Peachtree Creek, he turned left to cruise by the park and up the street past Sandy's house. They rounded the curve to see some boys in the park playing pickup football and Carter honked, acknowledging them.

One of the boys waved and was immediately tackled because of the distraction. Carter laughed and pointed to the boys as they drove past.

"That one who got tackled is Clark Barfield. I grew up playing with him and his brothers."

The car radio was playing and Jessie saw Carter tapping on the steering wheel keeping time with the beat but never losing sync with the rhythm. She knew from her piano lessons about proper beats and thought his talent unique as the music continued. The pleasant fall afternoon was a welcome addition to her comfort being with him.

They arrived at Springlake and pulled into the dirt and gravel parking lot at Springer Grocery next door. The parking lot was almost full, but Carter found a space for the larger Buick. When Carter saw that the spot was so tight that Jessie's door wouldn't open wide, he looked at her with an outstretched hand and helped her out through his side. The warmth of his hand sent the same feeling washing over her that she'd experienced outside Coach's classroom.

On nice days like this one, the pharmacy glass door was propped open. Inside to the left was shelving for convenience items and to the right were a couple of booths and a long marble top soda fountain with round chrome and black vinyl-covered bar stools. The cash register was at the end of the counter—all sales were rung there by Dr. Ellis, a clerk, or sometimes a student taking orders at the fountain.

When Carter and Jessie sat down in a booth, Dr. Ellis walked over and tapped him on the shoulder. "Hi, Carter! I hear the team is looking good this year." Jessie was impressed that Dr. Ellis knew him by name.

"Yes, sir," replied Carter. "We're hoping for a good season."

Dr. Ellis glanced over at Jessie. "What can I get you, young lady?"

"I'd love a Coke float."

"Make it two," added Carter.

Dr. Ellis said he would get their order ready right away. Once he'd turned around, Carter leaned forward and said in a low voice, "Sometime, we'll go to the Varsity downtown. Their orange floats are the best."

"*Sometime…?*" thought Jessie. She envisioned a future date at the downtown hangout and the security of Carter by her side as the server took their order on the upper deck.

"Do you have a lot of homework?" she asked.

"I have a study hall fifth period, so I get my homework done then." He smiled warmly. "I'm glad you came to practice today. And don't worry about Coach. He wants us to be our best in everything. He keeps talking up my potential. College scouts and all that."

"That's great! Mrs. Laney has been encouraging me, too. You know, to be my best. I love her business classes. Teaching has to be so fulfilling. I'm thinking about a Business Education degree someday." She opened the paper on her straw to sip the drink Dr. Ellis had brought to the booth. The long-handled spoon slipped through a large scoop of vanilla ice cream, and the whipped cream topping was perfectly arranged with a maraschino cherry. Her eyes brightened as she took a sip.

Jessie looked over to see a girl glaring at Carter from a booth nearby. There was a distance between them from across the seating area, but the chill was obvious. "I think someone wants your attention," she said.

Carter glanced in the direction of the girl and back at Jessie in frustration. He leaned in and whispered. "We probably shouldn't have come here. If I had known…"

The next moment they were interrupted by the girl, now standing over Carter. "I have waited for you to call me." She placed her hands on her hips and looked at Jessie. "I guess I know why, now!"

Another girl joined her and grabbed her arm. "Let's go, Carla."

She snatched her arm away from the girl and gave Carter an angry look. "I'll go when I'm ready!"

Dr. Ellis looked up from the pharmacy counter and shook his head in disapproval. Jessie felt it wise to excuse herself from the conversation and headed to the restroom. As she walked away, she could hear the girl speaking louder in a strange sort of voice. When she returned, Jessie found Carter waiting for her alone. She could already see the apology in his eyes. He had finished his soda, paid, and held her unfinished float in a paper cup.

"I'm sorry about all that," he said. "I think we should go, okay? I need to explain what just happened to you."

The clerk and Dr. Ellis gave them both a friendly wave as they passed through the open door. Jessie walked with Carter to his car, both unaware of the girl and her friend talking to an individual in a car near the back of the parking lot.

Carter rolled down the window of the Buick for some much needed air and waited to place the keys in the ignition. He stared straight ahead. "I guess Fran hasn't told you everything about me."

Jessie assumed he was referring to the loss of his parents and the car accident, so she was surprised when he turned to her and said, "I play in a band."

"A *band?*"

Carter nodded. "It started at a talent show at our church and grew from there. We play around town at other school dances and at a few schools out of town when we can work our schedules around my football. We're called The Playboys. Not my choice on the name, but it's good money to put aside and cover things."

Jessie was startled and amused. *How could Fran have not told me this? She told me about his family and not this? Did Carter think it would matter somehow to me? Does it matter to me? The Playboys? What does that mean?*

Carter studied her reaction and waited for her to speak. "I caught you off guard, I guess."

As she thought about it, Jessie realized nothing mattered about it because she already knew they had something special. A smile slowly appeared on her face and she giggled. "The *Playboys*? Tell me about it."

Carter's shoulders dropped as if a weight was lifted. He turned to her with a look she would never forget—a mixed look of trust and relief. "Yeah, the Playboys. Like I said, the name was not my idea." He put his hands up in self-defense and grinned. "There are four of us and I play the drums. The girl back there is Carla. She was at one of the dances a while back and she has started following us around. At first, we took it as a compliment that someone enjoyed our music that much. Now, it has gotten out of hand. She has some kind of problem because she bugs us, bugs *me*, like that," he said, gesturing with his head toward the drug store.

"She is a little strange. What do you think is her problem?"

"I really have no idea. Just my luck to run into her here and with you." He took a deep breath. "We've all tried to ignore her. The guys in the band said she knows where we live and where we hang out. I thought Springlake was safe. Who knows what she'll do next? Oh, and don't be mad at Fran. I asked her not to tell you about the band because I wanted to tell you myself."

"At least now you answered my question about how could you possibly keep such a great beat to the music on our ride here from school!"

Carter started the car, pulled out on Howell Mill and turned down Collier Road back toward Jessie's home. He reached out and touched Jessie's hand. "Will you go out with me Saturday night? The Fulton game is tomorrow, and Pete has scheduled us to play for a Fulton dance after the game. I promise Saturday will be better than this afternoon."

Without thinking, Jessie said, "Yes." There was no way she would miss attending the Northwest game and seeing Carter play. The thought of William never entered her mind.

They turned on Longwood and stopped in front of her house. Jessie saw her mother through the window over the kitchen sink as she waved goodbye to Carter and walked up her flagstone sidewalk.

Her mother met Jessie as she entered the house. "Who was that? Obviously, you didn't go riding with Sandy."

Jessie unloaded all her ammunition at once. "That was Carter. He is the one who called yesterday. Fran knows him and he's on the football team. Coach O'Connor says he has real potential. He gave me a ride home from school, and we went up to Springlake first for a Coke float. He's very nice."

Madeline raised her eyebrows and wiped her hands on her apron. "Supper will be ready soon when your dad gets home. Much homework tonight?"

Jessie was surprised yet grateful at the limit of her mother's questions. "Not much. Mrs. Laney gave me some information about the Education Department at Georgia today. They have a Business Education major that I want to read about."

DINNERTIME WAS IMPORTANT FOR THE REYNOLDS family to spend time together around the kitchen table talking about the day. The evening meal was always perfectly prepared by Jessie's mother, who had grown up on her family's farm in Alabama and made wonderful balanced home cooked meals. She kept her kitchen spotless and always used nice dishes for serving their meals. As a rule, her dad washed the dishes in appreciation.

On this particular night, though, the subject of a new "friend" named Carter never came up. Jessie decided to wait for the perfect time to introduce the Saturday night date as she made her way upstairs to finish her homework. She especially wanted to be prepared for Coach

O'Connor's class tomorrow and started there on her assignments, but it was hard to concentrate on much other than Carter.

Normally she would have dashed upstairs to call Robin or Sandy, but this was different. Jessie wasn't quite sure why she wasn't ready to divulge her innermost feelings with them about Carter. She knew that telling her friends about him would mean her words would be spread to the group before she even got to school the next day. Everyone pretty much always had shared each others every thought.

It was different with Fran, though. She managed to keep most of the details about her and Mike to just the basics as if there was nothing special to share. The group all knew better.

Jessie didn't hear the phone ring and was startled when her mother called up the stairs. "William is on the phone."

She paused for a second acknowledging the pleasant sound of her mother voice when referring to William. She reached to pick up her extension.

"Hey Jess! How's it going? Sorry it has been awhile since I called."

"Oh, it's going good. Busy with school and all."

She continued the conversation, surprised that her displeasure at William's lack of communication had melted away. After their time together this summer, she'd thought he was the perfect guy for any girl to have as a boyfriend, but she was beginning to think she'd been wrong.

"How about a movie Saturday? Robin and Mark are going to the Fox," he asked.

"I'm sorry, William. I have plans for Saturday night."

It was quiet on the other end of the phone. "Oh. Sorry. I didn't know."

"Well, it sort of just happened this afternoon. I wish I had known sooner about you and Robin and Mark." Jessie tried to sound disappointed, but she realized she wasn't at all. "It is a big game weekend you know, and everyone is making plans and several parties going on. Some other time?"

"Sure. See you later. Sunday afternoon after choir practice?"

"Yes. I'll see you Sunday." Jessie's head was spinning as she ended the call. She had known William now for a long time. She had wished that they would become more than friends and her wish had finally come true. But now she was about to throw all that aside—for someone who saw her in the school cafeteria, took her to Springlake for a Coke float, and...played in a band!

Chapter Nine

Jessie woke early Friday morning enthusiastic about seeing Carter again. It was all so new with him and the excitement was building for the big game that night.

Claire and Missy were the school friends she trusted most. Jessie had not had a chance to tell them about her afternoon with Carter or her upcoming Saturday night date, and she wanted so much to share her news.

On their ride to school, Missy told Claire and Jessie all the things she needed them, as Pep Club members, to do in preparation for the game. Missy's big heart and love of life had drawn Jessie to her as long as they'd known each other. Plus, Missy's brother Billy was like the brother she never had. He had a way with words and wrote scripts for their childhood plays performed in the Davis basement.

Missy's family also had the perfect pet—a Cavalier King Charles spaniel named Betsy who sat quietly watching over the children while they played. It was if she had been trained as their nurse maid—when a friend was hurt or upset, Betsy would move to their side to comfort them.

The dog's first litter of puppies was the center of the neighborhood friends' attention. Mrs. Davis taught them about the wonders of birth and an appreciation for life by talking about how Betsy would feed her young and how to handle the pups gently.

When the girls got to school, Carter was waiting for Jessie in the hallway. They made plans to see each other at lunch. She turned to see Sandy and asked about Josey. "She's fine," said Sandy. "Christy is going to help me groom her this afternoon."

"Great! I hope she likes riding bareback! Do we need to talk?"

"Maybe later. I might have jumped the gun about Rick and other things. He keeps asking when we are all going to the Zesto again. As you know, Jack is not a fan of Rick's, but he never really tells me why. When we were at our lockers yesterday, he told me to be careful when it came to Rick."

Jessie opened her mouth to speak, but Sandy shook her head. "I know. You and Carter have a thing. Fran thinks she is a matchmaker now."

Jessie ignored the reference. "Jack's a good friend. Maybe you can come watch him at football practice sometime." She had always thought Sandy would be a great match for Jack anyway.

"Maybe," she said. "You and Fran have that in common now with some of the other football players' girlfriends. I'm not sure about Jack with Rick and all."

"I understand," said Jessie. "This is still all so new with Carter."

She still wasn't ready to broadcast her feelings for him, let alone the world. It took no time for something like that to come out in the *Social Limelight* newspaper column. Some of the girls enjoyed telling stories at the lunch table as if they were privileged with the big scoop of the day. Jessie knew it would happen eventually anyway but didn't want to give it a boost at this point. There was much more she wanted to learn about Carter first.

The bell rang and the day was off and running. Jack raced in the door past the girls and beamed at Jessie. Although classes moved along at a regular pace, Jessie thought the lunch bell would never ring, but food was the last thing on her mind.

Fulton High was adjacent to the Northwest school zone and was one of their biggest rivals. The intersection of the Buckhead Zesto and Peachtree Street was the dividing line between the two schools—visits to the Zesto during rival weeks were closely monitored for any sign of trouble.

The cafeteria was more crowded than usual. The hype was building for a special rally that afternoon. The players were circulating through the lunchroom tables and the cheerleaders were already dressed in their uniforms for the regular Friday morning pep rally, but a change of schedule had been announced in homeroom. Instead, the pep rally would be in place of sixth period which meant all other classes would be shortened.

Jessie saw Carter coming toward her across the cafeteria. She smiled and waited as friends stopped him, wishing him a good game. Finally, he reached her. They instinctively walked toward the windows to move out of the whirlwind. Carter looked at her and grinned. "You look great! Glad it's Friday. We still on for tomorrow night?"

Jessie's blush acknowledged his compliment. "I'm excited about the game tonight. I know you will do great...and yes, we are on for tomorrow night."

"That didn't sound so convincing."

"I haven't exactly told my parents that we are going out tomorrow. We'll see each other tonight at the game, won't we?"

"Everything okay with your parents? I mean, about our date?"

"It will be fine. There just hasn't been time for me to tell them," she said.

"Okay," he said. "Try to sit near the front of the student section. I'm number 21. We'll have a tough defense from Fulton. But I have to admit that I won't just be thinking of Fulton because you will be on my mind."

Jessie was well aware of his jersey number. She had done her homework on the team with a special interest. Carter was so different from anyone she had ever known. It felt good to have someone tell her she was on his mind—but she was not accustomed to such direct comments. "I'm glad, but—"

Carter laughed. "Coach has been giving me the lecture about keeping my head in the game." Jessie could see what Fran had been talking about when she'd mentioned Carter's distinctive laugh. It revealed his upbeat and confident spirit. She was drawn more and more to his charm and openness.

He rattled on about the game. "Our team has the better record against Fulton, and we all want to keep it that way! Coach said they have a great passing defense, so it will likely be more of my running game."

"I know the players sit on the front row at the pep rally. I will look for you there. Good luck tonight if I don't get another chance to tell you. And…be careful. Okay?"

Carter welcomed Jessie's concern, although it was an unusual feeling for him. "I'll be fine. After the pep rally, we go straight to the locker rooms. Coach is bringing in a special dinner for us. Somebody said steak! It's going to be crazy tonight with the band playing for the dance at Fulton afterwards. I wish you could be there, but it wouldn't be much fun for you since we will be playing the whole time."

Jessie imagined hearing Carter play. "Maybe soon?"

"Yes, very soon! Pete said the guys will do all the set up and for me to just get there as quickly as I can after the game. I want you to meet the band, too."

Jessie wanted to ask him if that girl Carla would be at the Fulton dance, but she was determined not to show any sign of the jealousy she was feeling. She knew from past sleepover confessions that jealousy almost always ended badly and she was surprised at how much she wanted nothing to stand in the way of her having a relationship with Carter. "This will be a long day and night for you. Call me in the morning and we can talk about our date."

He walked away with a big smile and then turned back with a look Jessie read as "I'm looking forward to it." She felt a flutter in her stomach—she was really looking forward to it, too.

The bell rang and Jessie hurried to algebra class. As she walked past him at the door, Coach looked down the hallway. She wondered if he was looking for signs of Carter.

Finally, the coach closed the door and walked silently to his desk. He gave the class an assignment and took a seat at his desk near the window. Jessie noticed his behavior was different.

During class, Jessie looked up several times, finding the coach staring out the window. A sports jacket with the Northwest emblem sewn on the pocket hung on his chair. It was obvious he took great pride in the team he coached. Carter had told her how the coach worked out alongside the team, which explained why his tan was always perfect and he was in such good shape. A touch of gray hair along his temples was one of only a few signs of his age. *Maybe Coach O'Connor isn't so scary after all*, she thought.

She remembered that Mrs. Laney had told her that both he and she had been named Teachers of the Year, a signal that both had gone above and beyond to help some students in tough situations. She wondered if Carter had been one of them.

Jessie finished the assignment and looked up at the clock. It was almost time for the pep rally. When the bell rang, Coach lifted the jacket from the back of his chair and put it on. "Have a good weekend!" he said to the class.

Everyone excitedly headed to the field behind the school. Jessie wanted Carter to do well in the game, but more so, she found her hope was for his safety and not getting hurt. How different that felt—she'd never worried about things like that with the other boys she'd dated—even William.

IT WAS A COLORFUL FALL AFTERNOON and the pep rally spirit was incredible. The band performed. Booster Club parents gave out popcorn and sodas at an improvised concession stand. As usual, each of the classes sat together and competed to see who could show the most spirit.

Jessie sat with Sandy, Christy and Claire. When it was the junior class's turn to cheer they stood and yelled: *Raise some hell, we want more kicks! Hooray for the Class of Sixty-six!* The stands were rocking as the team, dressed out in their football jerseys, walked onto the field. Behind them walked Coach, whose expression was a serious one.

The team sat in folding chairs along the sidelines facing the students. Jessie could tell by his smile when Carter located where she was sitting. Mike, the senior team captain, came to the microphone to rally the crowd. Jessie turned to find Fran behind her and saw that she was beaming with pride as Mike spoke. And she saw Sandy wave to Jack as he made his way to his seat not far from Carter.

Then someone appeared from nowhere and came bounding down the bleacher seats carrying the school banner high over his head. It was

Rick! Jack typically carried the school flag, but since he was on the team, Missy had asked Rick to fill in. When he got to the junior section, he stopped to wave the flag back and forth while everyone cheered. Jessie avoided his gaze, pretending she didn't see him staring at her.

The cheerleaders led cheers, and everyone sang at the top of their lungs as the school band played the spirit songs and alma mater. After Terry, the quarterback, stepped up to ask for the support of the school at the game that night, Coach O'Connor came to the microphone. He stood silently for what seemed an eternity, gazing over the crowd and then the team. The student body finally quieted.

"Someone said to always challenge the limits rather than be limited by the challenge," he said. "Your years at Northwest and beyond will have its challenges. Never let those challenges limit you. Work hard. Meet them head on and your success as students, your success as players…" he looked back at the team seated behind him, "will never be limited! We are a team that faces all challenges. We are a team who trusts each other. We have worked hard. We are a team that will never be limited!"

The crowd came to their feet cheering, and the volume of his voice increased. "Go Tigers! Beat Fulton!" The students went wild, and the band played the fight song while the cheerleaders danced their routine. Jessie couldn't take her eyes off Carter. His smile gleamed as he stood and looked her way. The other players stood too, acknowledging the student body's support.

Everyone happily climbed over and down the bleacher steps and headed toward home to prepare for the game. Jessie looked back at the field and saw Coach talking to Terry, Mike, and Carter. Jack and the other players joined them. They looked at him seriously with obvious respect for what he was saying. Nodding their heads, they headed back to the team locker room. Jessie watched Coach's eyes follow Carter—he was important to Coach.

Carter caught Jessie's eye as they both walked to their separate destinations, and she beamed at him. In his hands was a jacket she didn't think she'd seen before.

Fran trotted up behind her. "Isn't it great? Carter earned his letter jacket. Coach gave it to him before they came out for the pep rally!" She bounced away to catch up with Mike.

It would be no problem for Jessie to sit where Carter had asked her to. At games, the Pep Club always sat together in front of the cheerleaders on the track. They held the school banners and made noise to boost the team. Everyone wore the purple and white team colors and a special student carried the school flag when the team entered the field. Club members passed out pom poms at the ticket gates and other tasks Missy assigned.

JESSIE HAD BEEN HESITANT WHEN SANDY told her that Rick would be picking them up to ride to the game, but decided that since Sandy would be along, it would be all right. But when Rick drove up in front of her house alone that evening, she was extra uncomfortable.

It was already chilly outside and Jessie was carrying her school blanket along with her Pep Club pom poms. She had spent extra time getting ready that evening, thinking only of Carter.

"You look amazing," said Rick. He took the pom poms and blanket from Jessie and placed them in the backseat.

"Thank you. Are we picking up Sandy next?"

"No. She is picking up the rest of the group. Something about they had somewhere to go before the game. They will meet us there."

Why didn't I know about this? thought Jessie, but she said nothing. Rick opened the door to his car with a courteous bow and her antenna went up even higher.

She saw her mother look through the kitchen window and acknowledge Rick's wave from the driveway. "I like your mom," he said. "Wish I could say the same for mine."

Rick had never talked much about his parents, but he had made sure to introduce himself to everyone else's parents and always displayed perfect manners. Jessie questioned his sincerity but had shaken it off.

When Jessie and her friends had entered high school, their parents had made a covenant. The girls had grown up together and their parents had come to know each other and had created their own special system for keeping up with the latest on all the girls and their potential dates. Some of the group made jokes about the parents and their rules. But everyone also knew that their rules often allowed them to blame their parents when they needed an excuse to avoid trouble.

So far, the group rules had worked, although some suspected they were not totally observed by everyone. There was no mention, for example, of "going too far" in the rules, but every parent had taken the lead in teaching his or her own daughter how to handle herself properly with a boy.

Jessie searched her mind for some help from the rules, but none had prepared her for a situation like this. Would the group have really planned something before the game without telling her?

Just then, she saw a movement in the corner of her eye. It was Claire standing in her yard. Jessie knew she was going to the game with Missy to help her with Pep Club duties, but she stepped away from Rick's car and walked toward her driveway. "Hey, Claire. Heading to the game? Need a ride?"

"Sure! Can Missy come, too? She would love to not have to drive!"

Jessie glanced at Rick, whose face had begun turning red. When Claire reached the car, Jessie pointed to the front seat. "There you go. I'll sit back here."

Missy joined them in a few minutes carrying a box of signs. "Great! Rick, I need your help with this box, and I found out we are short with help at the gate selling game programs. What a lifesaver!" Only Jessie could see Rick's glare in his rear-view mirror. Missy rattled on with all the details to expect about the game upon their arrival, while Rick brooded in the front seat.

All the Northwest football games were played in North Atlanta at Grady Stadium near Piedmont Park with overflow parking down neighboring streets. Except for Cheney Stadium on the south end of town, Grady was the only stadium in the area with lighting for nighttime games. The stadium was bordered with high walls with concrete seating flanking both sides of the field.

Posters were displayed on the fences promoting game sponsors and team banners. The largest Northwest sponsor banner was that of Dr. Frank Caldwell. Dr. Caldwell's son Tom was president of the junior class. When they approached the stadium, they could hear the band playing. Jessie could feel the excitement in the air as people filed through the gates from every direction. Parents, some wearing their son's jersey numbers on large lapel buttons, carried stadium seats and blankets.

Missy led Rick toward the stadium entrance carrying her box of programs and spirit ribbons to sell. Sandy and Christy, who had parked nearby, were walking toward the stadium. They met Jessie on the sidewalk, obviously upset. "Are you kidding me?" Christy said. "You asked Rick to tell us to meet you both here at the game tonight? Did you not think about how Sandy would feel?" Sandy stood silently beside her.

Jessie whirled around. "What? He told *me* you all had somewhere to go before the game and would meet us here!"

They turned as one to watch him walking ahead with Missy. But more conversation about Rick would have to wait. The Northwest High players' bus turned in through the back gate and the girls headed to their seats.

The Fulton team was getting off their bus and making their way toward the visitors' sideline. Once the players had finished their pregame warm up, there would be a formal entrance onto the field for both teams.

The girls made their way to the Northwest side where Rick and Missy were standing at the gates. A red car drove up near the ticket office and a woman jumped out of the car and dashed toward where they stood. Frantically waving her hands, she advanced on Rick, obviously in protest. Rick handed Missy the banner and walked away. The woman continued to make circles around him. Sandy leaned over and whispered to Jessie. "That's Mrs. Fields. Rick's mother. I met her last week."

The team began to amble onto the field. As each player stepped onto the sideline grass, they came alive and began to jump and stretch, and the fans could sense their energy. Jessie was excited to see Carter and she stood up to make it easier for him to find her in the stands. Carter smiled and waved and turned back toward Coach O'Connor, who was giving the players instructions. Jessie saw Michael and Robby warming up on the sidelines, too. She was proud to see her childhood friends in the starting lineup.

Also there were other assistant coaches, student trainers, Dr. Caldwell, who was also the team doctor, and the team chaplain, Rev. Hamilton. Dr. and Mrs. Caldwell were both involved with the school PTA and Booster Club and Rev. Hamilton had become close to the whole team— his presence was a calming influence among the players and their parents. Mike and Terry circled Carter and Jessie could tell they were anxious for the game to begin. Carter appeared calm, stretching and bending in preparation for the kickoff.

The band began to play again, and Jessie glanced around for Rick. He would need to take his place with the flag soon and she needed to keep an eye on him. About that time, Missy skipped through the crowd with Steve, another neighborhood friend. He was carrying the school flag instead. Rick was nowhere to be seen. Missy waved toward the Pep Club seats as the cheerleaders began to rev up the crowd. The stadium was full, and late arrivals were scrambling for empty seats.

The game finally kicked off, and as halftime approached, it was clear that Carter would be the star of the night. Every time he ran off the field, Coach ran to him, patting him on the helmet, and then Mike would join them to plan their next move. Jessie could hear Fran cheering for Mike several rows over.

At halftime, Fran made her way over to her. "See that guy near the press box in the white shirt with purple sleeves? That's Carter's brother, Bobby. He's always at Carter's games." Bobby sat alone high above the student section. Jessie kept an eye on him during the second half, glad someone from Carter's family was there to see him play.

The game ended 17-0. Northwest had held Fulton to a shutout, Carter had scored both touchdowns, and his yardage in the game had broken a school record! Jessie looked around for Bobby and found him on the sidelines with Rev. Hamilton.

Coach was still talking to the players as fans left, honking their horns in victory. Some Fulton students were angry, but others congratulated the Northwest fans. Missy shouted to Jessie and Claire for them to wait for her while she gathered her box of pep club items. "Rick's mom had a fit and she made him go home," she said when she reached them. "So, Steve is going to give us a ride home. There's a victory party at Tom

Caldwell's house. We're all invited and the team will be there." Claire and Tom were dating, and she was excited about being with him at his home.

It was hard to match the Caldwell family's love for Northwest. Their Arden Drive home sat on a large lot. Perfect for parties, school meetings or any large gathering, it had a beautiful kitchen opening to a large den with plenty of outdoor entertaining space. Plus, their position with the school, the PTA and the Booster Club checked all the boxes on the parent-approved parties rules list.

Jack waved at them from the field as the team headed toward their bus. Carter's brother Bobby jogged beside him. She was disappointed that Carter hadn't seen her, but at the last second, he turned back toward her. He mouthed the words "Tomorrow night!" and disappeared onto the bus.

Jessie turned to Missy and Claire. "Will y'all drop me off at home?"

"Don't you want to see Carter?" asked Missy, teasing her. It was obvious that a rumor about Jessie and Carter had begun to circulate.

"Yes, but I already know he won't be there." Jessie paused. "I'm sure glad we don't have to worry about riding home with Rick, though."

Missy pulled Jessie aside. "Rick's mom said something about a medication he hadn't taken. He got very defensive with her and I could tell she was upset with him. I walked away from both of them, but I could tell that neither of them was happy. Both eventually stormed away and got in their cars."

Cars waving purple and white flags in victory were slowing leaving the stadium and Jessie stood in the parking lot, reflecting on all that had happened—the evening had been a night of mixed emotions. Her day had begun with excitement for the future with Carter. He'd received his letterman jacket and been the star of the night. But Rick's erratic behavior had left her uneasy. And she was disappointed that she wouldn't be able to celebrate with Carter at the Caldwell's but she would celebrate with him the next night.

The friends slowly made their way to Steve's car. They waved at Fran as she passed by, heading to pick Mike up back at school.

"*They* won't be at the Caldwell's, either," said Claire.

"Why not?" asked Jessie. "I thought Mike and Tom were good friends."

"They are. But when it comes to Fran…those two seem to always have their *own* kind of party." She exchanged glances with Steve, who said nothing, but nodded his head knowingly.

He helped load the Pep Club's supplies in his trunk. "That was a great game tonight! And Missy, thanks for asking me to carry the flag. That was fun. I bet Fulton will be upset with another defeat by us. Some of their guys were looking for trouble after the game."

CARTER SAT IN THE BACK OF the bus as the team headed back to school. He knew he would have to shower quickly and then rush to Fulton to play in their band. He thought about Jessie and smiled. Seeing Jessie cheering for him in the stands—and the way he'd played—made the night extra special. Little did Jessie know how much she had had to do with how well he had played.

Coach made his way down the aisle complimenting each player. "Amazing night, Carter! Way to keep your head in the game!"

"Thanks, Coach. It's a special weekend in a lotta ways!"

STEVE DROPPED JESSIE OFF AT HOME and took off with Missy and Claire back up to Howell Mill for a shortcut to Tom's. Her parents, who had heard the news of the Northwest victory on the late news, met her at the door.

"You rode home with Steve?" asked Madeline. "What happened to Rick?"

"He needed to head home, so Steve gave Missy, Claire and me a ride." Jessie knew that her parents and Steve's were good friends—there wouldn't be any more questions.

She headed up to her bedroom and lay awake for a while before dropping off to sleep. Saturday would not come soon enough.

Chapter Ten

Jessie woke the next morning to the aroma of bacon and biscuits drifting up the stairs. She heard her parents talking and knew her father was helping her mother in the kitchen—unlike some of her friends' fathers, he had made a commitment to be home with the family on weekends.

Jessie pulled on her robe and went downstairs to find her mother's "special breakfast" on the table. She made her plate with two pieces of bacon and one of her mother's buttermilk biscuits, which she took from a basket lined with a floral cloth napkin.

"Who's doing the devotional this morning?" asked Madeline. A thoughtful start each day was a foundation for the Reynolds family.

Ladd read a passage from a small book on the table and bowed his head. Along with the blessing for the meal, he prayed for loved ones and those with special concerns—including their church staff. Jessie secretly said a prayer for Carter and hope for their day ahead. She still wished she could have gone with him to the dance at Fulton.

She took a bite of the bacon and smiled at her father, who had opened the morning's Atlanta Constitution. He flipped through the pages and finally settled on the sports section. Jessie glanced at the paper. At the top of the page was a headline: *Powell Sets Record at Northwest.*

Jessie almost dropped the pitcher of orange juice. "That's Carter! I have a date with him tonight!"

Her father lowered the paper and looked at her. "You what?" Madeline stepped behind her husband to read the article.

"*You* know," said Jessie. "He was the one on the phone this week. Fran introduced us."

Just in time to save her, the phone rang. "I'll get it," said Jessie. She jumped up and ran to the hallway table. Hoping it was Carter, she answered as happily as she could.

"Hello and congratulations! You were amazing last night!"

A low voice answered back. It wasn't Carter at all. It was Rick. "I just wanted to let you know I am leaving school. I thought you cared, and I know you don't think *I* am amazing, but you will! This is not the end of us. This is not the end." Before she could speak again, Jessie heard a dial tone.

Her mother appeared in the hall. "Who was that?"

Jessie swallowed hard. "It was Rick. He said he was leaving school." She left out the part about his creepy voice and saying he would see her again.

Mrs. Reynolds frowned. "I wonder what that's about."

Jessie shrugged. "I'll ask Sandy. She'll probably know."

Her mother stepped back and looked at her. "So, this Carter you say you're going out with tonight. He plays football and Coach O'Connor seems to think well of him. What else do you know about him?"

"Well, he's a senior. He got his letter jacket at the pep rally on Friday."

She figured it was not the time to say anything about his parents...or his band.

Jessie's father came to the door of the kitchen. "What time's your date?"

"Six o'clock, I think?"

"You don't know? That doesn't sound very respectful," said her mom.

"Yesterday was a whirlwind at school. You know, with all the excitement of the game. We kept being interrupted at lunch by Missy and others wishing him good luck, so we never got to settle on a time."

Once again, the telephone rang. Jessie's relief that it was Carter was immeasurable.

"How about dinner tonight?" he said. "Pick you up at six?"

"Yeah, that's fine."

"You don't sound very happy. You okay?"

"Sure. My day is perfect now that you've called." She paused. "By the way, my dad was reading the paper this morning. Coach said some nice things about you. How are *you*?"

"Actually, I'm a little sore, but we can talk about that tonight. Yeah, it was a pretty good game. Coach said there was a scout from Grady at the game. We play them next week." He paused. "Seven Steers okay for tonight?"

Jessie smiled. "Sure, I love Seven Steers. The one on Roswell?" Her thoughts immediately turned to what outfit she would wear.

"Yes. And after that, sort of a surprise. I want to take you to one of my favorite places." Jessie could almost feel the warmth in his voice.

Seven Steers was a popular restaurant in Atlanta with seven different burger choices. There were two locations—one in Buckhead where Roswell met Peachtree near the Zesto and one downtown on Peachtree not far from the Fox Theater. Jessie thought they would probably have to wait for a table on a Saturday night.

The afternoon went by and soon the countdown to six o'clock began. Jessie didn't want to keep Carter waiting even a second. She jumped in the shower, put on her makeup, and donned a skirt, blouse and sweater that coordinated perfectly with navy flats newly purchased at Davison's. She removed a pearl necklace that her parents had given her from her jewelry box and slipped her Grandmother Danby's pearl ring on her right hand.

She thought about Rick's phone call that morning and then put it out of her mind—she would check with Sandy later. She glanced out her dormer window just in time to see Carter's Buick pull in front of the house. The doorbell rang and Jessie ran out of her bedroom door, stopping on the stairs to go back and grab her purse. She headed down the stairs again to hear her dad's surprised voice.

"Wow! That's a shiner!"

As she stepped into the living room she saw Carter offer his hand to her dad. "Carter Powell," he said. "And, yes, sir. Things got a bit rough last night." There was a small bandage over Carter's eye and Jessie winced when she saw him. *When had that happened?*

Carter nervously touched his brow. "I'll need to duck a little faster next time."

Jessie's father gestured for Carter to enter. "Come in. And congratulations on the win."

Bandage and all, Jessie had never seen him look so handsome. She joined him near the front door and looked at her father.

"You two be careful tonight then," he said. "Don't be out late." He glanced at Carter. "It looks like you could use some rest."

The engine hummed as they pulled out of the neighborhood. The long front seat of the Buick seemed endless—Jessie slid closer to Carter as they took a left onto Northside and Carter cleared his throat. "We have lots to talk about, Jess. I know my eye didn't make the best first impression on your parents."

They made their way down Paces Ferry and took a short cut into the Seven Steers' parking lot, which was packed. Jessie straightened her skirt as Carter walked around to open the passenger door. She felt the gentle touch of his hand on her back as he guided her toward the entrance.

People were sitting, standing, waiting everywhere for their name to be called for a table. Jessie searched for a place to wait when the greeter approached them. "Right this way, Mr. Powell. Your table is ready."

Carter grinned when he saw her surprise. "My friend Lucas works here," he said. Lucas had made all the arrangements for Carter including choosing a table that would be just right for them. The red checkered tablecloths and candles glowing on each table were a perfect setting. A single red rose in a beautiful glass vase adorned their table.

Carter held the chair for Jessie and she took her seat, looking up at him to see him wink and smile. After the hostess left their menus, Jessie couldn't wait any longer. "What happened to your eye?"

About that time, a voice boomed across the restaurant. "Carter! Great game last night! How you doing, man?" They looked up to see Dr. Caldwell coming toward the table. "We missed you at the house after the game," he said. He smiled at Jessie. "You too, young lady."

He looked back at Carter and stopped. "Whoa, what happened to you, Carter? I know that didn't happen at the game."

Carter sidestepped the question. "We missed being at the party, too, sir. It was a tough fight but glad it turned out like it did for the team."

Dr. Caldwell placed his hand on Carter's forehead and pushed his head back. "Let me take a look at that. You might want to come by the office on Monday and let me check it."

"Yes, sir, I will."

Dr. Caldwell waved the server over. "Give them whatever they want. It's on me."

"Thank you, sir, but—"

"It's the least I can do since you missed the party and big celebration." The doctor went back to his table. Carter shook his head in disbelief.

Jessie smiled. "The table is perfect."

Carter shook his head. "I'm, sorry Jess. This was not how I imagined our date."

She smiled warmly. "I'm not sorry. Nothing could change my feelings about tonight. You know I want to know what happened to your eye, though. You were pretty quiet driving here. Does it hurt?"

"Not too much. Last night was a great night. That game was amazing, and Coach was proud of us. That was important to me. He has been more than a teacher and coach." Carter touched his eye. "I got this after the game. I went to the dance at Fulton all pumped to play with the band, but a crowd of Fulton guys met me in the parking lot. They recognized me from the game and things got a little rough. It was as if they were waiting for me." Jessie nodded in concern and gestured for him to continue.

"The guys from the band were just inside preparing for the dance to start. Fortunately, Pete had come out to grab another amplifier when he saw the pack. The rest of the band was out there in no time to back me up, but not before I got this sucker punch out of nowhere. There were some teachers and parents maybe, and an off-duty policeman. They broke it up before things got out of hand. A parent saw the whole thing and one Fulton guy is in some major trouble.

"It was tough to go inside as if nothing happened and do our set, but we did. I have to admit it was not our best performance." He paused. "I know this will get back to Coach. He keeps preaching to the team about keeping our noses clean, but I couldn't avoid it."

Jessie wanted to give him a hug right there, but she just sipped her water and listened.

"I'll talk to Coach about the fight on Monday. I didn't want to bother him over the weekend and take away from our win."

"I'm sure once you tell Coach what happened, he'll understand."

Carter placed his hand over hers. "Hey, let's change the subject. Let me tell you about my favorite place."

In her mind's eye, Jessie imagined a special park or spot by the river. Several places on the Chattahoochee were known to be the hangout these days for the senior class. She was surprised when he said, "It's called the Crow's Nest." His eyes lit up.

"Our band has three great guys. They've already finished high school. Crow goes to Clemson and Pete is at Tech. Larry works for his dad. They needed a drummer. Bobby knows Larry and told him about me playing drums. After they heard me play, they called me in to join them last year. We practice when we can, and Crow makes it all happen. You'll meet him tonight at the Nest."

"Crow?"

Carter laughed at her expression. "Some neighborhood kid started calling him that when they were kids and it stuck."

Once their food arrived, the two settled into their own world. They talked about everything—friends and school, the game, his drums and her dream of being a teacher. They talked about music and how she had taken piano for so many years and loved singing in the church choirs and chorus at school. He talked about teaching himself to play the drums on a practice pad in his basement, the pick-up games at Memorial Park with the Barfield brothers, and his relationship with Coach. Jessie listened intently to Carter's every word. She had so much to tell him and so much to learn about him.

"And Bobby?" she said, although she already knew much about him.

Carter learned back in his chair. "Oh, he's my older brother. We live together now since my Grandfather Crawford died. The three of us were very close. Bobby and I still are." Carter talked some about growing up and fishing with his grandfather. "We called him Papa Ford." He said nothing about his parents.

When Carter asked for the check, the server told him it had already been paid. They looked over to thank the Caldwells, but they were already gone. He stood to help Jessie with her chair and picked up the vase with the red rose. "This is for you."

"For me? It's beautiful!"

On the way to the car, Carter put his arm around her, and she wrapped her arm around his waist. He squeezed her gently and Jessie thought of how safe she felt with him. Carter seemed to have a maturity greater than other boys his age. His manners, his thoughtfulness, his courtesy and respect were evident. She smiled and mentally added a few more check marks on her "list." *Had he been enrolled like she was in Mrs. Bruner's sixth grade ballroom dance and etiquette classes?*

They headed back by way of Peachtree Battle. For an instant, she thought he had changed his mind and was taking her home, but they passed Longwood and turned onto McKinley and then Wilson. The Crow's Nest was just one street over from her house!

Carter parked in front of a brick cottage-style home with yellow mums in planters on the front porch. Several other cars were in the driveway and more stretched down the street beyond. As they approached the house, Jessie heard the faint sound of music. A woman waved at Carter through the living room window.

He waved back. "That's Crow's mom. She's the best. So is his dad. You're going to love them."

They made their way down the driveway toward the basement level. The back yard was neatly cut. Pruned shrubbery ran along a privacy fence. The music became louder and she could see people slow dancing inside.

There was something official in the way Carter took her hand and escorted her through the doors. Hugs and hand slaps greeted them. "Man, you look better than you did last night!" said a guy who jumped up from the couch to join them.

Carter grasped Jessie's hand and introduced her. "This is Crow."

"Glad to meet you," said the young man. "You sure you know what you're getting yourself into with this guy?" His joking lightened Jessie's uneasiness. "Welcome. Carter is family, and this is home for us."

She surveyed the room. Above a large white sectional sofa in the corner was a wooden sign on which "Crow's Nest" had been painted. On the opposite wall was a shelving unit with a stereo and gigantic speakers. Posters of famous bands were tacked on other walls with more shelves accommodating an impressive number of LPs, 45s, and reel-to-reel tapes. An alcove housed a refrigerator beneath steps that led to the upstairs. In the middle of the room were instrument cases, amplifiers, microphone stands, and a set of drums. Two small windows near the low ceiling opened to the base of the driveway through which it was easy to see when someone was making their way around to the entrance.

Pete, another of the band members bounded up, and Carter introduced Jessie to him. He pointed to Carter's eye. "You should have seen the other guy!" he said.

The music began to play again, and Carter whispered in her ear. "It's not as bad as it sounds. I'm still trying to handle this whole football and band thing. Playing on Friday nights isn't easy."

A girl came over and introduced herself. "Hi, I'm Brandi."

"This is Crow's other half," said Carter appreciatively. "She looks after us guys." Carter explained that Brandi and Crow had been dating for several years. Jessie could tell they were the couple everyone loved and trusted, whatever the situation.

Brandi showed her around the room, even showing her a small corner bathroom. "Crow's parents wanted everyone to have a safe place to go whenever they wanted to hang out. They helped Crow fix it up with full permission to invite any friends who would behave and be respectful of it. The band practices here, and the neighbors never complain. One neighbor even donated the white sectional over there."

She pulled Jessie aside. "I wondered when Carter would find his match. You should know that he has *never* brought a date here before. He's very much his own person, you know."

"I am beginning to get that impression," said Jessie.

"We have all tried to fix him up with someone, but he always gave the same answer. 'I'll know when the right person comes along.'"

Someone put a Righteous Brothers album on the stereo and couples went back to quietly dancing. Jessie's heart pounded when Carter came to her and took her hand. He leaned over to touch his cheek to hers and they fit together perfectly. They swayed back and forth to the music, neither missing a step. When the song ended, Carter led her away from the floor to a corner.

"How do you like the Nest?"

"I love it! I see why it's your favorite place."

Another half-hour passed and people began to leave. Jessie and Carter lingered to help clean up. On the way out, she told Crow she wanted to thank his parents. Crow looked at Carter and back at her. "You'll be able to thank them later. I have a feeling we will be seeing a lot more of you here."

The night air was cooler. When they got into the car, Carter leaned over to the backseat and retrieved the letter jacket he had proudly received the day before and placed it around her. They were soon stopped in front of Jessie's house. The yellow porch light was on and she could see light coming from the dormer in her room. They both sat staring into space—both obviously wished the night would not end.

Jessie looked down at the rose in her hands. "I've never felt like this before. The dinner. The rose. The Crow's Nest. Like I've always known Crow and Brandi. Like I've known you forever."

Carter touched the vase. "Papa Ford taught me and Bobby that women should be treated like flowers. Gently and respectfully. He taught me a lot of things." He reached out and took her hand.

"What else did Papa Ford teach you?"

"To make my own way in this world and never take anything for granted. And so much more. I wish you could have known him."

"Me, too." Jessie glanced toward the front door. She knew her mother would not sleep until she heard her key in the lock. She slipped the jacket from her shoulders. "I better go in."

Carter walked her to the door. She glanced at the porch light—they silently agreed that their first kiss would not be in a spotlight. Carter softly released her hand and backed away. "Sleep well."

As she watched him walk toward the car, Jessie thought about a discussion of Kismet they'd had in English class. Until now, she had not felt its clarity. The stars were surely smiling down on them. Carter glanced back several times and she returned his smile as she closed the door.

Jessie turned off the lamp on the stereo, the signal to her parents and the neighbors that all was well. She glanced out the living room window and observed a car on the street slowly pass the house. She heard her parent's bedroom door open with a creak.

"Everything okay?" said her mother.

Jessie felt a warmth wash over her. "Everything's more than okay," she whispered, and headed up the stairs.

Chapter Eleven

Jessie woke in a cocoon of happiness and got out of bed to get ready for church and an afternoon ride to Woodstock to visit Granny Reynolds, her dad's mother.

She turned to see the pink stuffed dog from the fair. William would be at church. Their usual routine was to sit with Robin and Mark in the balcony during the worship service. What would she say to him?

Her thoughts turned to Carter. She had told him about her Sunday routine and was glad to hear that church was important to him as well. He'd talked about the football team chaplain recruited by Coach O'Connor she had seen on the sidelines at the football game. Rev. Hamilton was also the minister of the church he and Bobby attended.

Jessie could see Memorial Park from her third-floor window. The leaves on the trees were falling now—making the view even better. Carter had told her that he planned to join some friends for a pickup football game at the park after church and finishing his chores at home. She would check for signs of a game when she returned home from church.

Robin stood waiting for Jessie before the beginning of Sunday School and waved at her as she approached. "We missed you at the movies last night. William said you had other plans. What's that about?"

Jessie looked around to see Mark standing near the door to the church and leaned toward her friend. "I don't know," she whispered. "Things changed once school started. He didn't call every night like he did this summer, and even when he did, we never talked about anything important."

"But you and William were the talk of the group this summer. All through our choir tour week in July, and even on the hayride to Stone Mountain!"

They looked up to see William join Mark and started walking toward them. When they entered the church, she followed Robin and Mark to the balcony. William stayed behind and chose a seat on the opposite side of the sanctuary.

Jessie joyfully sang the hymns that morning, full of the contentment she felt about Carter. A message of love and hope selected by the minister seemed chosen especially for her.

After church, Robin walked with Jessie to the parking lot and Jessie told her about Carter. Robin laughed. "Why not date them both? I would!"

Jessie thought for a moment. Dating more than one person at a time was not for her. "I couldn't do that to either one. It's not that simple," she said. "Would you really do that?"

Robin smiled. "Naw. But it sounds fantastic, though! Boys do it all the time!"

"I hope William and I can still be good friends."

Robin stopped her. "So, you've already made up your mind. You've had more dates *and* boyfriends than I have. I guess it's like my sisters say. You know when you know."

Jessie turned toward the car where her parents were waiting. "I think your sisters are right. I've got to go, but I'll see you at choir this evening. Who knows? William may be relieved!"

"Yeah, right. But I don't think so."

On the way to Woodstock after Sunday dinner, Jessie's parents were full of questions about Carter and their date. She told them about eating at Seven Steers and the special rose and vase Carter had waiting for her. They were impressed that Dr. Caldwell had insisted on picking up their tab. Jessie kept her explanations short to avoid any negatives—she would wait to bring up the Crow's Nest.

Jessie's father was the eldest son in a large family of six brothers and two sisters. Most of his siblings still lived close to their homeplace in Woodstock. His mother now lived with Jessie's Uncle Gid and family on the town's Main Street, and there were always lots of cousins of all ages at the Sunday gatherings to play and wave at the passing cars.

One of the older among her cousins, Jessie sat dreaming on the porch swing, watching her younger cousins play tag. An amazing week lay ahead and she hoped Carter would call before she left for choir practice.

WHEN THEY GOT BACK HOME, JESSIE ran to her upstairs window. A few cars remained at Memorial Park, but Carter's wasn't among them. There was just enough time to change before leaving for Sunday evening activities. His call would have to wait until later.

Jessie grabbed the car keys from the hook in the hallway as she rushed out the door. Her parents had cautioned her to always be smart when driving alone downtown. Having made the trip to church many times, she knew all the one-way streets and shortcuts, but this time she took the longer way so she could think about what she would say to William. No scenario would make the end result any easier.

After parking her car, Jessie gathered her thoughts and made her way up to the rehearsal room. Robin met her outside the choir room when she arrived. She seemed upset.

"Are you okay?" asked Jessie.

"No. Mr. James is going to make some kind of announcement tonight. The rumor is he is leaving the church!"

Mr. James came out of his office next to the choir room and walked to the director's stand. Robin went to her seat in the alto section, and Jessie took hers at the front of the soprano section. William and Mark had joined the basses in the back.

The director struggled to smile. He took a deep breath. "Choir. This has been a difficult day for me and my family. You have been so special to me, and I asked the staff to please let me talk to you first before I announce this to the whole church." Jessie turned to look at William and he met her gaze with a similar look of concern. She glanced over to Robin and could see tears welling up in her eyes.

Mr. James continued. "Being here with all of you has meant a lot to me. As many of you have already learned, I have made a hard decision. There are and will be hard decisions to make in your lives too. Your future and your dreams will be filled with them, and you will have to trust your head and your heart.

"You have taught me a lot and I will forever be truly grateful. But one of my dreams has always been to teach music on the college level. Out of the blue, I've received an offer in North Carolina to do that. It was not something I had pursued, believe me, but it is an unexpected dream. After much prayer, I have accepted the offer…with the stipulation that I not begin until January. We have some beautiful music to share for Christmas, and you have worked so hard to learn it."

The mood in the room shifted from enthusiasm to gloom. Jessie was sad. She had learned so much from Mr. James about music and so much more. He shared such a zest for life! At the same time, she could relate now to his words of making life's decisions and trusting her head and heart.

The room was quiet. Several of the girls next to Jessie began to cry softly. Mr. James opened a notebook on the music stand in front of him. "There will be times for goodbyes later, and I want to stay in touch with each and every one of you. Okay? Let's make this a celebration. Your folders are under your seats. Let's work on the carol arrangement."

Everyone slowly took out their folders. Jessie made eye contact with Mr. James and managed a smile. He was the person who had more than encouraged her music interest and singing and made choir so much fun. She thought about what it would be like after he left. What would happen to the choir?

When practice was done, everyone lined up to hug Mr. James as they left the room. He wrapped his arms around both Jessie and Robin. "We'll talk soon, okay?" They both nodded and headed to the stairwell.

Mark caught up with them at the bottom of the stairs. "Let's meet up at the drugstore." The drug store at the Howell House, just a block up Peachtree was the hangout for many of the teens from church, a central place they could easily get together. Robin went to Cross Keys High near Brookhaven, Mark attended Grady High downtown, and William went to Dykes High, in different directions from Jessie's school district. In the past, many of the choir members had gone to the drugstore to skip church. When Mr. James had joined the staff, he'd encouraged them to be in their proper places and meet there after church.

Jessie stopped. "Somehow, it just doesn't seem right going to the drugstore tonight. I can only think of Mr. James now when I see the Howell House."

Robin pulled Jessie aside. "Well, let's go somewhere else. I think William is already thinking the two of you might not be a thing anymore."

"I don't think I can deal with that right now. I'm sad about Mr. James leaving."

"I know. Me, too. But William read a lot more into you already having plans Saturday night. He told Mark he realized he had probably waited too long to make things work with you. This might be your best chance to make things right!"

Mark and William joined them. Turning to them both, Jessie said, "I'm sorry. I need to go home. I hope you understand."

William followed her. "Jessie, wait. I'll call you. Mr. James has been a good friend to me, too. I sure thought tonight was going to be different."

She opened her car door and turned to face him. "Mr. James was right about decisions and making hard choices and we need to listen to our heads and trust our hearts." She paused. "Sorry, but I've got to go, William."

Warm tears flowed down her face as she drove toward home. Were they tears of sadness about Mr. James or of saying goodbye to the relationship she had known all along had only been one of friendship with William? Or something else?

She turned at 14th Street and pulled into the parking lot of the Waterworks. Wiping the tears from her face, she looked at the lake near the picnic shelter, and remembered flirting with William there at the youth cookout. Although she felt sure of her relationship with Carter, she felt strangely sad too. The emotions of the day and weekend had caught up with her.

Tears welled up again in Jessie's eyes when she told her mother the news about Mr. James, and Mrs. Reynolds put her arms around her daughter. "Jessie, you will find that so much in life will be about change. One thing for sure is that change will come, and it's not always bad. So often it can be good. Think about it. You are growing and changing every day. All our experiences change the way we see the world."

"Thanks, Mom," said Jessie. She thought of Carter. "Any phone calls while I was gone?"

"Oh, yes. I think it was a girl named Fran."

Jessie felt her hopefulness deflate. "Did she leave a message?" Her mother shook her head.

When Jessie reached her room, her eyes fell on the vase on her dresser and she smiled. She would have to wait to talk to Carter. She would see him in the morning, and everything would be better.

Chapter Twelve

The Reynolds family sat around the breakfast table. "I'm sure we will be discussing at the next deacons' meeting what to expect about the change in the music ministry, Jessie," said Mr. Reynolds. "We will miss Mr. James. At least he will be here through Christmas."

"Let's have him and his wife for dinner before he leaves," said her mother.

On the way to school, Jessie wanted to share her feelings about Carter and Mr. James, but Claire talked non-stop about her weekend with Tom. They parked in a student lot near the Northside Methodist Church and made their way into school. "Our next game will be even more exciting with Grady," said Claire. "Tom says their defense will be tough on Carter."

"I know Coach will probably have some intense practices this week," said Jessie. "I'm sure Carter is up for it, though."

The hallways were buzzing. Jessie saw Jack and several players on the team in what seemed to be a serious discussion, but Carter wasn't among them. She searched the hallway but saw no sign of him.

She made her way to her locker and felt a hand on her arm. It was Sandy. "Something's up. No one has seen Rick for several days."

"That's strange," said Jessie. "He called me Saturday morning and told me that he was leaving. I thought maybe he was calling you and all the group." A shiver ran down her spine when she remembered of the sound of his voice on the phone.

Sandy frowned. "No, he didn't call me. What did he say?"

"Not a lot. Just that it wasn't the end. I was *sure* you would know what he was talking about."

The morning announcements trickled out over speakers in the hallway. Coach O'Connor whisked by the girls. His face was solemn and Jessie assumed he had seen Carter's eye by now and word had reached him about the fight at Fulton.

Mrs. Laney and other teachers followed Coach into the faculty lounge, along with Principal Kelley. That's odd, thought Jessie. Faculty meetings are usually *after* school.

Fran rushed up. "I tried to call you last night! Why didn't you call me back?"

"You didn't leave a message for me to call. We had something happen at church and..."

"Well there was something happening here, too! Jessie, Carter is in trouble. Big trouble."

Jessie and Fran entered their homeroom and took their seats. Jessie shook her head in confusion. "You mean the fight Friday night?"

"No. It's not about any fight."

Mrs. Horton stood in front of the homeroom. She held a piece of paper in her hand. "Class, I need your attention."

Jessie wanted to ask Fran what she was talking about, but Mrs. Horton continued. "Our Monday announcements will be delayed so we can have a discussion. It seems there was some damage at Fulton High School over the weekend. Some windows were broken and paint was thrown on their activity bus." Fran found Jessie's eyes.

"The police are investigating, so if anyone knows anything about this, it will be best if you see Mr. Kelley right away." She surveyed the class, making eye contact with every student.

Jessie looked around the room in disbelief. She couldn't imagine who would do such a thing. Northwest had won the game. Why would anyone want to cause trouble?

The first period bell rang and Fran hurried to Jessie's desk. "Jessie, they think Carter did it."

"I was *with* Carter Saturday night. He told me about the fight at Fulton Friday night and how those guys jumped him at the dance."

As she walked toward her next class, Fran stayed with her. The two girls turned toward the main office. Through the windows, they saw Carter standing inside with his brother Bobby beside him. "Carter has been *accused* of doing it, Jessie," said Fran. "That's why I tried to call you!" Just then, Dr. Caldwell passed by Jessie and went straight through the principal's door, closing it behind him.

Numb, Jessie made her way to art class. She could hear the talk and whispers about Carter and the vandalism and finally, Mr. Baker clapped his hands. "All right, class. I know our week is starting off with some excitement, but let's see if we can make some sense of it all with your projects."

Jack motioned Jessie to their work table and she took her place across from him. He leaned toward her and whispered. "Carter wouldn't have done it, Jessie."

Mr. Baker walked down the aisle and stopped by their table. "What is your direction, Jessie?"

Jessie looked down at an abstract piece on canvas. It was one she had begun to paint when Mr. Baker had asked the students the week before to "listen to the silence." Jessie looked up at Jack, searching for words.

"Jessie is working on something special," he said.

Mr. Baker looked at Jack and then at Jessie. "Yes, I'm sure she is."

The teacher went on to the next table and Jessie whispered back to Jack. "You know about Carter?"

"Yes, Jess. And he's innocent. The whole team knows it. Coach will get to the bottom of it, but it doesn't look good for Carter playing this weekend."

Mr. Baker reappeared at the table. "I was in the meeting in the faculty lounge this morning. I read in the *Tiger Tales* newspaper about you and Mr. Powell in the *Social Limelight* column, Miss Reynolds. Word travels fast around here." He paused and made sure he made eye contact with her. "We have to face our problems. Otherwise, they will consume us."

Jessie nodded and he continued. "Once things settle down a bit, you'll have a better perspective." Mr. Baker pointed to the framed newspaper article about the Paris plane crash. "That visual on the wall is a daily reminder to me. Whatever we encounter in life, find someone, or some *thing* that will help you keep life's ups and downs in perspective."

When the bell rang, Jessie put away her art board and wandered into the hall, almost bumping into Mrs. Laney. Her adviser pulled her to the side. "I heard you and Carter Powell are dating, Jessie. He's accused of the windows and the paint at Fulton."

Jessie's defense was quick. "Carter wouldn't do such a thing. He just wouldn't."

"Mr. Kelley was called and told about the fight before the dance. Then some girl called the school and said Carter damaged the Fulton property."

"What girl?"

Mrs. Laney seemed to ignore her question. "They think it happened late Saturday night. Someone started talking about a fight at the school dance, and Carter's name came up. They found some purple paint on Carter's letter jacket when the police went to his house yesterday. It was in the backseat of his car." She looked at Jessie with sympathy. "I know this is disappointing to you, Jessie."

"No, Mrs. Laney!" I *held* that jacket Saturday night. He is so proud of it and had just received it from Coach before the pep rally. The team would know how proud he is of it. He would never risk getting paint on it. I know he didn't do it!"

"Just wait and let's see how the day goes. Carter's brother is here and it sounds like Dr. Caldwell has spoken to the police and is looking into it, too. You know how much he cares about the team. Try not to worry. These things always work themselves out."

Jessie knew pleading Carter's case to Mrs. Laney wasn't going to help. She made her way to Miss Spearman's gym class. She changed into her PE uniform and lined up with the others to stretch and choose teams for volleyball. When a match began, Jessie watched the gym door hoping to see someone pass the doorway for a clue of what was happening to Carter. The net was high for Jessie's short frame, but she worked hard to make the plays for her team. She took her frustrations out on the ball.

Miss Spearman teased her about her hard returns. "When do you want to try out for the team, Miss Reynolds? You are playing exceptionally well today."

Jessie walked to the back line to serve and saw Coach walk briskly across the gym. Carter followed him through the door and headed toward the athletic office. He caught Jessie's eye and raised his hand, signalling for her not to approach him.

Jessie headed to the locker room to change and could hear the girls on the other side of the lockers whispering about Carter. *This can't be happening*, she thought.

Sandy was waiting for her in the hallway. "Rick's not here."

For Jessie, the situation with Rick paled in comparison to the accusation about Carter, but she tried to focus on her friend.

"I don't understand it," said Sandy. "Everything was fine and all of sudden, he is like a different person. That story about meeting us at the game and picking you up? Friday night, he acted as if he hardly knew me."

Jessie walked at a zombie-like pace toward the cafeteria. "Sorry, Sandy. There are a *lot* of confusing things happening right now."

The football players were grouped at the team table deep in their discussion. Fran waved her over to her table. Jessie laid her lunch sack on the table and sat down. "How did *you* find out about it?"

"Mike called to tell me the police showed up at Carter's house. That's when I called you."

Jessie shook her head. "I need to talk to Carter."

What a difference a day made! Jessie thought lunch on Monday would be a celebration over the Friday victory, but the mood was subdued throughout the cafeteria. The team was huddled as if it was fourth down with yards to go. After a few minutes, Jack left the team table and came over. "We haven't heard anything more, Jessie." He glanced at her uneaten food. "You better eat. The bell will ring soon."

Jessie stared at her lunch. She couldn't eat a bite.

When the B session lunch bell rang, Jessie headed toward Coach's algebra class. He watched her as she approached and stopped her at the door. "No use asking me what's going on, Miss Reynolds. Carter is under suspension and won't be playing Friday night. I thought I knew him better." His voice matched the disappointment on his face.

Jessie looked up at the coach. "There's got to be another explanation. Carter wouldn't do those things. I know it. Those Fulton guys came after him Friday night, and he was fine Saturday night. He was so proud of his jacket and excited about this week's game." She struggled to keep the tears from filling her eyes. "He wouldn't do anything to disappoint you. I just know it!"

Warmth flooded the coach's eyes. "Dr. Caldwell is handling things with Principal Kelley and the police. They'll get to the bottom of it, but until then, he is under in-school suspension. Come on into class. We are late getting started."

Jessie looked out the window toward the courtyard between the main building and the ROTC building. She could see Carter sweeping and picking up trash. She thought about Mrs. Laney's comment about some girl making the call. She needed to hear what he had to say. But when class was over, Carter had disappeared. Jessie stopped Terry coming out of his last period class. "Have you seen Carter?"

"I think someone said his brother picked him up. We need him in that game Friday night, Jessie. He and I have worked hard with Coach on plays. We'll have to come up with new ones in a hurry if he's out of the game."

Mike joined them. "Carter would never risk the team. I told Coach he wouldn't do something like that."

In the car on the way home, Missy and Claire talked again about Rick and his strange behavior at the game. "It was strange how his mother came to the game to find him," said Missy. "All of a sudden his mother was making him leave. I totally forgot to tell you, Jessie, but Rick said to tell you he'd see you later."

"How did he sound when he said that?"

"Why?"

"I don't know. Something doesn't add up. You know when I called to you to come ride with us to the game? I could tell he was furious with me. He told me Sandy and Christy were going to the game separately and they told me that he said the opposite! Then, he called me Saturday morning and sounded so strange."

Missy was silent for a moment. "You know that group home where I do my community volunteer work? I may be wrong, but I think he has some personality issues that could possibly require help. Medication even. He shows a lot of the same symptoms I see in the residents at the home. Unpredictable at times. Sometimes they really want your attention, and go out of their way to get it."

Things were starting to make sense to Jessie. "Well, there *was* an incident at the Zesto. He climbed the radio tower and didn't come down until I told him to."

Claire chimed in. "You know, he *did* ask me a bunch of questions about Carter last week when he saw the two of you talking at lunch."

They pulled into Jessie's driveway. "Let me know if you think of anything else, okay?"

Jessie's mother was on the phone when she opened the front door. Her conversation sounded intense. "Did you report it to the sheriff's office?" Mrs. Reynolds listened for a moment and then responded. "Good. Have you called the Holloways next door? Okay. Let me know if you hear anything, and I'll be watching too."

She hung up and acknowledged Jessie. "Well, it has been a day around here! Quite a bit of excitement."

Jessie could only think she was talking about the incident with Carter, and prepared to defend him. "Excitement?"

"Yes," said her mother. "That was Mrs. Crosby down the street. She said several of the neighbors reported a car cruising our street this weekend. It was reported to the police, and she is just spreading the word to be on the lookout. You didn't see anything Saturday when Carter brought you home, did you?"

Jessie shook her head. "Not really." She paused. "Wait. I *did* see a red car drive by slowly when I turned off the lamp in the living room."

"It's a red car that has been reported. It could be the same one. We can't be too careful, honey. You never know what someone is up to."

Jessie went upstairs to look over her homework. She was trying to make sense of her assignments when the extension next to her bed rang. It only had to ring once before she picked it up.

"Jessie," said Carter. "I just wanted to hear your voice. I don't have a whole lot of time."

"I wanted to hear from you, too! Carter, how could this happen? I know you could never do anything like that."

"Crow is here with me. We're just going over everything from Friday night. Dr. Caldwell has hired an attorney for me, and Bobby just talked with the police. Are you okay?"

"Am *I* okay? Don't worry about me. I saw you with Coach at school. He told me you have in-school suspension."

"The paint on the jacket is a killer, Jess. I swear I don't know how it got there. We had such a great time Saturday night. The only thing I can figure out is that when I got home Saturday and parked in the carport, I didn't lock the car."

"Mrs. Laney said a girl called in to report you."

He sounded hopeless. "Yeah, I know. None of it makes sense."

"Hey, I've got to go. Rev. Hamilton just drove up and the police investigator is here. We're going to go over everything with him. Bobby said he is a good guy and will look into everything carefully." He paused. "What do your parents think?"

"They don't know yet. Mother was on the phone with a neighbor when I got home talking about some car cruising our street this weekend." Jessie started to cry.

"Don't worry Jess, okay? Don't cry. There's got to be a way to make this right. I will try to call you again soon."

Jessie lay on her bed staring at the ceiling. She glanced over at Carter's rose on her dresser. The bud had slowly started to open, its beauty changing shape each day. Her eyes wandered over to a greeting card on her bulletin board. She'd been drawn to it last summer in a shop on the pier at the beach. The front was a painting of a white beach with waves rushing up to shore. Three swaying palm trees leaned in the wind. She got up and pulled it from the board and laid back down to read the back description again. The artist was a quadriplegic who painted with a brush in her headband. She flipped it back and gazed at the painting again, amazed at the detail by someone with such challenges. There it was—the visual she needed like Mr. Baker had said—it would help her keep all things in perspective.

After dinner, Claire called and the two friends went over the events of the day—Carter's call, their conversation on the way from school, and the neighborhood watch report. "Do your parents know?"

"Not yet. At least it didn't come up at dinner. The conversation was all about the strange car in the neighborhood."

"You know?" said Claire. "About this whole police report and your mother's description of a red car thing. Is it just me or am I the only one who remembers that Rick's mother drives a red car? You don't suppose..."

Jessie finished her sentence. "You don't suppose Rick had something to do with all this..."

"It's worth checking out. Did anyone get a license tag? You know Rick had been asking those questions about Carter... and about the two of you. Then there was that whole fiasco of the ride to the football game."

Claire paused. "You know, Tom's dad is trying to help Carter. I'm going to call Tom—maybe there is something to this."

Morning came and Jessie woke with the beach card laying beside her pillow. She showered and dressed for school, all the while hoping the conversation at breakfast would be limited. She was anxious, too, to hear if Claire's theory had proven to be true.

Jessie felt the glare from her dad as she entered the kitchen. She instantly knew he had heard the news about the Fulton incident and the allegations against Carter. She pleaded for her parents to hear her out. "He is innocent. I know it. Everyone thinks so. He wouldn't do such a thing!"

Her father raised an eyebrow. "Everyone? You hardly know him, and we don't know anything about his family. This is serious, Jessica, since it involves someone you are associated with. We won't allow it!"

"Dr. Caldwell is helping him, and I know Coach O'Connor is, too. You know, too, about that car that was seen cruising our street. There is talk that it might be some connection to the Fulton incident."

Her father pushed back his chair and stood up. "What possible connection could there be? That sounds pretty far-fetched. I'm not in favor of any more contact between you and Carter." Her mother nodded in agreement.

Jessie's mind ran wild, searching for a way to negotiate the directive she knew was about to be laid down. She reached for her books to walk to Claire's house for their ride to school and turned to her parents. "I promise I will do the right thing. You've always taught me to 'do unto others' and about second chances. I know the truth will come out soon."

Jessie's mother finally spoke. "When you leave this house, you carry a responsibility to yourself and your family. You have too much ahead of you to let anything or anyone change that. Anything beyond a phone call is not an option until further notice. You understand?"

"Yes, just phone calls. Claire's waiting."

Claire's car was in the driveway and Jessie stood beside it with her books in hand. Sandy drove by and stopped when she saw Jessie waiting. "Need a ride? I have some news. I saw Brandi at Springlake last night. Our parents go way back and it didn't take long for us to make a connection with you. She asked how you were doing. She said that Crow and Carter's brother might have some new information from the police about what happened at Fulton."

Claire appeared and waved to Jessie. "Go ahead with Sandy. Still no news from Tom's dad yet."

Jessie ran to Sandy's passenger side and jumped into the front seat. "What? What information?"

"Brandi told me she was concerned that this whole thing about Carter had gotten out of hand. She graduated from Fulton and still has connections with people there. She has a hunch that some girl from Fulton named Carla Peterson might have something to do with it all."

Jessie remembered how Brandi had responded when she had told her about Carla's behavior toward Carter at the pharmacy. "How annoying!" she'd said. "I would know that high pitched voice anywhere. She calls here all the time trying to talk to Crow and Carter when they're practicing."

When the girls arrived at school, word circulated that Rick was still absent. Rumors about the Fulton incident had intensified, and Jack waited for Jessie outside art class. "The team is getting more and more anxious about this week's game with Grady. Coach is trying to keep us optimistic about our chances—even without Carter."

Announcements for the morning had included reminders for juniors and seniors to check with the school counselors about college planning and SAT testing. Mixed reactions about the announcement could be felt in the hallways. College was the last thing on Jessie's mind. She saw a young man named Phillip. Everyone knew he had nothing to worry about with perfect grades and high SATs. Tom and Claire leaned against her locker looking at a brochure together. With Tom's parents' connections, Jessie knew he could go anywhere. Claire had her eye on a school in North Carolina.

Mrs. Laney saw her protege leaving Mr. Baker's class. "You have your appointment scheduled with Miss Clay, Jessie?"

Jessie shook her head. "Not yet. I will stop by her office this afternoon."

"Keep your focus, Jessie. You've worked hard to get to this point."

"I will, Mrs. Laney, and thanks." She could only think about how the suspension would affect Carter's chances on his college prospects. Carter had told her of Coach's interest in helping him get a football scholarship, but all of that was in question now.

At lunch, Claire told Jessie that Dr. Caldwell had reported that the police had interviewed people at the Fulton dance. "All of them—so far—said that Carter didn't start the fight. Tom's dad also said that no paint was in Carter's car other than on his jacket and that it was odd that the paint on the jacket was on the back, not the front."

On Wednesday night, Carter finally called Jessie—with his suspension, she'd only caught a glimpse of him at school. Jessie was grateful her parents allowed his calls.

Carter began to tell Jessie more about his family and how his parents had not been in the picture since he was in first grade. He explained how Papa Ford had been the only parental influence in his life and how important their church attendance had been to his grandfather. He talked about Bobby, how close they were, and how his brother had stepped in after their grandfather's death to look after him as best he could—with the help of Coach O'Connor and Dr. Caldwell.

"I sometimes feel like an orphan, Jessie. But Bobby has made the difference in making us a family." Carter paused. "I've got to go, Jess. Rev. Hamilton is coming by. I will try to see you after school tomorrow."

After she hung up the phone, Jessie thought about the deep conversation with Carter. It had opened her eyes to the fact that the world was not the same for everyone around her. Despite the current tensions with her parents, Jessie felt even more grateful for her family. She knew there was never any doubt about their love and care for her.

JESSIE SAT ON THE FRONT PORCH steps while her mother prepared dinner. Her dad pulled in the driveway. Since their breakfast conversation, his daughter's best interest had been on his mind. His long day leaning over his drafting table had taken a toll and he searched for a way to bring peace that evening instead of the struggle that began their day.

He loosened his tie and removed his coat. "Play the Irish Lullaby for me, Jess?"

They walked into the house and Jessie moved to the piano in the den. She searched through the stack of choir music representing years with Dr. Sellers and Mr. James that fed her love of singing. She lifted the piano bench filled with years of sonatas, Broadway musicals and scores her piano teacher, Mrs. Kerns, had provided and finally retrieved the well-worn lullaby piece. She positioned herself at the keys and began to play for her father and—this time—for her own comfort as well. She glanced at the stacks of music at her side. Her dream for a brighter tomorrow now included hope for a drummer in a band named The Playboys.

Chapter Thirteen

A police detective, Lt. Casey, had been assigned to investigate both the Fulton vandalism and the report of a car cruising through the Longwood neighborhood. He was beginning to think the cases might be connected since Carter Powell had been in the neighborhood with Jessie on that same Saturday evening.

After a conversation with Crow, the lieutenant drove by the Springlake Pharmacy and stopped for a soda. He took a seat on a stool at the counter, and spoke to Dr Ellis, who was working behind the counter.

"Lt. Casey, Fulton County police. I'm checking on some trouble over at Fulton High. There's been some questionable activity in a nearby neighborhood too. Just wanted to see if you could help with any information about a student, Carter Powell?"

Dr. Ellis looked at the officer's badge. "Oh, Carter! He comes in fairly often. What a nice young man. He and my grandson play for Northwest." Dr. Ellis pointed with pride to a Northwest pennant behind the counter.

The officer paused. "Well, the Powell boy has been accused of vandalism over at Fulton. You say he comes in often. Any recent visits or information that might help the case?"

"Well, let me see. He was here just last week with a nice girl. Both of them ordered Coke floats. Sat at the booth right over there."

The lieutenant reached for his notebook and began to write. "You remember what day that was?"

"Maybe Wednesday...or was it Thursday? Not sure, but I do remember two girls sitting in the corner booth over there. One of them obviously wanted Carter's attention and came over talking real loud. I kept my eye on them because she sounded pretty angry. Thought I was going to have to break things up if she didn't pipe down."

"Angry?" asked Lt. Casey.

"Yes...and demanding to know why he hadn't called her. Her voice carried throughout the store. I think I heard her friend call her Carla something. The young lady with Carter excused herself because the girl was making such a scene." The pharmacist held his head as if he had a headache. "I won't forget her or that high-pitched voice of hers."

"Anything else? Did you see the car she was in. Anything?"

"No, but come to think of it, I heard that same voice the following Sunday afternoon. You know, up front at the pay phone. I forgot about that until now."

The lieutenant continued making notes. "Did you happen to hear anything she was saying?"

The pharmacist paused. "Yeah, I remember a little. I heard her say 'Carter Powell did it.' That high pitch came out when she said his name. I thought it strange at the time."

The officer stood and shook Dr. Ellis's hand. "Thanks. You've been very helpful. I think I have what I need." He reached for his wallet and the pharmacist raised his hand. "No charge, Lieutenant. I hope you can help that young man. He has always been polite here."

Claire and Tom sat together in the Caldwell den. She had mentioned the reports of a strange red car in her neighborhood to Tom before, but it had seemed unrelated until now. Dr. Caldwell passed by the den and stopped when he heard Claire's voice. He stepped into the room.

"Excuse me, Claire. Would you mind telling me more about this car? You live up the street from Jessica, right?"

"Yes. They said it was red. I know there are probably a lot of red cars, but the only one I know about belongs to the mother of a guy named Rick. I saw it when she came to the Fulton game and made him leave. He and Sandy were dating for a while, but we think he has a thing for Jessie and is jealous of Carter."

Dr. Caldwell considered what Claire had said and then headed to the kitchen. "I have to make a phone call," he said.

Jessie was upstairs when the Reynolds' doorbell rang. She heard her parents talking to someone in low voices and looked out the window to see Dr. Caldwell leaving. She ran downstairs just in time to see her mother close the door and shake her head.

"That was Tom's dad. The police ran the information on Mrs. Fields' car. Lt. Casey compared the report they had from the neighborhood with those from the Fulton High incidence report. They went to the Fields' with a warrant, and to make a long story short, they found purple paint in their basement. It was also on some of Rick's clothes, and *he* has now been charged with the Fulton vandalism. It seems he had convinced a girl named Carla Peterson to be his accomplice. Both apparently wanted to cause trouble for Carter."

Jessie's excitement could not be contained. "I've got to go. I've got to find Carter!" She looked at her mother, who just turned and handed her the keys to her car.

Mr. Reynolds shook his head. "How are you going to find him?"

Jessie smiled at her parents. "I have a pretty good idea where he is, and it's not far away." She sprinted to the car and drove straight to Crow's house. The green Buick was parked in front. She pulled in behind it, hopped out of the car, and ran down the driveway straight into Carter's arms.

He broke into a wide grin. "You heard?"

"I heard!" She kissed him over and over and Crow, who was standing in the doorway to the Nest, stepped back inside and politely closed the door. After a few minutes, the two stopped to look at each other. In unison, they said, "Coach!"

Carter went inside the Crow's Nest to call the coach. He'd already heard the news and invited Carter and Jessie to come over to his house in Garden Hills. This would be Jessie's first visit to a teacher outside of school.

Coach O'Connor met them at the door. He shook Carter's hand in obvious relief and grinned at Jessie. "Come in. Come in. The phone has been ringing off the hook!"

While he and Carter talked, Jessie looked around. The O'Connor house was neat and well kept. Living room shelves were filled with books, memorabilia, and framed sports articles from the *Atlanta Journal*. Evidence of a woman's touch was everywhere.

A lamp glowed on a table next to a leather chair with an open book revealing Coach's current reading. An upholstered chair in a purple and white floral pattern, was opposite it. Its side table had a blue Chinese vase with a few stems of delicate purple iris. Over the arm was draped a beautiful purple knitted shawl. A cinnamon aroma wafting from the kitchen added to the noticeable cozy atmosphere. It was not at all what she expected.

"I just pulled some pumpkin bread from the oven for us. I don't bake much, but my wife Ann always made it this time of year."

There was artwork on all the walls, including several paintings by Mr. Baker. One in particular, a sunrise painting in the entry hallway, had a plaque with a French proverb: *Gratitude is the heart's memory."* Jessie read it again and savored the words.

Without her notice, Coach O'Connor had quietly joined her. "The sunrise was one of Ann's favorites. After the Paris crash, she dedicated much of her time to the grief recovery program at the museum."

It was clear to Jessie that all of the pieces held double memories of those Coach had lost—in Paris, like Mr. Baker—and his own dear wife.

The three sampled pieces of Coach's pumpkin bread and celebrated the good news of Carter's innocence. Jessie's skeptical feelings about Coach at the beginning of school had quickly turned to ones of appreciation. Getting to know him in such a way that night was a gift Jessie would never forget.

The coach's phone continued to ring. Word had reached the football team that Carter was in the clear. "Yes, yes, it's true," he confirmed with each call. "It's a go. He is clear to play."

The trip back to Crow's to retrieve Jessie's car was a joyous one. Questions still remained about what would happen with Rick and Carla, but for now, there was relief and appreciation.

Carter followed Jessie home so he could speak with her parents. After a brief conversation, he squeezed Jessie's hand and headed to the door.

The Reynolds were impressed that it was important to him that they would have no doubts of his respect for them and his feelings for Jessie.

Jessie followed Carter out to his car. The evening hours had brought a chill to the air so he turned to face her and stopped to warm her arms. Words could not describe his relief. He grasped the lapels of her jacket and pulled her closer to him. "You know, that was a special kiss earlier in Crow's driveway. It came with a lot of happiness."

Jessie nodded. The mood changed between them when he leaned in and pressed his lips to hers, she felt a warmth she had never before experienced. It was the kiss she had always dreamed of.

The two stayed in each other arms not wanting to let go. Carter lifted his head and placed his forehead against hers. "Thank you for believing in me," he said.

Jessie looked into his eyes and responded with a warmth all her own. "I will always believe in you."

Chapter Fourteen

Until this year, Thanksgiving had been the only November holiday Jessie and her family celebrated, but Veterans Day was special to Carter and she wanted to spend it with him. She had noticed how he stood straight and tall when the national anthem was played before football games and she had come to know how important the ROTC program was to him. When she had asked him why he joined the program, Carter had told her it was a way to honor his grandfather, but she knew, too, that it was more than just an elective to him, and she was proud to be at his side when he was dressed in his freshly pressed uniform.

Carter's church in Sandy Springs was planning a Veterans' Day service with lunch on the grounds afterwards and she had jumped at the chance to attend with him. Her parents had no reservations about her attending his church with him—they had come to appreciate Carter more and more, particularly after so many had come to his defense over the Fulton High incident.

Carter pulled into the Reynolds' driveway at 9:30 sharp and was dazzled by her. In honor of the holiday, she had worn a new navy-blue dress and carried a red cardigan. He helped her into his car and settled into the driver's seat. "Thank you," he said softly.

"For what?"

"The dress. You. Being here with me."

As they entered the sanctuary, the sun shone through the windows. A reverent spirit was obvious as members found their seats without the usual pre-service chatter. Carter held Jessie's hand and led her down the center aisle to a specific row on the right side. Jessie sat and opened the program an usher had handed her and read the lengthy list of names. Some had a small cross beside them, denoting that they were now deceased. She found James Crawford's name quickly.

Just before the bells chimed that it was 11 a.m., Bobby joined them. Jessie glanced around. The church was much smaller than her church. She noted the floral arrangement and one lighted candle on the communion table. She listened as the pianist played an arrangement of *God Bless America* and felt an unexplained peace.

After the service, several men came to speak to Carter, and Bobby invited her to come with him to the end of the pew and look at the adjacent stained-glass window. He smiled and pointed to the plaque below it. Jessie read the inscription aloud. "The Inviting Christ Welcoming All God's Children, given in memory of Mr. and Mrs. James *Carter* Crawford." She looked up at Bobby and he nodded his head and smiled.

They returned to where Carter was standing and the three walked down the aisle together toward the back. When they reached the door, Rev. Hamilton wrapped his arms around both Carter and Bobby.

"Welcome, Jessie," he said. "I have a great love for these young men. And I've heard a lot about you from this one."

Carter blushed and she smiled as the reverend continued. "Jim's boys are a special part of this church."

Part of the day's celebration was a lunch on the grounds and instead of heading to the parking lot, Jessie and Carter joined a group of people waiting in line. Bobby excused himself to talk to a young woman serving iced tea.

"That's Marie," said Carter. "They've been dating for at least three years, maybe more." Jessie and Carter each served themselves a plate of home-cooked vegetables, fried chicken, salad, and dessert and he steered her to two chairs in a shaded corner of the grounds.

"I'm glad you are with me today, Jess. There are several times during the year when I feel especially close to Papa, and this is one of them. He meant a lot to me."

"You were named for him," she said.

"Yes. Veterans Day is always meaningful because he served in World War II and received many medals and honors for his bravery and service."

Jessie nodded. "Two of my mother's brothers also fought in World War II. I remember Uncle Emmett and Uncle Travis's stories about the war at our Alabama family gatherings."

Carter moved the food around on his plate. "Papa was always there for me. My parents brought me into this world, but Papa gave me my life." He pulled his keys from his pocket and showed her a set of dog tags that had belonged to his grandfather. "They're on my key chain to remind me every day of Papa."

He glanced over at his brother, now eating with Marie. "Growing up, Bobby bore the brunt of times that weren't the best. With him being older, he protected me from what I've heard were tough times with my dad. I learned much later that Papa protected me, too. The most!"

He took a sip of iced tea and continued. "My parents died in a car accident when I was six. I barely remember them except in flashes, but Bobby remembers. Papa took us both in and raised us. He taught me a lot."

Jessie squeezed his hand. *How different his life had been from hers.*

Carter glanced over at Bobby and Marie again. "It works best for us to remember Papa and all the good times we had together with him. We really don't talk about the accident. Grandmother Crawford died at an early age too and left my mom to grow up without a mother just like me. But she *did* have a dad who loved her very much." Jessie watched as tears welled up in his eyes. "It's great to see how close you are to your mom, Jessie. I never had that." She took Carter's hand and noticed it had begun to tremble.

"I don't think there is anything I wouldn't do to make Papa proud," he said. "Reverend Hamilton was one of his good friends. Since Papa died, he's helped me understand a lot of things too."

As the days and weeks went by, Carter and Jessie spent more and more time together and their relationship grew stronger. The football team went on to have a winning season and Coach O'Connor was named Coach of the Year for the city. Dr. and Mrs. Caldwell held a celebration for him at their home and all the team and faculty were invited along with many parents and friends.

The team enjoyed the glow of success and the recognition for their coach. Jessie watched from across the room as Principal Kelley made a toast to Coach with Carter at his side.

She was startled by the appearance of a cup of punch in front of her and looked up to see Jack standing beside her. "You doing okay?" he asked.

"Yes. Why do you ask?"

"No reason. Just checking on you." Jack touched her punch cup with his. "Cheers to the rest of our year!"

After the toasts ended, Carter rejoined Jessie. He pointed to Dr. Caldwell and Rev. Hamilton, who were talking to Coach O'Connor. "Coach says that the three of them have been playing golf together for quite a while. I owe all three of them a lot for taking up for me. Someday, I hope I can repay them."

Other seniors on the team meandered over to where they were standing, all talking about whether they'd heard from college recruiters. Carter had set records and had made the sports page throughout the season, and there seemed to be no doubts of his receiving multiple scholarship offers. Even so, Jessie never heard him brag or get caught up in all the hype. When asked about his success, his comments always pointed to the team.

Before he left the party, Rev. Hamilton took Carter aside. Jessie saw him placing his hands on Carter's shoulders and looking squarely into his eyes as he spoke. Jessie turned to Carter as she got into the Buick. "It was good of Rev. Hamilton to come to the party."

"Yes. He's not just our team chaplain, but for me, he's like family."

They pulled away from the Caldwell's and turned onto Wesley. When they reached Memorial Park, Carter parked and turned off the engine. "I need to tell you more about my family, Jess." He touched the keys hanging from the steering column and his grandfather's dog tags rattled. Then he placed his arm on the back of the front seat and she moved closer to him.

"All my life," he said, "I never felt like I deserved anything. I guess I'm more like my mom—Bobby says she seemed sad all the time." He paused. "And...my dad favored Bobby over me. He wanted nothing to do with me. Bobby tried to make up for it by taking me everywhere he went." He gazed through the windshield at the stars. Jessie moved closer.

"The car accident happened when I was barely six and Bobby was ten. My first real memories of Papa are from then. Mama Ford had passed away before the accident. Rev. Hamilton performed her funeral…and the ones for my parents. Papa moved in with us after the accident and kept the family going. He made sure Bobby and I went to church. He gave me my first set of drums and encouraged me to love music along with sports and school and everything in life. He told me about ROTC and the things the military taught him." Jessie could see tears in his eyes, but a twinkle appeared there too. "I always knew when there was something special he wanted to talk about. That was when he would take us fishing."

He paused again, as if carefully choosing his words.

"On one of those fishing trips, it was just him and me. I was probably eight years old. He told me he would rather have waited but knew the truth would come out sooner or later. He said it was for darn sure that no one else would tell me but him. What he told me answered a lot of questions, though."

"What was it?"

Carter took a deep breath. "The man I thought was my dad wasn't my dad. Bobby and I had different fathers."

Jessie sensed that he thought this news might be of concern to her. "Did you think that would matter to me?" She stopped and thought. "You were given Bobby, Papa Ford, Rev. Hamilton, and Coach. All fathers in their own way, don't you think?" She leaned over to kiss him and laid her head on his shoulder.

Carter checked his watch. "It's getting late. I'd better get you home."

Chapter Fifteen

The Playboys grew in popularity and with the Beatles' fame at their height, the band capitalized on their songs. Arrangements of "*She Loves You*," "*I Want to Hold Your Hand*," "*From Me to You*," and "*Love Me Do*" were favorites and often requested by their audiences. Jessie now joined Brandi at all the band's engagements and loved watching Carter play. She could see a twinkle in his eyes as he played and the crowd cheered wildly following his solos. He would catch her eye and smile at her when they sang certain song lines—his winks told her that the words were meant just for her.

Christmas was now approaching, and it was time to buy presents but Jessie's income from babysitting, even with her allowance, wasn't enough. She'd taken Mrs. Laney's typing and business courses, so she jumped at the opportunity when her dad asked her to work part-time at his office after school. The extra earnings would help her afford a meaningful gift for Carter.

JESSIE AND JACK STOOD NEAR THE front of Mr. Baker's art class with a group of other junior students.

"I just don't know what to do," said Jessie. "None of the ideas for our holiday display feel right."

"I agree," said Jack. The other students nodded their heads as well.

Holiday decorations were appearing throughout the school, and each class would be judged on their displays. Confidence was high that their class committee would be the most creative, but so far, no one had been able to determine a theme that seemed to connect with everyone.

The senior class always had the best display spot—at the front entrance near the main office. The sophomore class had the area outside the gym and the freshman class had the bulletin boards adjacent to the parking lot's lower entrance. The junior class was assigned to the bulletin boards outside the cafeteria main entrance.

Mr. Baker passed by the group on the way to his desk. "I overheard some of your discussion," he said. "Would you like a suggestion?"

"Yes," replied the group in unison.

"Consider making your display about others."

"Others?" asked Jessie.

"Think about it." Just like many of his art class assignments, Mr. Baker threw out a vague statement and left the rest to the students' imagination.

Within a matter of minutes, the group had decided that children should be at the center of the junior class decorations and not just any children, but those who were patients at Egleston Hospital. It made perfect sense—the high school had adopted a sponsorship of the children at Egleston. It didn't take long before the group had settled on a plan to make the hospital the centerpiece of their display. Jessie was appointed to call the hospital and ask for a visit. The administration welcomed the students and she arranged for Coach O'Connor to drive them in the school's van that afternoon.

Jessie climbed into the front seat with the coach. She smiled inwardly as she thought about how nervous she had been about him at the first of the year and how those feelings were now long gone. Now they had a special bond.

As they made their way to Egleston, Coach told them that his late wife Ann had been a major volunteer and what he knew of the hospital's history through her. When they arrived, the group was given a tour. The staff, seeing Coach O'Connor with them, told the students of their love and respect for his wife. He beamed as they spoke of the literally hundreds of blankets and caps she had knitted for infants and children treated there. Jessie recalled the purple shawl she had seen at Coach's cottage the night she and Carter had visited.

The tour soon took them to the hospital activities room. Jessie and her friends joined the older children to work on their art projects together. When they were done, the children gave the students the finger paintings, and Jessie told them they would share their special creations with all their friends back at Northwest. Coach gathered the students and children to take pictures of everyone.

The junior class display was entitled "Ann's Gratitude Tree," in memory of the coach's wife. Adorned with a large Christmas tree in the middle, small colorful knitted caps were collected as decorations. At the bottom of the display were the pictures Coach had taken of the children with a note that said the caps would be donated to Egleston's infant wing. When he saw the display for the first time, Coach tearfully gave the students a group hug. The holiday spirit reached a new level that afternoon with a competition win by the juniors and an unexpected connection with their coach.

The next day, Jessie stopped at the coach's desk when class was over. "I'm trying to find the right Christmas gift for Carter, but I haven't come up with anything. I would love to give him something special since the whole Fulton thing, you know."

Coach smiled. "You'll think of the right thing. Ann taught me that gifts from the heart always mean the most."

Jessie left the room and contemplated her gift shopping. She ran into Fran on the stairs.

"Jessie, what are you going to wear to the Snow Ball dance? I already have my dress."

Jessie shrugged her shoulder. "I don't know yet. Mother and I are going shopping this weekend." She didn't share how special the shopping trip would be—in the past, for most occasions, Jessie typically chose from the carefully preserved formal dresses her older sisters had worn. Mrs. Reynolds had recognized that this dance with Carter was special and decided it was time Jessie should have her own special wardrobe.

The next day at lunchtime, as she had for weeks, Jessie sat down with Carter. Both had dispensed with the "rules" of who sat where and had eaten together every day since his in-school suspension.

"What are your plans for Christmas?" asked Jessie.

"Marie has invited us to her family's home for Christmas dinner. The last few years we have gotten together with Rev. Hamilton at some point, too. It has become a tradition for me and Bobby, I guess. But the Snow Ball can be *our* special time, right?"

Jessie nodded and smiled. "My mom is taking me to find a dress this weekend. I can't wait to find the perfect one!"

Carter looked around and leaned in closer. "The perfect dress for the perfect girl!" he whispered.

She whispered back. "For the perfect boy."

"Now what's going on here?" The low voice of Coach came from above them. Both peered up to see him looking down at them. "Glad I saw you, Carter," he said. "There's going to be a team meeting after school on Thursday. Be sure and be on time."

Once the coach had gone, Carter turned to Jessie. "I've gotta leave early. I have an appointment with the school counselor," he said.

"What about?"

"Just regular stuff. College. Scholarships. Future plans." He finished his lunch and then stood and smiled at Jessie and headed for the hallway.

When the bell for the end of the lunch session sounded, Jessie headed to her algebra class. Coach waited at his doorway as usual and saw Carter down the hall approaching them. He quickly asked her to stay for a moment after class.

When Carter reached them, the coach shifted into his practiced grumpy image. "Christmas holidays will be here before you know it. The team meeting Thursday afternoon is important, so don't forget. Dr. Caldwell will be there." He winked at Jessie as he turned toward the classroom. "Don't be late to my class, young lady."

Jessie noticed Carter seemed distracted. "How was your appointment with Miss Clay?" she asked.

He shrugged his shoulders. "It was fine. My grades still could qualify me for a scholarship. Just a lot to consider. I better get to my class. See you after school." He brushed her cheek with a kiss and continued down the hall.

When the class was over, Jessie hung back until the other students had left the room and stepped up to Coach's desk. He was grinning from ear to ear. He pulled a large white box from behind his desk. "I think I have the perfect gift for Carter." He opened the top to show Jessie a brand new letter jacket with the same signature white leather sleeves and purple wool front panels. The large "N" letter had a small gold football pinned to it. It was just like the one Rick had destroyed with purple paint.

Jessie matched the coach's grin. "I can't believe it. It's perfect! After the purple paint ruined Carter's other jacket, he said he knew he would never have another one."

"I pulled some strings. Frank Caldwell helped, too. You know he was always in Carter's corner during that whole mess."

"Carter will be so surprised. What a wonderful gift from you both!"

Coach looked the jacket over. "Well, it will be from the school. The team deserves another time to celebrate its great season every chance we get. Some of the players are receiving college bids to play next year, and we will celebrate that too. The whole thing with Fulton, believe it or not, really brought our team together. I think they will stay close for years to come. Their commitment to each other makes me proud."

ON THURSDAY AFTERNOON, THE COACHES AND Dr. Caldwell threw a special celebration for the team and all those who had played sports that season. Jessie's act of surprise was believable when Carter told her about the new jacket. She listened to Carter tell how Coach had given an unforgettable speech about support and commitment throughout their lives. As he talked, Jessie searched his face.

She wasn't sure it was gone, but whatever was troubling him seemed lessened.

Chapter Sixteen

The night of the Snow Ball was bitter with a forecast of snow. The holiday spirit was everywhere in the Reynolds home from its Frazier fir wreath on the front door to the tree decorated with cherished ornaments to the holiday candles burning on the dining room buffet to the scents of almond and vanilla in the air.

The doorbell rang and Carter was greeted by Jessie's father. He stood with his Kodak Instamatic in hand as his wife arranged Jessie's new stole.

A light appeared in Carter's eyes when he saw Jessie in the blue and white designer dress. He handed a box to Jessie's mother.

"Would you mind?" he said. "I'm not very good at pinning them on."

"Of course not," said Mrs. Reynolds. She took the red rose bud and baby's breath corsage and attached it neatly to the shoulder of Jessie's dress.

"Jessie, go and stand by Carter," said Mr. Reynolds. He lifted his new camera. "Say cheese!"

When the photograph session was over, Mrs. Reynolds invited the couple into the kitchen. There, cooling on the table were six pound cakes and several tins of pressed cookies decorated in red and green. "The pound cakes are to die for," said Jessie. "Mother makes them from scratch every Christmas by my Grandma Reynolds's recipe." Her dad beamed.

Madeline picked up a tin of cookies and handed it to Carter. "Merry Christmas. These are for you and Bobby." Jessie didn't miss the look in Carter's eyes as he took the gift from her mother. It was a look that told a story only a motherless child could express.

Jessie's parents sent them off through the doorway arch of multicolored string lights with words of caution about traffic, curfew and warnings of predicted snow. Carter turned to Jessie's father as they started down the steps. "We'll be careful, sir."

Carter opened the door of the Buick. "Perfect," he said. Jessie held her dress with care as she slid onto the front seat of the car. Next to her on the seat was a school blanket and a white package with red ribbon. He moved the package to the back seat without a word and spread the blanket over her. She slid over, moving closer to him, and placed her arm through his as they drove toward Paces Ferry. "Perfect," she responded.

By the time they arrived at the Civic Club on the Chattahoochee River, snow had already begun to fall. The seniors traditionally took the lead in decorating for the Snow Ball in winter, while Jessie's class would do the same for the Junior-Senior Prom in spring. Carter was proud to have Jessie on his arm when they walked inside. The club's ballroom was decorated with artificial snow, as it seldom snowed in Atlanta. Each time the door opened, the cold from outside rushed in to chill those nearby.

Fran and Mike had already arrived and had saved chairs at a table near the stage for them and for Tom and Claire. Sandy, Christy and Jack, who came together to the dance, filled the rest of the seats. Fran and Jessie meandered through the room showing off their dresses as others streamed in. Carter checked out the band as they set up on stage and

Mike joined him there. The Playboys had been asked to play for the dance, but the group's bookings were already through the roof. They had declined anyway, as Carter would be there as Jessie's escort.

The band began to play and Christmas spirit filled the room. Faculty members, led by Mrs. Laney, acted as chaperones and joined in the fun. Students took tinsel decorations from the large tree and wore the glittery pieces around their necks as they danced.

Jessie glanced back toward their table and saw Carter talking to Mike. The look on his face was serious. She waited until she saw Carter head for the refreshment table alone and then joined him. "Is Mike okay?"

"Not really. He and Fran are going through a tough time right now."

"Fran seems fine to me," Jessie said. "She hasn't mentioned anything about a problem."

The band took a break and Carter and Jessie returned to their table. Mrs. Laney went to the stage and stood at the microphone. She thanked the seniors for the decorations. "If we only had known it was going to snow, we could have spared a lot of expense on our decorating budget!" she said joking with the audience. Then she cleared her throat and the crowd quieted. "And now, it is time to announce our 1965 Snow Ball King and Queen! This year's Snow Ball Queen is…Missy Davis! And our King is…Mike Martin!"

Everyone applauded. Neither winner was a surprise. Missy did everything for the school and was liked by all, and Mike had always been known as a leader on the football team. Missy bounced up the stairs. Mike, on the other hand, was slow to move. Emotionless, he finally stood, and with a nudge from Carter, followed Missy onto the stage.

Fran clapped and cheered. Jessie noted that her expression and Mike's couldn't have been more different. She was grateful to Fran for connecting her with Carter, but she knew little about the girl's relationship with

Mike. Fran had always, even with her, kept conversations about him limited in detail, only saying they were serious and in love.

As Mike stepped up to the microphone, his face told the story. Being the Snow Ball king was not what he wanted or needed on this particular night. Carter put his arm around Jessie and hugged her. She could feel an unusual vibe from him as they both watched Mike and Missy thank their classmates for their votes. Each left the stage with their crowns to another round of applause and hugs from others in the crowd. Fran made her way to meet Mike and followed him back to their table as the celebration continued.

After another half hour, the chaperones cautioned the students of increased weather concerns and couple by couple, they began to leave. Mike and Fran were among the first to go, disappearing through a side door. Carter placed Jessie's stole around her shoulders and they lowered their heads to hurry toward his car.

The winds had increased and the temperature outside had dropped. Once inside the car, they embraced, and Carter briskly rubbed Jessie's arms. He started the car and turned on the wipers. "I didn't expect we would have this tonight."

Jessie placed her hands over the car heater and waited as the engine warmed. "I have to ask. What is with Mike and Fran?"

"Let's keep tonight about us," Carter said, and when Jessie didn't press, he changed the subject. "How about we go by the Nest? It's not too late, and I need to check the band schedule anyway. We're booked solid all the way to New Year's."

Jessie agreed, but was disappointed. She was searching for an opportune time to give Carter his gift and she knew other people would be there. Her mood changed, though, when Carter pulled down the driveway, contrary to their usual pattern of parking on the street. No other cars were around.

A glow radiated through the windows inside the Nest. As she stepped from the car, she took Carter's hand, and with his other, he reached in the backseat for the white box. "What's going on?" she asked.

Carter slowly opened the door to the Nest, where Jessie could see the lights of a simply decorated Christmas tree inside. They were alone. From behind, Carter wrapped his arms around Jessie's waist and slowly guided her toward the tree. Next to it were a dozen long-stemmed red roses in a cut glass crystal vase.

Carter pointed to the flowers. "These are for you. And *this* is for you." Still with his arms around her, he turned her so they faced the entryway. A large hand-painted sign hung over it. "*To Jess. I love you.*"

Jessie was speechless. Carter had planned with Crow to make sure they would have the Nest all to themselves. "Carter," she whispered, her face glowing in the light. "I love you, too."

Carter turned her toward him and lifted her chin. "Jess, I have loved you from the minute I saw you. I have loved you more each day and cannot believe you would want to be with me. I wanted this night and this moment to be special. To be perfect. Like us."

Jessie could not believe the lengths he had gone to create the moment. Joy and happiness overflowed as she searched for the words in her heart.

She reached for her purse and he stopped her. He reached for the white box she had seen in his car. With a questioning look of excitement, she opened the box to find another smaller blue box, one that seemed familiar. It was Carter's senior ring. She had never seen him wear it.

"Oh, Carter. Your ring."

"I bought this before we met, but I was thinking that maybe someday I would give it to a girl who meant the world to me. Like you do, Jess." Inside the white box was a delicate gold chain. Many of the girls like Fran wore their boyfriends' rings on their hand using molded wax to better fit their smaller fingers. Jessie had seen other girls wear their boyfriends' rings on chains around their necks. She would now be one of them.

"Will you help me?" She placed the ring on the chain and carefully handed it to him. Turning her to look up at the sign again, he gently moved her hair to one side to close the clasp at her neck.

"Papa told me," he whispered, "that one day I would find someone that would have my heart. In spite of whatever went on with my mom and my dad, Papa always talked about how I should treat girls, and he told me that one day I would find the perfect someone. You have my heart, Jessie, and you always will. I want you to always remember that, with my ring close to your heart." He kissed her neck, then her ear, then her cheek, and then her lips and he held her close. Feeling his heart beating against her chest, Jessie was filled with happiness. The tree, the roses, the sign, and only the two of them in their favorite place alone.

"Wait!" said Jessie. "My purse!" She reached in and pulled out a Maier and Berklee box. "This is for you." She had taken Coach's advice to find a gift from her heart.

Carter hesitated. "I didn't expect anything."

Jessie made a face at him. "Open it."

He lifted the top from the box to see a gold medallion key chain inside. On one side was engraved "*Forever*" and on the other, "*All my love, Jessica.*" He tried to speak, but she stopped him, placing her finger over his lips. "You told me you looked at your keys every day as a reminder of your Papa with his dog tags. I wanted you to have a reminder of me every day, too."

Carter looked at her again in disbelief. He turned the medallion over in his hand. "I love you more than you can know, Jessie."

She reached for the ring around her neck. The medallion would be with him always, just as his ring would be for her. Carter was her forever and she was his perfect love!

Carter attached the medallion to his key chain and then kissed her again. He left her just long enough to put a Johnny Mathis album on the turntable to play. She rested her head on his shoulder and they danced to "*Chances Are*" in front of the warmly lit tree.

After that, their kisses were endless, and Jessie knew that like her, Carter wished their embrace could be something more. But time was getting late and the weather was still deteriorating. And she knew how responsible Carter was. He had promised her father that he would return her safely.

"I need to take you home before the weather gets worse," he said.

"I wish tonight didn't have to end."

"Me too. I want to stay here with you, forever. If only we could." His true desire was emphasized in the heat of their final kiss.

"I will always remember this," she said. "This time, this night."

The snow was falling more heavily and sticking to the ground and car. Jessie's heart was full as Carter took down the sign and carefully folded it for her. She watched sadly as he turned off the tree lights. From her introduction to the Nest on their first date until now, their love had blossomed from a single rose to a beautiful bouquet.

Jessie wrapped her stole tightly over the sign and the ring around her neck. The snow fell on the rose petals as Carter carried the vase to the car. He opened her door, helped her manage her dress, and then reached for his keys. He gazed at them, reading again the engraving on the medallion, and then secured the blanket over Jessie and pulled her close to him.

It was a gesture he would repeat many times.

Chapter Seventeen

Jessie slept blissfully until the morning light peeked through her window. Throwing back the covers, she opened the curtains and looked outside. Icicles hung from the branches of trees and everything was covered in white.

Shivering, she put on her robe and slippers and went downstairs to the kitchen where her mother stood over their gas stove.

"Sit down and relax. Look at the snow!" said Mrs. Reynolds. "Church services have been canceled." As usual, Atlanta drivers were unprepared to handle the slippery road conditions.

Jessie's father stood inspecting a couple of flashlights. A small bunch of candles and the massive Sunday *Atlanta Journal and Constitution* he had rescued from the sidewalk lay on the counter beside him. He picked up the paper and joined Jessie at the table.

She listened to the soothing hum of the heating system keeping the house warm. During some of the city's rare winter storms, ice-weighted trees had fallen on power lines, sending much of the city into darkness.

It's a good thing our stove is a gas stove, Jessie thought, and then smiled. *Even if we lose power, Mother can still make us hot chocolate.*

Her thoughts soon drifted to Carter. They had talked about walking up to the Bobby Jones Golf Course in the afternoon—if he could get back to her house in the snow. The golf course was "the place" to meet on days like this. Children, teens, and families would gather any semblance of a sled, including trash can lids, to experience the joy of sliding down a snowy hill.

Mrs. Reynolds lifted a pan from the stove and put the breakfast eggs into a bowl on the table. "How was the dance?" she asked. At this, Jessie's father peered over the paper.

"It was wonderful. The seniors did a great job decorating the club, and everyone *loved* my dress," she said looking at her mother, "and Mike and Missy were voted this year's Snow Ball King and Queen."

"Did Carter like his key chain?"

She searched her mother's face for a clue to what she was thinking. When Jessie had asked to use the car to go to Maier and Berkele, Mrs. Reynolds hadn't questioned the gift when Jessie told of her plan to order one. She had been busy doing Christmas baking for the family and friends and Mr. Reynolds had gone to the farmer's market to buy fresh fruit for her gift baskets. It had obviously not occurred to Jessie's mother to ask about any engraving.

Jessie nodded, offering no additional information. "Yes. He really did."

Her mother slid the bacon onto a plate and set it on the table. "So, did Carter have a gift for you?"

Jessie felt her face warm. "Roses. They're upstairs on my dresser." Before her mother could respond, she added, "And his senior ring."

At this, Jessie's father put down the paper. "What?"

"Carter gave me his senior ring," she repeated.

Her mother stopped and looked at her. "Jessica, you haven't known Carter very long. I am concerned the two of you are getting far too serious too quickly."

Jessie winced. She had hoped that the fact that her sister, Meredith, had received the same gift from her boyfriend while in high school would temper her parents' response, but apparently it hadn't. She took a deep breath. "I knew you might feel that way. I hope you will trust my judgment and decisions like you always have. You know some of the boys from church you've always wanted me to date were not ones that I could like as a boyfriend. Carter is different, and I hope you will keep getting to know him." She looked out the window at the snow and then back to her parents. She knew she was taking a risk to continue the conversation, but neither they nor she was going anywhere.

Mr. Reynolds cleared his throat. "Let's eat breakfast first. Then I think we need to talk more about this." He reached for the small transistor radio next to the table and turned the dial to WSB for a weather report.

In Jessie's family, coming-of-age subjects were not often discussed, so she knew her parents were serious when they spoke of their need to talk. Most of her knowledge about growing into maturity had begun with classes arranged through her sixth-grade scout troop. Mothers joined their daughters at the classes as the girls listened to "foreign" information about things like menstruation and visual aids of male and female anatomy. Intimate subjects were left to the parents' discretion beyond those classes.

Jessie had learned much more through conversations with friends and at slumber parties. A lot more than what those awkward scout classes taught, she thought. They had all depended on Claire to educate the group. "Her parents tell her everything!" said Missy.

131

After breakfast, the family moved into the living room. Mr. Reynolds pulled up the blinds to admire the snow and watched as it quietly continued to fall. Jessie found her mother's afghan folded neatly in the basket next to the fireplace and settled in on the Chippendale sofa facing out toward the street in front of the house. A cardinal looking for food on the front porch caught her attention. Its red feathers stood out against the pure white blanket of snow. She was transported to Alabama and a summer visit to her Grandmother Danby's farm.

The two of them had been in her grandmother's rose garden when a cardinal had landed on a bush nearby.

"Oh, look, Jessie," her grandmother had said. "Someone is thinking of us from above. See a red cardinal and it's a sign that those we've lost miss us. They're telling us they are still with us in good times and bad, especially when we need them the most."

JESSIE WAS DISTRACTED FROM HER THOUGHTS by her mother taking a seat in the wing chair near her father. "Now, what's this senior ring mean, Jessie? We think Carter is a nice boy but we know so little about him and his family. Lord knows we were glad that whole Fulton situation turned out the way it did."

Jessie thought for a moment before answering. "It's not like an engagement ring or anything. But it *does* mean we'll be known as a couple at school. What can I tell you more than that? Maybe he can come for dinner so you could get to know him better."

Mr. Reynolds, who was generally more stern when it came to his daughters' dates, leaned forward in his chair. "He is not my son and I have no authority over him and what he does. But I *do* want to know you are making good decisions about how and with who you spend your time. Coach O'Connor has been quoted as saying some good things about Carter, and that's a start. And our parent group from the basketball games seems to think he is a nice young man." His voice softened. "It's just you're the baby, and I'm having a hard time thinking you are growing up so fast."

The phone rang and Jessie got up to answer it. She was glad to hear Robin's voice. "You probably already know, but the choir won't be singing this morning."

"I figured as much," said Jessie, a little disappointed. She had hoped to show Carter's gift to all her church friends. At least she could tell Robin about the night and the ring.

"Are you kidding me?" said Robin. "How romantic! I can't imagine Mark ever planning something like that!"

"Carter's the one, I think. I know you wanted William and Mark and you and me to remain couple friends, but—"

"It's okay, Jess," said Robin. "And just so you know, Mark told me that William is dating someone from his school." Jessie was glad to hear this news. She'd certainly never set out to hurt William and she hoped he was happy.

SCHOOL WAS OUT FOR THE HOLIDAYS, signaling a string of busy days leading up to Christmas. The few remaining choir practices with Mr. James were sad, but Jessie reminded herself that college teaching had been his dream—just like teaching was a career she'd thought about too. After practice one evening, she was rearranging the sheet music in the library when Mr. James asked her to stop by his office when she was finished. She replaced the last notebook and stepped around the corner to where Mr. James was sitting.

"How's it going?" he asked.

"That is a better question for you, isn't it?" said Jessie, smiling.

He pointed to the chair in front of his mahogany desk. "Have a seat. "How's your holiday going? Your family having a big celebration?"

"The holidays are good," Jessie said, in a low key manner. It was difficult to mask the joy of her forever love with Carter as she reached to touch the ring at her neck. She knew there was something else on Mr. James's mind—he'd never been one for much small talk.

"Tell me about this Carter fellow. Could that be his ring on the chain you are wearing?"

"Have you been talking to Robin?"

He leaned back in his chair. "No. Actually his name came up in a conversation with your parents. It sounds like you two are pretty serious."

"Yes," she said calmly, though not surprised by her parents' concern.

"You know, you are one who has made my work and ministry here so rewarding. I have enjoyed this choir so much. Working with young people and seeing them experiencing the joys of life gives me such a joy for life myself. I wanted to say thank you for that." He leaned forward to rest his arms on his desk. "But I also want to say, believe it or not, that life is short. Make the most of everyday and surround yourself with good people. Take one day at a time and pass some of that joy on to others around you whenever you can."

Jessie didn't miss a beat. "My parents are worried about me and Carter, aren't they?"

The music minister first looked surprised and then laughed. "I'm impressed. I didn't think I was being that obvious! I'm going to have to sharpen my counseling skills before I leave for North Carolina."

Jessie took a deep breath. "Well, Mr. James, they don't have to worry. I know where I am heading and I haven't forgotten my goals. Carter Powell is like no other boy I have dated. The first time I met him I had that 'you just know' feeling people talk about."

Mr. James leaned back in his swivel chair. "So, tell me about him. What makes him so special and different from the others?"

Jessie answered without hesitation. "He is humble and respectful. He can have fun and appreciate the little things. He is a member of Sandy Springs Methodist Church and he's in the ROTC—both church and country are priorities for him." She paused for a moment, thinking about the school blanket. "He is protective and yet not overbearing. He listens and is open and honest. He loves music and sports and he's good at both. He's had a harder time in life than anyone I have ever known, but he *loves* life and I know he truly cares about me."

"Wow," said Mr. James. "That's certainly a list of wonderful characteristics." Jessie had surprised even herself with her ability to list so many of Carter's qualities without thinking.

Mr. James gazed at her for a moment and smiled genuinely at her. "Well, Jessie, I know you have always had your head on straight and your heart in the right place. You have a foundation given to you by your parents and—I can say—your church, will see you through. Always trust it and your heart will see you through every time."

Chapter Eighteen

Jessie got out of her car and walked toward Carter and a group of guys from the football team who had gathered to play a pickup game.

"Hi, Catch!" said Carter.

Jessie tried to look serious. "Catch? What's that about?"

He grinned. "With all the other guys in the world, I still can't believe I caught you!"

Later, when they were with friends, Carter whispered his new pet name for her in her ear. Others noticed the beam that radiated from Jessie, especially Fran. "Okay, you two. What is that whisper about? You know it isn't nice to tell secrets!"

"No secrets," he said. "Just a hello for my girl!"

Over the holidays, there were movie dates at the Rhodes Theater, the Fox and the Piedmont Drive-In. They spent happy times at The Crow's Nest, and cozy evenings in the Reynolds rec room. Jessie knew her time with him was precious—she was already dreading the uncertainty of how they would maintain their relationship after Carter graduated.

The Playboys were booked a lot too during the holidays, including one performance at Carter's church for their youth Christmas party. Jessie was glad for the opportunity it gave her to become more acquainted with Rev. Hamilton. She stood in the back watching and listening and saw the energy and enthusiasm Carter's drumming inspired.

The minister approached and handed her a soda. "You know, the Powell and Crawford families have come a long way and overcome many obstacles. It's good to see Carter happy and doing well."

A Georgia Tech fraternity had called months before to ask The Playboys to do their New Year's Eve event. The pay was too good to refuse, so Crow suggested a New Year's Day party the next evening to cap off the year's successful run. Brandi and Crow both wanted to hear Jessie's description of the Crow's Nest surprise Carter had pulled off.

The foursome arrived early for a private toast for the good things to come. "To many years ahead with the love of good friends and each other. To us!"

Fran and Mike were invited and last to arrive. Jessie had not seen them together since the Snow Ball but the stressed looks on both of their faces were hard not to notice. Almost immediately, Mike pulled Carter aside.

Jessie searched the room for Fran and when she saw her in another corner of the Nest, she joined her. "Are you and Mike okay?"

Fran barely acknowledged her. "We're fine," she said. And then, "I heard Carter gave you his ring."

"He did. As a matter of fact, he gave it to me right here after the Snow Ball." Before Jessie could continue, Fran turned and ran toward the bathroom and Brandi appeared from nowhere.

"Fran and Mike have something going on," she said.

"I have no idea what it is. Maybe an argument, but I think it's more than that. They were like this at the Snow Ball."

Brandi gestured toward Carter and Mike. "Carter has to know. You can tell by the way he is talking to Mike."

"I think I need to check on Fran," said Jessie.

"That's probably a good idea."

Jessie found Fran crying in the bathroom. "I'm sorry you're so upset," she said. "What's wrong?"

Fran wiped tears from her eyes. "Oh, Jessie. I've been so stupid. And Mike is so upset with me. I really can't talk about it. Not yet. I think we better leave. Will you ask Mike to get my coat?"

"If I can help, you'll let me know, right?"

"Yes."

Jessie delivered Fran's request to Mike and he drew a deep breath and headed to retrieve her coat. Carter reached for her hand. "Jessie, I promise to always take good care of us."

"What does *that* mean?" she asked.

Carter walked her to the dance floor and wrapped his arms around her. "Trust me. Always. I know we need to talk."

After the song was over, Crow's parents appeared. By the way Carter responded when he saw them, she could tell they included him like a part of the family. Brandi stopped the music and gathered the other couples together. Crow raised his glass to make a toast for the New Year. "To friends who are family and family who are friends. A happy and prosperous New Year for each of you!"

Everyone hugged and then cheered and the music began again. Jessie watched over Carter's shoulder as Mike and Fran slipped out the door. The party continued and soon all began to say their good nights.

Jessie learned over to pick up her coat and felt a twinge of dizziness.

She had shaken off a tired feeling earlier in the evening attributing it to all of the holiday activities.

In the car on their way home, Jessie placed her head on Carter's shoulder, only raising it when they arrived at her driveway. Carter had been especially quiet. "I know you well enough to know something is bothering you," she said. "Is it Mike and Fran?"

He nodded. "I need to tell you what's——"

Jessie closed her eyes and took a deep breath and he stopped. "Are you okay?"

"The holidays have just been so busy. I guess I am just tired."

"Do you think your parents will understand if we sit out here and talk?"

"It's just Mom. Dad's out of town," said Jessie. She began to shake. "Carter, I don't feel so good. My head hurts and I'm feeling dizzy."

He felt her forehead and reached for his school blanket. "You're burning up. Here. Wrap this around you. Come on. We're getting you inside!" He ran around the car, swept her into his arms, and headed up the sidewalk.

Carter fumbled with Jessie's house key but, before he could insert it into the lock, Mrs. Reynolds opened the door, tying her robe around her. "What happened? Is she hurt?"

"I don't know," he said. "She seemed fine tonight at the party and then on the way home, she said she was dizzy and started shaking. Now she can hardly walk."

Like Carter, Mrs. Reynolds felt Jessie's head. "She definitely has a fever. Can you take her upstairs to her room?" She motioned to the stairs. "There is so much going around. I'm going to call the doctor's after-hours line."

Carter started up the stairs, and Jessie tightened her arms around his neck. "You're going to be all right, Jess," he whispered.

She pointed to the door of her bedroom and Carter placed her on one of two twin beds. He removed her shoes and then covered her with the blanket. She opened her eyes and watched him as he glanced around her room, taking in his expressions as he saw the bulletin board covered with newspaper clippings about his football performances. There were pep club ribbons surrounding his name, which was written in large letters in the middle. The roses he had given her at the Nest after the Snow Ball were pressed and carefully pinned to the board.

"Stay, Carter. Don't leave me," she said. He started to reassure her but looked up to see Mrs. Reynolds standing in the doorway.

"I reached the doctor's on-call line," she said. "The nurse says there is mononucleosis going around. That could explain some of these symptoms. They told me to watch her for the next several hours and, if her condition changes before morning, to take her to the emergency room."

Carter released Jessie's hand. "Jessie told me that Mr. Reynolds is out of town. If you need help during the night, Mrs. Reynolds—to get her to the emergency clinic or anything—please call me."

"Of course," said Mrs. Reynolds. "Thank you, Carter. And don't worry. She'll be all right. Call us in the morning. I'll let you know how she's doing."

"Yes, ma'am." Carter walked to the door and turned to say goodbye but went silent when he saw Mrs. Reynolds' face and her obvious care for her daughter. He continued down the stairs and let himself out.

As Carter started the car, a wave of sadness washed over him. He thought of all the doctor visits he'd had after broken arms and ankle sprains and cuts needing stitches, all sustained when Bobby and he and their neighborhood friends had played army. He'd always considered his bandages as badges of courage, like the heroes in Papa's military stories. He hadn't realized how much he'd missed in not having a mother's touch when he was sick or hurt until he'd seen the look on Mrs. Reynolds's face.

THE PHONE RANG SEVERAL TIMES. Jessie opened her eyes when she heard her mother's voice at her bedroom door. She raised her head, then lowered it. Her head and throat hurt. She was weak and her muscles ached. Her mother felt her head and pulled out a thermometer. Jessie obediently opened her mouth and allowed her mother to stick it under her tongue. She closed her eyes again and dozed until her mother spoke.

"You still have a fever."

"What is it? Is Carter here?"

"It is 103 degrees. You're confused, honey. Carter brought you home last night and then went home. That was him on the phone to check on you. This could be the flu or a virus or even mono. I spoke with the on-call nurse last night and have a call in to the doctor." Jessie's mom offered a sip of ginger ale, the age-old liquid of choice in times of illness.

Jessie groaned. It was hard even to think. "Claire said there was flu and mononucleosis going around school. This could last several days or several weeks!" She flopped back on the pillows.

Mrs. Reynolds reached for Jessie's gown on the closet door hook. "I told Carter maybe you could talk later this afternoon. For now, let's get you into your nightgown. Carter took off your shoes last night, but you were so dizzy, I let you sleep in your clothes. How about something to eat?"

"I'm not hungry. I feel awful." Jessie just wanted her dizziness, fever and chills to go away.

Afternoon rolled around and Jessie's mother came in carrying a wooden tray of chicken noodle soup and crackers with more ginger ale. She managed to slide up in bed and her mother lowered the tray across her. "I've spoken with the doctor. We have an appointment tomorrow. From your symptoms, he's pretty sure you have mono."

Jessie sighed. Claire had joked about mononucleosis. Everyone called it "the kissing disease." But this was no joke!

"The doctor said friends need to be careful about sharing soft drinks or food. We're looking at your possibly missing weeks of school."

"Maybe it's just a virus."

"Maybe," said Mrs. Reynolds. "But until we know for sure, you are to stay in bed and rest. Doctor's...and MY orders!"

It was late afternoon when Jessie heard the phone again. The dormer window alcove next to her bed was filled with a tissue box, thermometer, a glass of ginger ale and a plate of leftover crackers. Her mother had closed the cafe curtains to keep the light at a minimum so Jessie could rest. Mrs. Reynolds called up the stairs and asked if she felt like taking a call. "It's Carter," she said.

Jessie rolled over with some difficulty and picked up the receiver, placing it next to her ear.

"I'm so sorry, Jess." Hearing Carter's voice was like a magic potion to Jessie's spirits and she tried not to sound as bad as she felt. "Mother says my fever is a hundred and three."

"You had me worried last night, Catch. And everyone was asking about you at school today. I heard Mr. Kelley and Miss Clay in the office talking about the number of absences. Mrs. Spearman was even talking in gym class about being careful because it was so contagious."

Jessie pulled the phone cord closer and settled back on her pillow.

"I go to the doctor in the morning. I guess we'll know for sure then. Are *you* feeling okay?"

"I feel fine," said Carter. "But wouldn't it be something if the two of us were side by side in our sick beds! Your mom is the best. I know she is taking good care of you. By the way, that is some room you have."

"Yes, since my sisters are gone, I have the whole upstairs to myself. It's a bit of a hike for my mother to check on me right now, but nice and private when I'm talking to you. Thank you for helping my mom last night and carrying me up here."

"It was the least I could do. You had me worried. By the way, what's the story on the pink dog?"

Jessie looked over to see the stuffed dog still sitting in her slipper chair. "That was given to me last fall by the guy I was dating before I met you. You know, William, the one I told you about from my church."

"Oh, yeah, I remember."

"Don't worry. I keep it as a reminder of the difference between friendship and true forever love." Carter was silent and she imagined a smile on his face. "Is that a smile I'm hearing?"

"You got that right. I love you, Catch. I want you to feel better. Let me know how it goes at the doctor's office."

"I will. Claire is going to get my books and assignments for me. Tell Mrs. Laney and Coach hello."

After an evening of more chicken soup, crackers, and ginger ale, Jessie woke the next morning without much improvement. The fever had taken its toll. She teetered out of bed to look in the mirror and caught her breath at the sight. She searched for her hairbrush and hoped no one would see her in such a state. She got into the shower in hopes that it would make her feel better and look better for the doctor's visit. Once she'd accomplished that, she put on her robe and slowly descended the stairs toward the kitchen.

Her eyes fell on a red rose in a bud vase on the kitchen table. Her mother set a plate of cinnamon toast in front of her.

"It was on the front steps this morning when I went out to get the paper." Her mother looked closely at her. "How are you feeling this morning?"

Jessie beamed. "Much better!" She knew Carter must have left for school early to have dropped off the rose on his way.

The doctor confirmed that Jessie had mono and prescribed a major period of rest, medication and lots of fluids. Each day, Claire brought Jessie's school assignments and teacher notes. Carter met Claire daily to add special notes for Jessie to discover tucked in the pages of her assignments. His distinctive handwriting on the envelopes became her special medicine. His notes had silly drawings in the margins but always ended with sweet words of love and comfort. She put every note in the memory box tucked in her drawer. They were special, but nothing compared to hearing the sound of his voice each afternoon.

Robin kept her posted on the friends and happenings at church and Sandy called with other news. "I swear we saw Rick pass the Zesto, Jess. He drove by slowly then took off when he saw Jack." Jessie had managed not to think about Rick since the Fulton incident, and she was determined not to give him the satisfaction of another thought.

AS SHE BEGAN TO RECOVER, JESSIE's mother allowed Carter to see her when he delivered her morning roses as long as he kept a distance. When she returned to school, his face was the first to greet her when she arrived at her locker. "Am I glad to see you!"

Jessie turned to the face she cherished most. "This whole crazy place has been empty without you," said Carter. He leaned against her locker. "I even had to listen to Coach giving me a hard time about moping around acting all lovesick."

The homeroom bell rang, and Carter waved to someone behind her. Jessie turned to see Jack pass by on his way to their first class.

Carter gave her a squeeze. "Jack's a good guy. I passed him on your street several times when I was leaving your roses." He put his books under his arm. "See you at lunch? I can take you home after school. Coach said there is no track practice today."

When she got to art room door, Jack was waiting for her.

"Feeling better?" She was about to answer when Fran appeared beside them.

"Hey, Jessie! You're back!"

Jack signaled that he'd talk to her later and went on inside the classroom.

"Yes, I'm back! How's Mike?"

Fran raised her eyebrows. "You mean Carter didn't tell you? Mike and I broke up that night at the Crow's Nest."

"No, he didn't."

Fran flipped her hair over her shoulder. "Oh, it's no big deal. You win some and you lose some. But I'm sure Carter is glad to have you back."

Jack waited at their worktable and held Jessie's chair. She took her seat and smiled at him and pulled out her sketchpad to prepare for class. He retrieved her canvas from their storage cubicle. "Your project is just as you left it," he said.

"Welcome back to the land of the living, Jessica!" said Mr. Baker as he passed by the table. "Your roses were waiting for you." He pointed to the unfinished canvas. "It'll be good for you to get back to their development. It appears a bit complex between the abstract and still life."

He continued to the front of the class and made an announcement. "Class, the prom committee has asked for our help in their planning. I will have more details soon, but I want you to begin thinking how we can interject our works into the prom this year."

The idea sounded wonderful to Jessie. She remembered the single comment he'd given with respect to the junior class Christmas displays and how things had turned out. Jack gave her a thumbs up. "We got this," he whispered.

Mr. Baker continued. "I will be coming around and checking in with each of you this morning. We are getting close to the end of the year and I think we have some great possibilities for entries in the district art competition."

With the morning's eastern light, the large windows made creative impressions on Jessie's work space. She toyed with sketches of an impressionist design. Her abstract work from back in the fall seemed so elementary now. As with her experience of true love, her art had matured. Everything in her world now seemed more real, more vibrant and colorful.

Mr. Baker looked over Jessie's shoulder. "Your work this year has really blossomed. What is your secret?" Jack looked up from his drawing.

Jessie thought for a moment. "I suppose I have a deeper sense of myself."

"Interesting," said the art teacher. "I hope you will use that sense of self to produce a piece for the art competition. Maybe even something that would be useful for the prom. Do you have that inspiration in you?" He turned and spoke to the whole class. "Once the prom committee has a direction, I will share it with you and we will round table our efforts and work together on it."

Jessie glanced at Jack. He had been a constant for her since their early grade school years and yet, something seemed different—he seemed more reserved than usual.

"You okay?" He gave her a slight nod and returned to his work, so she did too.

Even with her inclinations toward business and education as a career, Jessie's artistic side was calling her. Her sketches that day involved roses of various shapes—still life, landscape scenes, and impressionist studies. Her direction was coming from deep within.

Lunchtime was a "welcome back" party. Fran waltzed by as Jessie headed toward Sandy and the girls. The next thing she knew, she heard, "Hi! I'm Carter. I believe you are my date?" The girls giggled as they watched him pull out a chair at the table next to them.

"Thank you, sir," she replied, moving over to take her seat.

Carter pulled his own chair close and whispered in her ear. "Welcome back, Catch." They pulled sandwiches from their lunch bags. Jessie had noticed that he always had a balanced lunch. Knowing that he and Bobby had to care for themselves, she was embarrassed that she had ever complained about her food.

"You have an apple today?" he asked.

It reminded her of what he had said to Fran about her the first time he saw her. She grinned and reached into her bag to pull out a shiny red delicious. "Right here! An apple a day keeps the doctor away." He laughed and leaned in to take a bite.

Mike walked by on the way to the guys' table. "You two look happy," he said. "Hope it will last." Jessie had not seen him since hearing the news of their break-up. She watched him as he continued on his way.

"Wish things were better for him," said Carter. "He's had a rough time while you've been out sick."

"Why didn't you tell me about him and Fran breaking up?"

"It's a long story. I thought it should wait until you were better."

Claire stopped at the table to speak to Jessie. "The prom committee is meeting after school. Mr. Baker said for you to join us. We are to meet in the library."

Jessie looked at Carter. She knew he had planned to take her home after school. "I'll wait for you," he said.

"Good," said Jessie. "My mom said she wanted to see you. She has something for you!"

When lunch was over, Carter walked Jessie to Coach O'Connor's class. "He's probably going to give me a hard time when he sees us together," Carter warned. "Our talks about next year have gotten a bit touchy lately."

"Why?"

"That's another long story. I've had a hard time not getting down on myself when it comes to college next year and all. Miss Clay has been helping me, but there's nothing so far. I bet Mrs. Laney will be anxious to see you, too."

"Hey, you two!" said Coach as they reached his door. She saw Carter's step quicken.

"She's back!" said Carter, giving Jessie a kiss on the cheek.

Coach put on his best scolding voice. "Mr. Powell! That will be banks for you this afternoon!"

"Yes sir, Coach. Thank you, Coach. I'll be there, Coach!" Carter backed away and headed to class. Jessie almost thought she heard him whistle.

Coach shook his head. "And you put up with that guy?"

Mrs. Laney was thrilled to see Jessie in her class. In her motherly manner, she cautioned her to not overdo. "I won't," said Jessie. "I'm just taking one day at a time until I feel better."

"Good. I have a folder for you from the Education Department at Georgia. I think you will like what you see. I want you to consider a visit to the department."

Jessie took the folder and assured Mrs. Laney that she would. She thought about all her friends and their future plans. Jack had always wanted to go to UGA and she thought sure he would. Terry knew a football scholarship was in his future—many college scouts had contacted Coach about him. Although Jessie loved art, Christy was Mr. Baker's top student and would head to art school in Savannah. William would follow in his father's footsteps and the family business. Robin and Mark had already made campus visits to West Georgia.

It was easy to name those who had defined their paths in one way or another. Like them, Jessie had never considered going anywhere other than Georgia. UGA and Athens had always been the goal just like they'd been for her sister, Meredith.

She thought about her father. Ladd Reynolds had told all his daughters the same thing. "You do your part and we'll do ours. You make the grades and get accepted into college and your mother and I will save and cover the costs." Jessie had made it part of her plan to work hard and achieve her dream to teach someday.

She looked down at the brochure, but she could only see Carter. She hoped his college potential would soon be recognized.

Chapter Nineteen

Jessie joined Claire and other junior class members at the prom committee meeting. She was happy to be back and able to participate. Mr. Baker opened the discussion noting the location had been decided. A ballroom had been secured at the Holiday Inn on Howell Mill near the Interstate 75 interchange.

The second order of business was decorations—and a band. When the Playboys were mentioned, Jessie tried not to react. In her heart, she prayed the group wouldn't be chosen.

Mr. Baker saved the day. "Even though the majority of the band members are in college, I don't think it is fair to Carter Powell to not be able to fully participate in his prom." Jessie breathed a sigh of relief.

"But they're the best around," said a girl across the room.

"Overruled, Maryanne!" said Mr. Baker. "I'm putting you in charge of finding another option." He paused. "Moving on. Now, for a theme, food, and decorations. Once we have all these items in place, we can determine a cost. Dr. and Mrs. Caldwell have already let me know they will sponsor the prom which will help to keep the cost per student down."

Jessie volunteered for the theme and decorations planning committee. As others left the room after the meeting, Jessie stopped to talk to Mr. Baker. "Could we have an art auction to raise money for the prom?"

The art teacher smiled. "What a wonderful idea, Jessica! I cannot think of a better idea, and it would encourage everyone to take their district art competition creations to a new level. I'll check with Principal Kelley for his approval."

When Jessie exited the school building, she found Carter waiting for her on the brick wall at the front entrance. "Hey! How was the meeting?"

"It was good," answered Jessie. "Maryanne Sharpe wanted to ask the Playboys to play, but Mr. Baker nixed it pretty quickly. I didn't say anything, and I don't know if you guys need the money or not, but I want us to be together that night."

Carter smiled. "That's all good. The guys all agreed long ago we wouldn't perform at events that we were personally connected to. I'm glad Mr. Baker took care of it. We would have turned it down anyway. Nothing will stand in the way of it being a special time for us."

Jessie told him about the art auction idea. She was already picturing ideas in her mind. "I am going to work on some sketches tonight to show Mr. Baker tomorrow."

They walked to Carter's car. "I know you need to go home to rest, Catch. But I thought we might go by the park and talk. I wanted to tell you something New Year's night but then you got sick."

"Okay. But remember, Mother has something for you."

The park's lawns had just been mowed and were pristine, their fescue signaling the Atlanta spring. Carter pulled over at their usual spot and removed his keys from the ignition. He held the medallion and Papa Ford's dog tags in his hand, and Jessie wondered what was on his mind.

Carter selected a tree near the creek bank and sat first, reaching for her hand so she could nestle in front of him. The water flowed quietly toward Howell Mill.

He moved her hair aside and wove several strands of her hair together. "Let's see. Is this how you do it?"

"More like this," she said, shifting in front of him so that she could show him how to braid her hair.

Carter wrapped his arms around her. "We have been together eight months, Jess. The best eight months of my life. I've never been happier."

Jessie heard a different tone in his voice and turned to look at him. "Me, too," she said. "I can't tell you how happy I've been."

He sat for a moment and finally spoke. "You asked me several times about Mike and Fran."

Jessie nodded. "Yeah, why didn't you tell me they broke up?"

"That's part of what I need to talk to you about. At the Snow Ball, Mike thought Fran was pregnant. I told him not to overreact until they knew for sure, but all Mike could think about was his plan for college and a football scholarship. He even talked about *options* if she was pregnant."

"What do you mean?" asked Jessie.

"Catch, life is very important to me. For lots of reasons. More than you think." He looked away and then back at her. "Mike was a wreck. He kept suggesting doing something to get rid of the baby if Fran was pregnant. I mean, I know it was their decision and I was trying to be supportive, but I thought I knew him better than that. He even accused Fran of *trying* to get pregnant so he would have to marry her."

Jessie looked out over the creek and thought about how many times she and Carter had already come close to taking their love to the next level and what might have happened if they had and what might happen if they did. "It has been enough time for them to know by now. What happened?"

"As it turned out, she was *not* pregnant, but they broke up when she pressed the whole idea of marriage anyway. Mike told me she accused him of taking advantage of her when they were together. That night at Crow's, he told her he was going to college to play football no matter what. It just got worse from there."

Jessie turned to face Carter and saw a deep sadness in his eyes. "At least Mike came to you as a friend and you told him what you thought. My guess is Fran went to no one. She certainly didn't come to me." She turned back to look at the water. "I knew you and Mike had something going on, and I knew you would help him work it out."

"I think he really loved Fran, but he saw a different side of her through it all. I'm just glad it didn't come to putting an innocent life at risk."

They were both quiet for a moment.

"Is there something else you need to tell me?" she asked.

"I just need us to trust each other and know we are there for each other forever. That our decisions will always be based on what's best for both of us. No matter what."

Jessie took his hand and placed it on her heart. "Forever. You and me, Carter Powell. Good times, bad times, happy times, sad times. I hope you know that." Carter held her tight.

The breeze picked up and Carter placed his jacket around her shoulders. "I better get you home. I don't want your mom to worry about you."

JESSIE'S MOTHER BROUGHT GREAT PLEASURE TO friends and families by preparing meals and treats for them and her home cooking was well known in the community. She felt it was a ministry for her to share food she made to warm their souls. Her father did his part, too, helping with the cooking, buying the baskets, and making the deliveries. His ministry was to provide the wit and humor to brighten the day of the recipients of his wife's special homemade gifts. That afternoon she'd been making a special gift for Carter to thank him for his help and concern when Jessie was sick.

When Carter and Jessie went inside, they were met with the aroma of roast beef with potatoes, carrots and onions. In the kitchen, they saw a dish with green beans and a Mason jar of homemade tomato jam on the table—next to a still-cooling pineapple pound cake. Carter's eyes grew big as Mrs. Reynolds opened the oven door and removed a tin of yeast rolls. She smiled with genuine pleasure. "Well, it's not red roses, young man, but I hope you and Bobby will like it."

Carter rubbed his hands together. "Yes, ma'am! Thank you!"

"Ladd has the baskets ready, and I will have this packed up soon. Jessie, hand Carter some of my TLCs to test."

Jessie laughed when she saw Carter's confused expression. She held a plate of oatmeal chocolate chip cookies in front of him. "Dad calls these her TLCs, her 'tender loving care' cookies. He tells people that she can make them with her eyes closed. And he's serious. Trust me, Mom never lets the cookie jar get low when Dad's around."

ON THE WAY HOME WITH THE FOOD, Carter felt his mood lift. He realized that the situation with Mike and Fran and what Mike had contemplated when he'd thought Fran was pregnant had been a heavy burden for him. This unexpected gesture from Jessie's mother, however, filled him with gratitude. He thought of how Papa Ford had shared vegetables with neighbors from his garden at the house on Moores Mill and his heart warmed. Jessie's mother's thoughtfulness gave him hope for a future with Jessie's family. Perhaps the Powell and Crawford families weren't that different from the Reynolds family, after all.

THE NEXT WEEK AT SCHOOL WENT by fast. Students were preparing for their final exams. The chorus held multiple practices for its spring concert and the prom committee met every afternoon. Jessie worked on her assignment at school and at home, sketching variations of roses. Her palette of reds increased with intensity as her drawings developed.

Mr. Baker was encouraging. "Very good. Keep on," he said as he stood watching her technique. "Have you thought about a theme for prom?"

Jessie looked up and grinned. "Can't you tell?" she joked. "Everything's Coming Up Roses!"

Mr. Baker's face brightened. "Straight from the musical *Gypsy*. You know, I think that is a great idea!" He reached for her drawings and looked closely at them. "How would we incorporate this into the decorations?"

Jessie was a step ahead of him. "I would like to create the backdrop for pictures at the entry to the ballroom. A large canvas of a rose. How would that work with lighting and a photographer?" she asked.

Jack, who sat in his claimed spot across the table, looked up. "I could help her. Maybe prep the canvas? It would have to be pretty large and Jess might need help to handle it," he said.

Jessie nodded emphatically. "Thanks, Jack!"

"I'm sure that would be helpful, Mr. Mason," said Mr. Baker. "We will do whatever we must to make it work."

He raised his hand to his forehead. "A photographer! I forgot to put choosing a photographer on the committee's list of things to do. I'll make some calls, and we can discuss it tomorrow at the meeting." He made a note in a composition book. "And I will order you a large canvas today. We will need to start on that piece right away."

The art auction received clearance from the school administration. To obtain greater awareness, word of the upcoming sale went out to the community. Mr. Baker suggested that it be a silent auction and that the school tie it to its annual Open House and final PTA meeting. Principal Kelley even told Mr. Baker to plan on the auction's becoming an annual event to highlight his art students.

The prom committee members were enthusiastic about Jessie's ideas and embraced the theme and decorations. During one of their meetings, Mr. Kelley stepped in to congratulate the committee. "The idea fits even better than you may know. Several years ago, before we changed to having the seniors wear caps and gowns at graduation, our young men wore suits and our young women wore white dresses. Each girl carried a bouquet of red roses."

Their brainstorming complete, each went out with assignments to implement. The large canvas arrived, and Jack found the best studio space for it so Jessie could work. Mr. Baker provided multiple shades of red paint. It took extra time after school, but the masterpiece slowly but surely came together. In no time, the florists were overrun with orders for rose corsages and boutonnieres. Roses were solicited from family gardens to create arrangements to decorate tables at the dance.

The silent auction for entries in the district art competition was scheduled a week before the prom. Mr. Baker was optimistic the funds raised would help cover the prom expenses. Members of the Art Council were solicited to judge the competition.

Jessie was astounded when she and Carter entered the auction. Her canvas was front and center. Mr. Baker was talking with a couple and pointing to other pieces around the room when he saw her come in. "Jessie," he called. "Come meet Judge and Mrs. Fields."

Upon hearing the names, Jessie looked at Carter. Carter hesitated but took Jessie's arm and began to guide her through the crowd toward Mr. Baker. "Don't say anything about me," he said. "This is *your* night. I have no interest in bringing up Rick with his parents," he whispered.

When they approached, the art teacher turned to Jessie. "This is the artist of the rose canvas you asked about."

Jessie extended her hand as her father had taught her to. "I'm Jessie Reynolds."

Mrs. Fields smiled. "Yes, we know. Your work is amazing. The proportions are spectacular."

Jessie managed a thank you and stole a look at Mr. Baker. Surely he knew Rick's Fulton prank had almost cost Carter everything.

"We will be very interested in seeing the results of the competition," continued Mrs. Fields, who glanced at her husband. "Dear, let's browse some of the other paintings." She turned back to the young couple and nodded at each in turn. "Jessie. Carter." They had never been introduced, but Mrs. Fields definitely knew who they both were.

Mr. Baker waited until the couple was out of earshot. "Interesting people." Jessie opened her mouth to speak, but he stopped her. "I know. I know. The Rick thing was disappointing and Carter, you have every right to be upset with them."

Carter shook his head. "No, sir. I don't hold any grudges toward them. I just hope their son has gotten some help."

At the end of the night, Jessie's canvas had been awarded first place and a "SOLD" sign was placed beside the blue ribbon. Mr. Baker rushed over. "One thousand dollars, Jessie! One thousand dollars!"

"We made a thousand dollars for the prom?!"

"No. Your *painting*. It brought one thousand dollars by itself! The owners will allow it to be used at the prom, and it will be delivered to them afterwards."

"Them?"

"Yes, the Fields. There was a lot of interest in your rose and Judge and Mrs. Fields told me they were not going to let anyone else outbid them. They said they have a perfect place for it in their home."

Jessie was speechless. She looked around, but the Fields were nowhere in sight. She saw Carter beaming at her across the room. It was clear he wanted her to bask alone in her well-deserved glory. "I don't know what to say," she said, when he finally reached her.

Coach O'Connor slid up beside them. "I dropped by to see what you art lovers were up to," he said. "And congratulations, Jessie. You must paint a smaller version for my gallery wall at home someday. My Ann loved her rose garden." He looked at Jessie and smiled with a hint of sadness. "You know, Miss Reynolds, a rose only blossoms once."

THE NIGHT OF THE PROM FINALLY came. In between her recovery and the extra canvas activities, Jessie's mom had managed a shopping trip with her. The powder blue dress with a chiffon ruffle that they'd found at Davison's complimented Jessie's eyes, and the a stop in the jewelry department had yielded the right accessories to add the necessary sparkle. She modeled the purchase for her father, who reminisced the many times she and her sisters had made "runway turns" for him in the past.

The doorbell rang and Mr. Reynolds opened it to find Carter standing on the porch in a tuxedo with a white dinner jacket. He saw the glow in the boy's eyes when he first saw Jessie and invited him in.

Mrs. Reynolds pinned a red rose boutonniere on Carter and a matching corsage on Jessie's shoulder. Just as on the night of the Snow Ball, Jessie's father took photographs of them in front of the fireplace while her mother stood next to him, instructing him in how to take the ideal shot. Jessie was amused at the whole interaction, but she took advantage of the moment to whisper to Carter how handsome he looked.

The early spring air was cool, and Carter winked at Jessie and took her hand when they reached the bottom step outside. He glanced back at her parents and knew their sleep would not begin until they heard their front door close later in the evening. They had extended Jessie's curfew to midnight.

By the time they arrived, the parking lot was already filling at the Holiday Inn. Carter reached to remove his keys from the ignition, thinking that Jessie would be anxious to join the others inside.

"Wait," said Jessie. Carter dropped his hand from the steering column and put his arm around her.

"I don't know how to say what I am feeling tonight," she continued.

"Are you feeling okay?"

"Yes. Not that kind of feeling. I am feeling like I want this night to last forever," she said. "I don't know. I guess I am sad about you graduating. It hit me tonight while I was getting ready. I don't know how to feel about not seeing you at school every morning at my locker. Not seeing you every time I enter the lunchroom. Not having you walk me to Coach's class or bringing me home after school."

Carter turned to face her. "I know how you feel. And there's one thing for sure. We will always have each other. Together or not. You will never have to question that."

As they entered the ballroom, they were pleased to see Jessie's rose canvas backdrop. The photographer was busy posing couples in front of it for their official photos. Carter and Jessie waited in line and then took their place. They could hear the band already playing inside and saw Coach O'Connor across the room. He gave them a silent thumbs up.

Mike had invited Missy and had reserved seats for Jessie and Carter at their table. Within minutes, Jack and Sandy joined them, along with Claire and Tom. Jessie waved at Fran when she arrived with her date, a boy from Fulton, and watched as she searched for a table across the room. Dr. and Mrs. Caldwell were there as chaperones, along with Mrs. Laney and her husband, and Coach. Mr. Baker circled the room, checking every detail with the prom committee members to be sure all was going well.

The dance was proceeding smoothly when a girl Jessie hadn't expected to see came in. Carla Peterson had somehow managed an invitation to the prom from a Northwest senior she didn't know. It had been months since the Fulton incident and Carla's part in the vandalism had been chalked up to sour grapes, but Jessie knew she and Rick had orchestrated the plot together. She was placed on probation and given community service hours.

When Carter saw Jessie's face, he turned to see the cause of her horror and frowned. "Never thought I would see her again. Especially like this," he said.

"How could she dare come here? She *had* to know you would be here. That *we* would be here."

"We will just avoid her. I am betting that guy has no clue what she was up to last fall."

Jessie was still upset. Carter was clearly more forgiving than she was. "Something tells me this is not over with her."

"It's over, Jessie. I'm sure of it. Neither the band nor I have seen any sign of her or heard from her since last fall."

Though still naïve in many ways, Jessie had been around enough to know the look she caught in Carla's eyes. Carter had always been so protective of her. Now, it was her turn!

Carter left the table to talk to the band members on their break and Jessie saw an opportunity to work her way over to Coach. She pointed to a table where Carla and her date were sitting. "Coach, I don't know if you know it or not, but that's Carla Peterson."

"Seriously?" said Coach. "That's *her*? *Here*? At our prom?"

"Yes, yes, yes, and yes." Jessie was pleased to see Coach's outrage.

"Don't worry, Jessie. I will be watching her every move. Bobby and Carter decided not to press charges, but I never heard the outcome of her community service. I'm not sure if there was any decision on any kind of 'no trespassing' notice at Northwest activities, but Mr. Kelley will be here soon and I will find out. She is treading on shaky grounds regardless. If something happens, it won't be Carter who will be making the decision about her future. It will be me!" Coach turned to look again for Carla on the dance floor, but she and her date had mysteriously disappeared.

Carter joined Jessie and Coach as the band began to play again. "I learned about their booking agent," said Carter.

"Their what?"

"Booking agent. The Playboys have been approached by several booking agents, and Crow asked us to consider the idea. I thought I would check out the agent for these guys." Jessie looked at Carter with a questioning look and he explained.

"Crow spends a lot of time getting our bookings and keeping track of things for the band. It would mean giving up a percentage of our take to the agent, but it would also mean we would get more bookings and work. Summer jobs have been a big discussion at practices lately. The guys need to earn as much as possible during summer breaks to help pay their tuition. The band leader gave me their agent's card."

With summer coming, it was time for all of them to make choices. Bobby had already asked Carter to work for his company during the summer. Pete had an option of an internship at Tech.

Once the prom wound down, Jessie and Carter stopped at the Crow's Nest to check in with the group and he shared the agent's card. Crow called his dad down to ask his advice.

"It's the big time!" exclaimed Larry.

"It's now or never," Crow said. "This is our chance."

Chapter Twenty

After the prom, time flew by as the Class of '65 graduation approached. The Playboys signed a contract with a booking agent and through Coach O'Connor and Dr. Caldwell, who was on the board of Bradford, a small college in Kentucky, Carter received a full scholarship to play football. Jessie, along with Bobby and Marie, planned a party to celebrate Carter's graduation.

Carter's cap and gown hung on his closet door beside his ROTC uniform. Bobby walked by the room and saw his brother pacing the floor. "Big day! You okay?"

His gaze on the uniform, Carter nodded. "Sure. Ready."

Bobby stopped. "Hey man, what's up? That look says something else."

"I don't know. I guess I was wishing Papa could have been here."

"Me too," said Bobby. "But he's watching. Nothing matches his pride for you today."

"Yeah, but both of you got me here. Thanks, Bobby. I know you've made a lot of sacrifices for me."

Bobby's squeezed Carter's shoulder in what had always been a quiet show of support. "*You* got you here. Keep it going. Not so serious now. Marie, Jessie, the Reynolds—they've planned a nice dinner for you. This is a time to celebrate!"

Carter smiled. He took one last look at the uniform beside his graduation attire and nodded. "Coffee's ready?"

"You got it, Bud!"

Jessie stole a kiss when Carter joined her in his car and headed to Chastain. His purple graduation gown hung on the backseat hook. "Hey handsome. You excited?" she asked.

"'Kind of hard to believe it's here," said Carter.

"I know. If only I was up on that stage with you too. But next year will go by fast and who knows? Claire asked me if I would change my mind and apply to Bradford."

Carter's look surprised Jessie. "Your dream has always been to go to Athens," he said.

"I know. But dreams can change."

The Chastain amphitheater parking lot was filling and Carter glanced toward the park nature area and took a spot near its entrance. "I'll meet you at the steps afterwards," he said and they walked toward the graduate staging area.

Jessie could see Coach welcoming the graduates as they filed in and found their assigned places in line. She watched as Terry and Mike circled Carter when he reached them and Missy took a spin in her white gown.

"He looks good," said Bobby to Marie, who was sitting to Jessie's left. Jessie's parents had joined them and sat on her right, along with Rev. Hamilton.

A large class crossed the stage that afternoon with many caps flying at the end of the ceremony. "Big Jim is looking down with a big smile today," said the reverend.

"That's what I told Carter!" said Bobby. "He was a little down this morning, but it seemed to pick up his spirits."

Jessie heard Bobby's comment to Rev. Hamilton and stood to stretch and wave to Carter, who was making his way to them and waving his diploma. She was pleasantly surprised to see her mother step up and grab the first hug. Carter's eyes lit up with Mrs. Reynolds's gesture and Bobby joined their embrace. Mr. Reynolds touched his shoulder and Carter turned to find Jessie. He wrapped an arm around her shoulder. "Whew! Wow! Thanks, everyone, for being here." Jessie slipped her arm around his waist.

Mrs. Reynolds headed toward the parking lot. "Coach will be joining us for dinner, so don't be too long, you two."

"We won't," said Carter. "We just have one stop to make."

When they reached Carter's car, he kept going. His step quickened and Jessie almost ran to keep up. He pulled her inside the tunnel and pressed her to the wall, kissing her more passionately then ever before.

"This couldn't wait," he said.

"I'm glad," said Jessie.

Carter placed his forehead to Jessie's. They gazed at each other, knowing their actions could go no further. Finally, he stepped back. "Come on, I want to show you something."

Once outside the tunnel, Carter hoisted Jessie up on a boulder and climbed up beside her. She glanced around at the view. "I love this Witches' Cave," she said. "In elementary school, I used to come down here with my Girl Scout troop." She looked back to the entrance of the tunnel. "And now I have another wonderful memory of it! "

Carter nodded. "I used to come here when I was a kid, too. I would pretend that I was the ruler of the cave." He smiled, remembering. "It was an imaginary fortress, but no one ever got hurt. In my kingdom, no harm ever came to anyone. Papa Ford brought me and Bobby here a lot to play. Bobby always said when we were here no one could hurt us." Jessie listened as his eyes wandered the park.

"Bobby told me our parents were always arguing," he said. "That is, when Papa Ford wasn't around. I was young and don't remember much, but I felt safe because I knew Bobby was always there to protect me." Carter lowered his head. "Later on, when I was older, I would come out here by myself and think."

He pointed toward an area in the distance near the stables. "Sometimes, I would see two girls riding bareback on a horse over there and wish that I felt as free as I imagined they were. Especially the one with a ponytail."

Jessie whirled around and grinned. "So *that's* why you asked Fran if I ever wore my hair in a ponytail!"

"Yep," said Carter, his eyes glistening.

Jessie pulled his face to hers and kissed him softly. "Carter Powell, you are free, and we are safe together. And today puts us one step closer to our life and future together."

THE SPECIAL DINNER PREPARATIONS AT THE Reynolds home were well underway when Jessie and Carter arrived. Marie was in the kitchen with Jessie's mother and there were cheers from Mr. Reynolds, Bobby, Coach O'Connor and Rev. Hamilton as the couple walked through the door.

Carter held his diploma high again. He was warmed by the welcome and the wonderful aromas coming from the kitchen.

Mr. Reynolds called for everyone's attention. "Some special hands have prepared our celebration dinner and I think it appropriate this evening to join all our hands for our blessing." The family and friends made a circle holding hands around the dining table and bowed their heads as he began the blessing.

"Lord, thanks and gratitude is without question today for all you have given each of us. It is with great joy that we gather together on this wonderful occasion to celebrate Carter's accomplishments. May we cherish today's memory within our hearts and remember the joy we are experiencing. With our joy comes the beginning of a new journey in his life. We pray that it will take him safely along a path of new hopes and dreams. With it comes our continued prayers and encouragement. Just as our hands are joined around this table, we ask your gentle hand of guidance in his plans, his dreams, his decisions and the work and adventures waiting ahead for him. Special hands prepared this food and we are grateful. Special friends are gathered in support and we are grateful. Special hearts are filled with love and pride today and we are grateful. We ask this prayer in the name of the One who fills us with hope and love each and every day. Amen."

"Thanks, Mr. Reynolds," said Bobby, when Jessie's father lifted his head. "All I can add to that prayer is this. I have known James Carter Powell since day one and he came into my life as a special gift. Carter, you have never given up on yourself. Humble, dependable, trustworthy, strong, caring and honest. Everything that Papa taught you to be. Keep showing grace and love to those around you and know that home and family will always be here for you. I could not be more proud of you than I am today." He raised his glass. "To Carter!"

A collection of gifts and cards were neatly arranged on the dining buffet, and after dinner, Mrs. Reynolds began handing them to Carter one by one. In some of the envelopes, there were checks to cover some of his future expenses. He was overwhelmed with the sense of family he felt.

After dinner and gifts, Jessie and Carter took Coach aside into the den off the living room. A small item wrapped in brown paper sat on the piano. Jessie picked it up and handed it to him. "You can wait until you get home to open this, Coach."

Coach looked confused, and she continued. "It's something from Carter and me. Besides so many other things, it's a thank you for being a big part of Carter's attending Bradford." Jessie hugged the coach and Carter wrapped his arms around the two of them.

CoACH O'CONNOR LEFT THE REYNOLDS HOME with food items from dinner that Mrs. Reynolds had wrapped for him. She'd included a tin of her TLC cookies. When he reached his home, he entered the darkened living room and turned on the lamp next to his leather chair. After placing the food items in the kitchen, he carried the package from Jessie and Carter and set it on the table beside his chair.

He sat for a moment and then picked up the package, turning it over in his hands. Thinking about the day's events, he carefully opened the wrapping. Inside, he saw the back of a small canvas with the initials JER crossed over JCP. He turned it over to see that Jessie had painted a rose.

But it was not just any rose. It lay on a purple shawl with a silver thread.

Coach looked at painting and then at Ann's shawl, still on the upholstered arm chair where Jessie had seen it the night she and Carter had visited. He returned his gaze to the painting and tears filled his eyes.

Chapter Twenty-One

Summer began with a busy schedule for the Playboys in and around Atlanta, and Jessie went to every engagement. It was hard for her to contain her pride when Carter's drum solos were featured.

One night the group were packing up their instruments after their final set. Brandi and Jessie were waiting to accompany Crow and Carter back to The Nest. They hadn't noticed a large item covered by a tarp at the corner of the parking area. The band members saw their agent, Perry Michaels, drive up to the stage door and step out of his Corvette. "I've got some great news, men. You are officially going on tour!" he announced. "A southern road tour and it starts on Friday!"

The band looked at each other in disbelief.

Perry stepped into the middle of the group. "We have gigs already scheduled in Asheville, Johnson City, and Bristol. I've invested in something you'll need to get you there." He walked to the back parking area and pulled a tarp off something behind them. It was a brand new van with The Playboys painted on the side. Larry gave Pete a high-five and leaped to open the door. Crow reached for Brandi and danced the jitterbug in excitement and Perry handed him the keys. Carter felt Jessie's arms around him and he whispered, "Catch." They knew their summer time together would soon be coming to an end.

Carter and Jessie spent Thursday having fun at Lake Spivey with a special dinner at Seven Steers that evening. It was the time they needed to express their commitment to each other and share their goodbyes.

On Friday morning, the band met at the Crow's Nest to pack the last piece of equipment in the new van. The agent was there to review the notes on the tour clipboard with Crow. Their first stop would be in Asheville, North Carolina.

Jessie stood in the driveway with Brandi, watching the band pack the van and prepare for their six weeks of separation. After hugging Jessie one final time, Carter climbed into the van. He touched the key ring and medallion that Jessie had given him in his pocket. The van pulled away from the curb and Jessie and Brandi waved as it disappeared down the street.

Brandi put an arm around Jessie. "They're going to be fine," she said. "We will just have to look forward to the amazing time we will have when they come home."

Jessie reached for his ring on the chain next to her heart. "I miss him already. I feel selfish not wanting him to go," she said.

"I know. Me too. But it is one of those times when down the road, they will never have to say 'what if' or 'if only'."

Jessie nodded in agreement. "You're right, of course. I would never want to stand in the way of something Carter wants to do or knows he should do."

BRANDI GOT A SUMMER JOB AT Rich's to stay busy while Crow was gone. Jessie's mother suggested that she consider a summer job as well. In addition to being a distraction from Carter's absence, it would give her some experience in business especially before she was required to declare a major in college.

The Reynolds were close friends with Mrs. Riley, a woman in their church who had formed Atlanta's first temporary employment agency. One of the city's first female business owners, she was a warm and caring, beautiful woman of integrity. When her parents suggested she apply with Mrs. Riley's agency, Jessie loved the idea of learning from her over the summer. She wasted no time in applying.

Mrs. Riley quickly saw that Jessie's energy and enthusiasm was contagious, and she put her to work right away. The office staff soon knew Jessie was more than qualified to move to an outside assignment, so when a new listing appeared on the office Rolodex, Jessie was the first person they thought of. The assignment was to provide campaign research for a man running for a state office in the next primary. The candidate's office was located not far from the agency's main office, and Jessie was due to start the next Monday morning.

ASHEVILLE WAS AN EASY DRIVE FOR the band, but they were booked for an 8:00 p.m. show and much of their time would be spent setting up in an unfamiliar venue. It would leave no time for practicing. Crow turned up the radio and suggested they sing to warm up as they drove into town.

Although they were from Atlanta, the Playboys' reputation—with help from their agent—had preceded them. When they arrived, a large line had already formed at the club entrance.

"Wow, look at that line!" said Crow. They made their first trip with equipment into the club and tried to shake off any nerves they were feeling. Carter had more to unload and returned to the van. Several young women waited at the side entrance. "What are you doing after the show, good looking?" said one young woman.

Carter was polite and smiled as he continued his route to the side door. He'd already decided that Jessie would be the only girl on his mind that night. But then, as he dodged the other women, he caught a glimpse of a familiar figure in the shadows.

THE FRIDAY NIGHT SHOW WENT WELL, and the band members woke up Saturday morning looking forward to their second show that evening. From there, they would stop for nightly concerts in Tennessee and Virginia and then back via the North Carolina coast.

Carter checked the clock in his room. He had enough time to dress and walk outside to find a phone booth nearby before breakfast. He dialed the operator and gave her Jessie's number before depositing the coins requested to complete the call. Jessie answered on the first ring.

"Good morning, Catch!" he said.

"Hey you! How did it go last night?"

"Good. There was a big crowd. Standing room only. Crow has already heard from the venue manager we could expect just as big a crowd again tonight. We'll probably make a few changes in our set. They liked our Beatles medley."

"I'm glad, but I'm not surprised. You guys are great!"

"What are you doing this morning?"

She used her most sultry voice. "I'm lying here looking at our prom picture. It arrived in the mail yesterday."

"Wish I had it with me—or better yet, you!"

"It turned out really good. We're both smiling and you look so handsome." She looked at the photograph again and touched it to her chest as if hugging it meant hugging him. "Tell me more. You know, about last night."

"Not much to tell. It was the usual setup and sets, breaks and all. The manager was real nice. Got a nice meal when we arrived. Perry said not to expect that much from some of the other places."

"I wish I could have been there."

"What else is going on?"

"Oh, Mrs. Riley is sending me to a new job on Monday. I will be doing some research for a man running for office."

"That sounds good. How's everybody else?"

"Well, I went with the group to the Zesto. Sandy and Jack and everyone said to tell you hello."

Carter looked up to see Crow waving at him to get off the phone. "The guys are calling me to go to breakfast, so I better go. I'll call you again when I can. You still have the schedule we gave you and Brandi?"

"Yes," said Jessie. "I know where you'll be. Be careful."

The guys surveyed the breakfast in the lobby and decided to go across the street instead. Perry had put the motel breakfast on their schedule, but given the looks of it, they opted for the Waffle House. They found seats side-by-side at the counter.

Once they'd placed their orders, Crow leaned up and looked down the row. "Okay, guys, what are we going to do about Carla Peterson's showing up here last night?"

Carter was quiet.

Pete shook his head. "Can you believe it? She's following us, and that can't be good!"

"Should we let Perry know?" asked Larry.

Carter felt Crow looking at him and just bowed his head.

"Carter, you know full well she can be nothing but trouble," said Crow. "We're going to need to watch ourselves and have each other's back. I'm still not sure she didn't have something to do with those guys jumping Carter at the Fulton dance. We didn't give her the attention she wanted, and now she's back."

"Maybe it was just for last night and she went back home," Pete said.

"Maybe, but I say we don't tell anyone back home," replied Crow. "And that includes Perry for now. I think we give a heads up to the venue manager tonight, and then see if she shows. No use upsetting anyone— if you know what I mean." He glanced at Carter, knowing how both Brandi and Jessie would take the news.

IT WAS SUPPER TIME WHEN THE phone rang and Jessie ran into the hall to get it.

"Catch," said Carter, "I just wanted to say I love you."

"I hoped it was you!" said Jessie. "I love you, too." She thought he sounded strange. "You okay?"

"Yeah. I can just tell it is going to be hard getting used to this kind of life. Got to find me a good book or something to do when we are just killing time waiting for shows and on the road. Crow and Pete are working on some new music. I thought I'd try putting down some lyrics."

"That's a good idea. I guess it's a good thing to find out if you are cut out for it, right?" she asked. "I bet you all have those crazy groupies that show up and make over you!"

Carter laughed nervously, but avoided the topic. "Hey. What are *you* doing tonight?" he asked.

"Oh, I don't know. Maybe going to a movie with Claire and some of the girls. It's a crazy summer. Everyone is looking for jobs. Sandy has a summer orientation to go to with her parents, and Missy went on trip with her family."

"If you get a chance, check in with Coach, will you? I know he's having summer practices at school. Let him know how it's going for us."

"What should I tell him? You haven't really told me that much." The phone calls from the road had been noticeably different from those when they were together. Jessie missed the opportunities to share their thoughts and dreams.

"Just catch him up on where we are," said Carter, "and hey, tell him to say good luck to the rising seniors for me. I'll call again soon."

THE BAND ARRIVED AT THE CLUB for their second performance and surveyed the crowd that had gathered. Carla was nowhere in sight. "Maybe we were concerned over nothing," said Crow. Carter wasn't so sure.

What they didn't know was that Perry Michaels had had a surge in new clients and the increase had called for additional staff. Looking for less costly solutions, he had hired a high school graduate who arrived unexpectedly at his office applying for a job. Carla Peterson had fit the bill—she'd convinced him that she could handle an opening on his "travel team" that sometimes checked in on clients.

The only problem was that the agent had been too busy to check her references.

THE BAND LOADED THEIR EQUIPMENT IN the van and went to breakfast at the Waffle House again. They split up to go to their rooms and gather their luggage. Crow had a message at the front desk to call Perry before they got on the road.

When he appeared with his luggage, Crow wasn't happy. "Can you believe it?" he said. "Perry seems to think our performances didn't go well. He said his contact gave us a sub-par rating."

"What does that mean? Sub-par? Did our contract include some rating thing? Who was this contact?" asked Larry.

"The venue manager told us he was more than pleased and wanted us back. Right?" said Pete.

"Yeah, that's right," said Crow. "I asked Perry if he had spoken directly to the manager, but it was as if he didn't trust what I was saying. He just said he would get back to me and for us to head on up the road."

Carter shook his head. "Something is not adding up. First Carla and now this?"

Larry climbed into the driver's seat and the band headed out Highway 19-23 toward Johnson City. Pete sat up front and the group continued talking about what the booking agent had said. Carter said nothing.

Crow leaned over to his buddy. "You alright? You've been awfully quiet."

"Just thinking about stuff. You know, about the band...training camp at Bradford."

Crow smiled. "And Jessie!"

"Lots to figure out," replied Carter. He glanced down and returned to scribbling song lyrics in his notebook and doodling as he thought about all what was ahead.

Crow was getting closer to graduation at Clemson, and Pete had great flexibility with his classes at Tech. Larry had full permission from his father to do whatever it took to find himself before he committed to running the family business. Carter had neither the stability nor the options of most of his band mates.

With Papa no longer around to advise and encourage him, his thoughts turned to Coach. He would call him that evening.

Chapter Twenty-Two

Jessie's first day at the Jacobs campaign office was an orientation for the days ahead. The campaign manager, Allen Monroe, showed her to a seat in his office to explain her assignment. He touched her shoulder and adjusted her chair before returning to his seat.

He took a large ring of keys from his pocket and laid them on his desk. He pointed to a folder in front of her. "This portfolio has a picture of Mr. Jacobs' opponent and pictures of his family." He shifted in his seat and straightened his tie.

"Now, young lady you are to spend as much time as needed to research the campaign and put together a collection of newspaper articles, documents, and materials for my review. Also, find everything you can on our opponent. I'm sure you know that our campaign needs everything," he stopped to emphasize the importance, "and I mean everything ... that will benefit Mr. Jacob's campaign."

He pointed to the portfolio again. "The public library downtown and other public record locations will have what you need. One thing is very important for the campaign. I want the assignment complete by the first of August. We need this information to properly prepare our campaign strategy."

Jessie nodded, her mind racing. The deadline meant she would have to miss the annual family trip to Grandmother Danby's in Alabama along with visits to friends in Luverne and Montgomery. She'd hoped the trip would be a distraction during the weeks of separation from Carter while he and the band were on tour.

She shook off her disappointment and followed Mr. Monroe to a desk in another room with a typewriter and telephone. A door to a large closet with file cabinets in the hallway was cracked.

"Who left that open?" he muttered to himself and closed it quickly.

Mr. Monroe placed a stack of papers in front of her. "This is a list of public officials throughout the state for you to contact. When you're in the office, that will be your primary duty." He laid another piece of paper on top of the stack. "This is the script you will use to ask each official to support Mr. Jacobs. I'm sure you can charm them for their vote, right, young lady?" Jessie smiled and nodded thinking she would not want to disappoint Mrs. Riley on her first assignment.

"But first, you need to spend time at the library gathering the news articles and information we need. Any questions you let me know." Jessie smiled and placed her purse in the desk drawer.

She spent the rest of the day organizing and planning her duties. The next day she would go straight to the downtown library to begin her research. When she got home that afternoon, Jessie worked out with her father a plan for her to ride to work and home with him each day. On "research" days, he would drive her to the Carnegie Library on Forsyth in the mornings, and at the end of the day, she would walk to catch the West Peachtree Street bus to her father's office for the ride home.

Jessie arrived on Tuesday morning to begin her research in the library basement caverns, where she quickly settled into a routine requesting years of public records from the clerk. She was excited to learn to use the microfiche reader and make copies of documents on the brand new copying machine there. The candidate Marcus Jacobs had served in public office for over fifteen years before being defeated. There were years of public records touting his prior service to be included in her research.

On alternate days, she planned to go to the campaign office, type up her notes, and organize the documents for Mr. Monroe's review.

COACH O'CONNOR STOOD IN THE KITCHEN making a fresh tomato sandwich when the phone rang. When he heard the long-distance operator's voice on the other end, he wiped his hands on a dish towel. The operator put the call through. It was Carter.

"Carter! Great to hear from you. How's the road trip?"

"It's alright. Missing everyone there, though."

Coach smiled. *Missing Jessie, he means.* "Still gonna be ready for the beginning of football practice at Bradford?"

"Yes, sir," said Carter. "It'll be tight, but I'll make it."

"Good, good. So, tell me all about it. What's it like to be on tour?"

"Oh, it's okay," said Carter. "Not what it's cracked up to be. The band seems excited and pumped. But it's not an easy life, being on the road and all. Not to mention some surprises along the way."

The coach sensed that Carter hadn't just called to catch up. "Surprises? What kind of surprises?"

"The band agreed we wouldn't say anything about this unless we had to, but I'm not sure what to do. Our first night on the road, Carla

Peterson showed up at our show. She didn't say anything to us, but she was there. We all saw her."

The coach leaned against the counter. "Wait a minute. She was there? In Asheville? At your show?"

"Yeah. On top of that, after that first night in Asheville—which went great, by the way—we heard back from our agent that he had gotten word that we had a poor performance. Coach, there's no way. The crowd loved us. The manager himself told us he was going to book us again. We're in Tennessee now and are getting ready to play tonight. We'll be fine. But we all agreed not to tell the girls."

Coach opened the drawer of a small desk below the phone and flipped through his address book, searching for the number of the police lieutenant he'd met with during the Fulton incident. "Sure, none of the girls need to know about this," he said. "Keep me posted and let me know if she shows up again. And hey, Carter, don't worry. I got this."

Jessie had gained a sense of maturity and took pride in the work she had accomplished. Learning more about the Atlanta political scene had opened her eyes to how the system, much less people, operated in the local government. Her trips to the library were coming to an end and she would spend the rest of her assignment back at the campaign office. She finished around noon and decided to go ahead and drop off the documents she'd gathered at the campaign office before going home.

As she entered the office, she saw several men walking toward the conference room. Mr. Jacobs was already sitting down inside and Allen Monroe was closing the window blinds. She signaled to her supervisor that she was carrying the documents and was surprised when he hurriedly crossed the room and shut the door as she passed by. She overheard Monroe say, "She's doing our research. You don't have to worry about her."

After dropping off her notebook and writing a note to him, she headed back up the hall to where Joan, the receptionist, sat. Joan glanced up at her, a strained look on her face. "Jessica, you should probably go on home," she said. "And, it might be a good idea in the future for you to confirm with Allen when you will be stopping by the office."

"I'm sorry," said Jessie, instantly uncomfortable. Minutes ago, she'd been so proud of having completed her research and now not so much. "I'm done with my research and ready to start making calls tomorrow. Should I call in the morning before I come?"

"That would be a good idea," said the receptionist.

Jessie went back to her office for her purse and dutifully left the office, and headed to the bus stop. She knew her father would let her wait in the break room at his office.

The ride gave Jessie time to think about some other things that had bothered her. Mr. Monroe always made sure the hallway closet was locked when he passed. And, there were the times when he'd commented on the dress she was wearing or asked if she had a boyfriend.

Chapter Twenty-Three

"Mrs. Peterson, this is Lieutenant Casey with the Fulton County Police Department. We met last fall about your daughter's involvement in the incident at Fulton High School."

"Yes?"

"I'm calling in reference to Carla. May I speak with her?"

For a moment, there was no response. "Lt. Casey, I don't know where my daughter is. I haven't seen her since graduation."

The lieutenant cleared his throat. "You remember, I think, that as part of Carla's probation she was required not to go anywhere near the boy she falsely accused. She has reportedly been sighted several times in the vicinity of Powell, including once in Asheville, North Carolina, just a few days ago."

"I am so sorry to hear this, Lieutenant," said the woman. Her voice broke and the officer thought that she might be crying. "You might check with my ex-husband. I understand he's back in town. And I am fairly sure that Carla's been in touch with him."

"I need to find your daughter, Mrs. Peterson. If she is not honoring the agreement made last fall, we will have to take further steps in the case. How can I contact your ex-husband?"

"I don't know, Lieutenant. I have had no contact with Carla's father since our divorce years ago because he moved away. But I can tell you his name, of course. It's Martin Garrett."

THE CROWD AT THE BAND'S NEXT performance was enormous. Larry and Pete were finishing the setup while Crow and Carter finished a sandwich in the back dressing area. Crow was upbeat, but Carter was subdued. "Have we heard anymore from Perry? You know. About our reviews?" asked Carter.

"No. It is kind of strange. I talked to my dad this morning, though. He said he got a call from Perry. He told him our first payment has been placed in our bank account and that he'd had to fire an assistant. Asked him if he knew of anyone who might want a job. Dad said Perry was going to make sure we had what we needed and that we were doing a good job."

Larry stuck his head into the dressing room. "Five minutes," he said. "Setup is good to go and sound has been tested. Great crowd out there!"

JESSIE'S MOTHER AND SISTER HAD GONE on to Alabama to visit with her grandmother. Her father, who said he had more than his share of work, remained home with Jessie. He had not visited the campaign office where Jessie worked, so he decided to surprise her and take her to lunch.

When he arrived, there was no one up front at the receptionist's desk, so he wandered down the hall. When he reached the door to the back office, he saw Jessie sitting at a desk and a man leaning over her shoulder much more intimately and far too closely for his liking.

The man looked up. "Hey fella. You're not allowed back here. This is a private office!"

Jessie glanced up. "Dad!"

At that, Monroe hurried around the desk to offer his hand. "Mr. Reynolds. Uh, I am sorry. I…uh…didn't know…uh…Was our receptionist not out front?"

Jessie's father ignored the man's outstretched hand. "No. I've come to take my daughter to lunch." He turned to her. "Jessie, get your purse?"

"Sure," she answered and reached in her drawer. She looked at her father and could only imagine what he might be thinking. She stepped cautiously from behind her desk and turned back to glance at Mr. Monroe. He said not a word as Jessie passed by him and her father took her arm.

Mr. Reynolds waited until he and Jessie were in the car to speak. "After you told me about the way you were treated when you dropped by the office unannounced, I have asked around about this Allen Monroe and there are red flags all over this guy. I didn't like what I saw just now, and I don't like your being alone in that office with him." She watched as red crept up her father's neck.

"You're not going back there," he continued. "I'm going to ask Helen Riley to transfer you immediately to another assignment." Jessie's father started the car, prepared to argue his case, but he met no resistance at all.

Jessie nodded. "Dad, I would love to tell you to let me handle it. But you're right. I should have said something sooner, but as long as I was doing the research out of the office, I felt fine. I guess when I know something just doesn't feel right, I shouldn't ignore it. Can we just go home for lunch?"

"You bet!" said her father. "Home, it is!"

After lunch, Mr. Reynolds placed a call to the temporary agency and Mrs. Riley had already reassigned Jessie when the newspaper article came out in the *Journal* the next day. Accusations were flying everywhere about the Marcus Jacobs campaign including allegations of corrupt activities. It seemed that the men who Jessie had seen in the conference room that day had included questionable Atlanta family "kingpins."

Mrs. Riley apologized profusely that she had placed Jessie in such a situation. Jessie added the experience as one more wake-up call and burgeoning awareness about life outside her world.

Coach O'Connor was sitting at his desk when the phone rang.

"Coach O'Connor, this is Lieutenant Casey at the police department about the Peterson girl."

"Yes, Lieutenant. Did you find out anything?"

"I would like to come by, if that's okay. Are you available?"

"Anytime. Now. Anytime!"

In less than an hour, Lt. Casey appeared at the athletic office door and Coach waved him in.

"I'm not really supposed to do this," said the officer, "but given my involvement with the Fulton vandalism incident, I know how much you care about the Powell boy." The coach nodded and gestured to the officer to take a seat and continue.

"I had no idea my investigation would lead us in this direction, but we discovered that Carla Peterson's mother hasn't seen her since her graduation ceremony. She pointed us in the direction of her ex-husband. It took some time but my partner actually located him. His name is Martin Garrett."

The coach was confused. "Should I recognize the name?"

"Peterson is the girl's *stepfather's* name. Martin Garrett is her father." The officer stopped reading and looked up at the coach. "But there's one other thing. There's a connection to Carter Powell too."

The color drained from Coach's face. "What are you telling me?"

"I am telling you we tracked down Mr. Garrett, and he has cooperated with our questioning. We learned that he returned to Atlanta approximately one year ago. When we interviewed him, he said he had stayed out of the picture with respect to Carla, but had wanted to make amends for not being a part of her life and the divorce from her mother when she was a child. He met up with her and had a very frank conversation with her. A frankness he now realized she couldn't handle.

"He told her that the reason he and her mother had divorced when she was a baby was an affair he'd had with a woman—and the fact that he'd fathered her child. She asked him why he'd left town and he told her that the woman he'd had the affair with had died in an automobile accident and that he hadn't been able to handle the grief. He left soon after and moved to New York."

The coach felt a chill run down his spine. "Go on."

The lieutenant paused. "The woman he had an affair with was Amanda Crawford Powell. Martin Garrett is also Carter Powell's father."

"What?"

"Garrett thinks his daughter blames Carter for his leaving and is out to make trouble for the boy. And I think he may be right. That was likely her motive in the incident last year at Fulton High School. And it's the reason she applied for a job with Carter's band's booking agent. He *did,* in fact, see her in Asheville. She's still trying to make trouble for him."

Coach rubbed his head and looked at the lieutenant. "What is your next move?"

"When I called Perry Michaels to talk to him and told him the story, he fired the girl. My guess is that might have triggered more trouble for Carter by her. I suppose we can make some sort of harassment case against her given the Asheville sabotage report and pick her up for violating the restraining order we put in place last year. All in all, though, I'd say this is an angry young woman who needs therapy or counseling, not jail. But some sort of intervention would be in order before she does something else."

After the officer left, Coach picked up the phone and called Rev. Hamilton. "Stephen, I need your help. Any plans for dinner?"

"Nope. Just leaving the church."

"How about my house? I'll put something on the grill. It'll be private."

"Okay," said the minister. "I have to run some errands, but I can be there around five."

When Rev. Hamilton pulled into the driveway, he found the coach putting away some gardening tools. The minister got out of his car and glanced around the yard.

Coach followed the reverend's gaze. "When I've had a difficult day, I usually head to the garden first," he said.

"Beautiful flowers. And your lawn could compete with the Cherokee greens! Let me know when you have another difficult day and you can come work on our church yard!"

Coach smiled faintly and opened the door to his house. "Come on in. The steaks will be ready for the grill soon. How 'bout a glass of wine?"

"Maybe in a bit. Looks like *you* could use one. Perhaps you should fill me in first on what's going on."

When the coach was done explaining the discovery, even Rev. Hamilton admitted he was stunned. Although he had been a close friend of Big Jim Crawford's and had been closely involved with his grandsons after the Powells' tragic accident, Jim had not divulged this kind of information.

The coach was distraught. "How do we tell Carter? Or better yet, *do* we tell him?"

Rev. Hamilton sat for a moment before speaking. "You know, I knew before James Crawford died that he had told Carter he had a different father from Bobby. I found it interesting when I discussed some of the details surrounding his birth with the boy, he never once asked about his real father. I believe he has attributed so much to his grandfather that he never seemed even one bit curious. I'm not so sure now is the time. It seems to me we need to first find this Carla and determine what we can do for her."

JESSIE WAS UPSTAIRS IN HER BEDROOM, putting her clothes away when her mother called up the steps. "Carter's on the phone."

She dropped the clothes on her bed and grabbed the phone. "Carter! I am so glad you called. How much time do we have?"

"Lots of time. The club manager offered his phone to us. Nice guy. I can tell he understands what it's like being out on the road. We arrived in Richmond this afternoon and got in early to do our setup. How's your job going?"

"Oh," said Jessie. "My dad came to my job yesterday to take me to lunch and he didn't like the vibes he was getting from my boss and he wouldn't let me go back." She told him more about the things Mr. Monroe had done and the way he'd responded that day in the conference room. "The bottom line is Mrs. Riley moved me to another job today."

"Way to go, Ladd! Your dad's the best. I need to hear more."

Jessie pretended to scold him. "No, you don't. You need to tell me how much you miss me! Because *I* miss you very much."

"I do miss you. I miss you a lot. In fact, that's why I'm calling right now. I was telling Crow after he called Brandi how much I miss you. He also heard from Perry that he might shift our schedule to bring us back there for some good openings that just came up and let us end the tour in Atlanta—maybe even this weekend!"

Jessie jumped up from the bed. "You mean it? Come home, Carter. Hurry home!"

Perry Michaels made good on his word. The Playboys tour had been extremely successful and, when the group arrived at the Crow's Nest that weekend, he met them with a reward. His office had connections throughout Atlanta and with the national public relations firm, Famous Artists. "Here you go, guys! Eight tickets to the upcoming Beatles concert at Atlanta Stadium. You deserve a reward for a great tour. Take your dates and enjoy."

The band's mood quickly shifted to jubilation. The group and songs that had brought The Playboys so much success were coming to Atlanta and they would be there for their concert! It would be a wonderful celebration of the band's end of their road tour. Crow asked everyone to give some serious thought to whether they would continue. The contract with Perry would expire at the end of the month. Carter lost no time going to Jessie's house and into her welcoming arms. She, of course, would accompany Carter to the Beatles concert.

At the concert, they couldn't believe they were hearing the wildly popular British band live. The occasion brought a renewed energy to the band and when the concert was over, they all returned to the Crow's Nest to talk. Crow put a 45 on the stereo and was about to drop the needle when Carter asked him to wait.

"You guys are the best," he said, and he reached for Jessie's hand. "You asked me to join you and be a part of something I will never forget. But I've got to say being on the road gave me a lot of time to think. My scholarship at Bradford has to be my choice going forward. It's what's best for my future." He glanced toward Jessie. "*Our* future."

Chapter Twenty-Four

Carter and Jessie stood in the Powell kitchen cooking dinner together. They often joined Bobby and Marie to cook and share a meal, but Bobby was working late that night. Jessie broke the silence between them. "You making enough to save a plate for Bobby?"

"Yep!" Carter turned to Jessie to find her studying his demeanor. "We don't usually have this kind of time alone in the kitchen, do we?" he said.

"You've been pretty quiet tonight," Jessie said. She was doing her best not to make their final days together sad ones. "One day we will be standing here doing this every day. We'll have all the time in the world to catch up on our busy days and sit by the fire at night together."

Carter felt a surge of appreciation for the young woman beside him. "Yes, we will." He saw the beam in Jessie's eyes at his response. His hands covered with the dinner preparations, he leaned over to kiss the top of her head. "I guess we'll have to put in a fireplace!" They laughed and continued to work side by side.

"You know, Bobby and Marie have an interest in this house just as much as we do. They'll come a time that Bobby and I will have to make some changes."

"What kind of changes?" she asked.

He pointed around the room. "Well, never thought before about how all this would look when Bobby and I both have wives and families."

"Wives and families!"cooed Jessie. She stepped up behind him and placed her head on his shoulder and wrapped her arms around him.

"Yes, wives and families...some day." He turned to accept her embrace and smiled.

"Oooh...big family dinners with cousins chasing each other," she said. She pointed to the dining room. "That dining table can seat a lot!"

"Yes, it can. Speaking of dining, we have two very important dates coming up soon. Your birthday and our one year anniversary. I'm sorry that reporting for football camp has me leaving before them both, but I thought we could celebrate early."

"There's not much time," Jessie said. "With our being apart most of the summer I'm trying very hard to not think about you leaving again so soon."

Carter heard Bobby's car pull into the driveway. "So I was thinking... the weekend is coming up and Bobby and Marie are heading to that wedding in Augusta, so let's go out for a birthday dinner Friday night. It's our anniversary too. Our place? Seven Steers?"

"That sounds wonderful!"

When they arrived at the restaurant, the hostess recognized Carter from his earlier stop. "We're ready for you, Mr. Powell," she said and led them straight to the same table they had sat at the year before.

This time the table was adorned, not just with one red rose, but a vase full of them. "They're beautiful," said Jessie. "They're like the ones you gave me after the Snow Ball."

"One more chance to let them tell you I love you like that night." He turned his head from side to side to observe the others in the restaurant. "And without any interruptions!"

Jessie laughed as she opened her menu. "I don't see Dr. and Mrs. Caldwell anywhere." She glanced up from her menu to find Carter staring at her.

"You look beautiful tonight Jessie," he said. "I mean you always look beautiful but tonight...amazing!"

She had loved the way he looked at her from that first time they'd met face to face in the school cafeteria. "I chose this sundress for tonight. Specifically for you," she said.

Their dinner continued without interruption. They talked about Jessie's upcoming senior year, what being on the football team at Bradford would be like, and how they would plan to see each other. When dinner was over, they left the restaurant and walked toward the car.

Carter helped Jessie with the vase of roses. "Here. Wouldn't want to spill anything on that pretty dress." The warm moonlit night's softness surrounded them. Their eyes conveyed the unspoken passion that had only grown during dinner.

"When did Bobby and Marie leave for the wedding?" she asked.

"Four o'clock."

Carter pulled out of the parking lot and instead of turning toward Jessie's house, he headed for Moores Mill. The evening, their frank conversations at dinner, and the pressure of his leaving soon had left him wanting Jessie more and more. He dimmed the car lights and pulled into the driveway.

Jessie touched Carter's ring around her neck as they stepped into the darkened house. He walked ahead of her, checking to make sure all was well. Jessie surveyed the kitchen with its sparkling clean counters and the ever-present bowl of fresh fruit. She could feel her heart beating faster.

Carter returned from the back of the house and slid his arms around her. He kissed her face and neck and then her lips and she responded with a kind of passion she had denied herself until now. After a moment, Carter held her away from him. "Is this what we really want?"

"I just want to be with you, Carter," replied Jessie. "I am so scared right now. Scared of this…but more scared of not being together anymore."

"You know how I feel about you, about us. Those nights on the road, being so far away made me think a lot about you and what I want for us."

"Sometimes at night, I pretended I was lying next to you," she said. "I still do."

"I may not be by your side for real, but I'll always be with you, Jess."

Carter took Jessie's hand and led her back to his room. She looked around the room. It felt different from the times they had spent at his house in the past. The double bed was made with its neatly tucked sheets and simple quilt with squared off corners. On the side table was their framed prom picture, next to a bedside lamp. Carter's ROTC uniform hung on his closet door. She saw the evidence of his packing to leave for Bradford stacked neatly in the corner.

She picked up Carter's trophy for breaking the city record and pretended to read its plaque as he closed the door behind them. When Carter hesitated, Jessie moved to his embrace.

He touched the thin straps on her dress as they kissed more passionately and Jessie turned her back to him. Words were not necessary—Carter gently pulled the zipper down on her dress, revealing her bare shoulders and back. She turned to unbutton his shirt and felt his heart beating.

Papa Ford's words of responsibility ran through his head. "I love you, Jessie," he said as he pulled her toward the bed.

Jessie lay next to Carter. The night had been an emotional one and her face was stained with tears. They had teetered back and forth between desire and tenderness neither of them had ever experienced before.

Carter kissed her on the forehead. "It's eleven o'clock," said Carter. "I need to take you home."

"I know," said Jessie. She moved the cover aside.

Carter sat on the bed watching as she stepped into her sundress and stood to help her with the zipper again. She turned and looked at him, tears streaming down her face.

"Jess, it's okay. We'll wait until the time is right." He moved his face to find her eyes and wiped a tear from her cheek.

"You're just saying that."

He leaned down so their foreheads touched. He wiped another tear from her face and pulled her close to him. "You know me better than that. I will never forget the love you showed me tonight."

"I *do* know you. And I want to know you in every way, but we stopped for a reason," she whispered. "You and I both know this may be our last time to be together like this before you leave."

"Tonight just made our love even stronger. Sit down a minute."

They sat on the bed together and he reached in the side table drawer for a square, unwrapped box. Jessie wiped her eyes again. "Open it," he said. Inside was a silver bracelet with Jessie's name written in script on the front. "Happy Birthday, Jess," he whispered.

"It's beautiful. I've never seen one like it."

"I found this little shop in Virginia while we were on tour and they were able to engrave it while we were there. It's for our anniversary too."

Jessie turned it over to read the inscription on the back. *All my love, Carter.*

Jessie placed her head on Carter's shoulder. He pulled the fallen strap on her dress back over her shoulder. "Now seems the perfect time for me to give it to you. I look at the medallion you gave me on my key chain every day and I want you to have the same words from me."

STEPHEN HAMILTON STOOD WAITING FOR PAUL O'Connor at the bag drop at the Cherokee golf course. When he saw the coach pull into the parking lot, he walked over to see if he could help. By the time they returned to the drop, two carts were waiting for them, and they drove to the first tee box.

"Heard anything about the young lady?" asked the minister, as he stepped out of his cart.

The coach nodded his head and stopped to pull the driver from his bag. "Lieutenant Casey located her in Marietta. Perry Michaels heard she was staying with an acquaintance there and he was right. Casey said Michaels signed a complaint against her and worked out an agreement to avoid any negative publicity for his booking agency. The Marietta police said she was not very pleasant, putting it mildly, when they picked her up."

"What will happen to her now?"

"That was Casey's question for me when this all started back up."

"It's in the air right now. I spoke privately with Principal Kelley and he has said he will back any decision I make."

"And Carter?"

"Kelley said to move forward as I see fit. Perry Michaels too, as long he can keep the integrity of his agency intact. That's where you come in, Stephen. Casey says that given her age now, it's up to her. He said she's old enough that she has a choice—accept some sort of court-ordered treatment plan to deal with her issues or spend some time in a less than desirable environment with jail time."

"So what can I do to help the girl make a good decision?" asked Rev. Hamilton.

"She's not going to listen to her parents. Casey confirmed that when he picked her up. Talk to her, Stephen."

CARTER PICKED UP JESSIE ON SUNDAY after church. "You take care, Carter," said Jessie's mother as the two walked out the door and got into the car to go for a drive.

Claire was sitting with Missy on her front porch. The girls jumped and shouted as they drove down the street and passed them. "Bye, Carter!" They knew Carter was heading to Bradford the next day.

When they drove down the street to Memorial Park, it was filled with cars from the players at the afternoon football game. Carter honked the horn and the Barfield brothers jogged over for a high-five from their friend. "You got this, man. Make a touchdown for us!"

Jessie wasn't surprised when he turned up Northside Drive and drove toward the familiar hangout on Wilson. "I saw the band before I picked you up," Carter said. "They won't be there now." He drove down the driveway and parked at back entrance of The Crow's Nest. He took Jessie's hand. "Come on."

Once inside, Carter set the needle on the turntable and the familiar music began to play. Jessie moved her hands from his arms to his shoulders to his neck as they swayed to the music. Once more, she wanted to feel the safety of his arms around her and he wanted to hold her and remember every part of each other they had come to know.

The time at his house Friday night and the engraved words they each held confessed their forever bond. They knew their world would look different tomorrow.

The next morning Carter's packing was almost complete when he heard a car in the driveway. When no one came to the door, Carter looked out his window to see Coach still sitting in his car. He watched as he finally straightened his cap and got out and headed to the door. Bobby let him in and sent him back to Carter's room.

Carter reached for a few more items in his drawer and turned to welcome him. "Thanks for stopping by, Coach."

"I just wanted to make sure you had everything you needed and to see if you had any questions…you know, about Bradford…and things?"

Carter looked at the folded shirts still waiting to be packed. "I'm almost ready," he said. "I think I've got everything I'm supposed to have. There *is* one thing, though."

"Sure. What would that be?"

"At graduation, I received a lot of checks from people and I put the money in the bank. I made sure to thank everyone for their gifts, but one envelope held a whole lot of cash and there was no card. Do you know anything about that? Who I should thank?"

The coach shook his head. "I have no idea who gave the gift, but they obviously know you are more than worthy. I'm sure they had their reasons for not letting you know who they were."

"I've saved a lot from the band job this summer, you know. I never wanted Bobby to do anymore than he already has. I'm good at making my own way, but this was a *large* amount of cash, Coach. I don't know folks that have that kind of money," said Carter.

Coach didn't ask how much he was talking about. "Well, just thank them by putting it to good use."

"I will." He turned to face the coach and extended his hand. "I can't tell you how much I appreciate all the support you and others have given me, Coach. Being there for me through all of this—the Fulton thing especially—has meant everything."

"Not many of your teammates could have withstood those difficult tests of character. Rev. Hamilton has told me a *lot* about your grandfather." His eyes glanced at the ROTC uniform still hanging on the closet door. "I know he would have been proud."

"Thanks. Jessie and I were talking about how so many people have supported us. My grandfather, her parents, you, Rev. Hamilton, and so many others. We couldn't ask for any more support in our corner. I have to admit that as exciting as going to college is for me, it's still hard to leave. So, will you do something for me?"

The coach patted Carter on the shoulder. "You name it, bud!"

Carter showed Coach the prom picture waiting to be packed. "Watch out for her. I mean, I know you can't play favorites at school, but will you watch out for her...for me."

Coach nodded and watched him while he placed the final items in his bags. He battled with himself about whether to say anything about what he'd learned about Martin Garrett. "Carter..."

Carter looked up from his packing. "Yes, sir?"

Coach searched for the right words, but couldn't find them. "You got your toothbrush?"

Carter grinned and reached in the side pocket of the suitcase. "Yep! Got it!"

The coach helped Carter carry his bags to Bobby's car and waved as he watched the brothers pull out of the driveway. *This will be a fresh start and a new chapter in his life*, he thought.

BOBBY HELPED CARTER MOVE INTO THE athletic dorm that afternoon and introduced himself to the coaches. He wanted to be sure his little brother was in good hands.

When they were done, Carter walked Bobby to his car for the trip back to Atlanta. "I'll miss our morning coffee starts to the day," Bobby said. He gave his brother their customary morning shoulder pat. "You know you've always been free to accept my brotherly advice or not."

"Of course. There hasn't been much though." Carter could only envision the many times Bobby had been his protector.

"You have your whole life ahead of you," continued Bobby. "This is one more step in getting to where you want to be in the future. Make Papa proud." Carter nodded and watched as his brother climbed into his car and drove away and then walked to an orientation session for new students. After that, he went over to the athletic facility to receive his locker assignment and gear. Trainers interviewed him and other members of the team, taking notes and checking every medical detail on their charts.

"Let me be clear, men," said the assistant coach at the team meeting. "You need to be on time and be disciplined. You freshmen—there will be lots of distractions on campus. You need to keep your head straight. Your studies, your practices, your training all take precedence over everything else. You hear?"

"Yes, sir!" exclaimed the upperclassmen. The freshmen followed their lead.

Carter was newly determined to stay focused and do the job he had come to do. So many had supported him for his scholarship and this opportunity. There was little time yet to get to know the other members of the team although several spoke of parties that would be taking place off campus.

After the team dinner he walked across the campus with the team. He passed a chapel near the library and fell behind his teammates. He saw a light on inside and walked to the door. Over the door was a sign: *"Welcome to all who enter. Find peace and comfort for your journey."*

The phone rang in Jessie's room later that evening. "Hey, Catch. I don't have much time. I just wanted to hear your voice."

Chapter Twenty-Five

In an effort to occupy herself while Carter was away, Jessie dove back into her church group. The youth minister announced a planning retreat with the leaders and she agreed to join Robin and Mark at the meeting. William came in late and took a seat next to Mark. Robin suggested the friends get together after the meeting. "Let's go up to the Howell House," she said.

Jessie looked at her watch and wondered if Carter might call that evening and offered an excuse not to go. "Well...it's getting late and..."

"Come on. It's our senior year. Besides, we haven't seen much of each other lately, " Robin answered. "We won't be late." Robin glanced over at Mark talking to William. "Oh, and, just so you know, William was staring at Carter's senior ring around your neck."

"I doubt that," replied Jessie. It was hard to believe that it had been a year since she and William had been "the couple" of the youth department. Robin and Mark had taken over that spot.

"You can say what you want, but I'm sure of it," said Robin.

Mark joined them and looked at William walking away. "Things sure are different from this time last year." He took Robin's hand. "So, are we heading to the Howell House?"

Before Jessie could answer otherwise, Robin said, "Yes, but Jessie can't stay long."

The soda fountain area was buzzing with the chatter of other teens new to the scene and flirting for attention. Jessie and Robin found an empty booth while Mark grabbed some menus. "Hey, was that us last year?" he said as he dropped the menus on the booth table. He looked at Jessie and snapped his fingers. "Jessie. Hey, girl. You look like you are in another world."

Jessie looked up at him and smiled with an excuse other than the obvious. "I'm sorry. I just thought about Mr. James. Has anyone heard from him? How's he doing?" Mark and Robin shrugged their shoulders, acknowledging they had heard nothing.

Jessie stood up and stepped out of the booth. "I think we should send him a card and let him know that we hope all is going well." She headed over to the drug store's greeting card section.

Robin and Mark sat together on one side of the booth and had their heads together while she was gone. "I *told* William it was serious. You know with Jessie and that Carter guy." He was about to continue when Robin elbowed him to signal Jessie's return.

"This card has a picture of mountains like the ones we saw on our choir tour last year in Tennessee," said Jessie.

"Yeah, it does," said Mark, recovering from Robin's elbow to his side. "I bet it looks like some mountains near him in North Carolina, too."

Jessie nodded in agreement. "Maybe we could write something that refers to what he said to us before he left." She still remembered Mr. James's words about passing joy on to others.

Mark made a face. "You girls seem pretty serious. Before he left, my conversation with Mr. James made me think he thought I was needing to not goof around so much." He looked at the girls. " Do I goof around?" Jessie and Robin both laughed.

They returned to the card. Each wrote messages to the former music director who made a positive impact on them all. Jessie wrote about his last words to her.

To Mr. James – Thank you for these unforgettable words that I will always remember...

'Life is short, believe it or not. Make the most of everyday and surround yourself with good people. Take one day at a time and pass some joy to others around you. Always trust your heart and it will see you through.'

I hope all is well...Love, Jessie

When Jessie began her nightly letter to Carter to tell about her day, she began it by quoting Mr. James's same words.

On the first day of school, Jessie entered the senior hall to, once again, find Jack waiting to greet her. She was glad to see him and gave him a hug. It felt good to be back for their final year together. "I hear you and Tom are co-captains of the football team this year."

"That's right. Coach announced it at our last practice. How was your summer? I didn't see you around much."

Jessie thought for a moment. "Interesting, I guess you could say. I had a job with a temp agency that I'll have to tell you about sometime."

Jack noticed a bracelet on Jessie's arm and Carter's ring around her neck. "There's a spot at the Zesto with our name on it," he said. "Anytime," he echoed, with a twinge in his heart as she walked on down the hall.

Jessie filled up her time as much as possible. She accepted a position on the Viking yearbook staff, agreed to be co-chair of the Pep Club, and took over as president of the Art Club.

Among the morning announcements was a reminder of the upcoming Sadie Hawkins Dance and Fall Festival, where the girls would ask the boys of their choice to the dance. Jessie agreed to help with the planning—there were pumpkins to carve, posters to make, and refreshments to collect for the dance.

After school, she arranged to go to Chastain with Sandy, and was glad. It was like old times. Jessie pulled her hair into a ponytail and was reminded of Carter's watching from afar. Sandy aimed Josey toward the Witches Cave, and Jessie's memories of time there with Carter flooded in.

"The Sadie Hawkins Dance is coming up soon," said Sandy. "Why don't we get a group and all go together?"

"I don't know," sighed Jessie. "I can't think about going to that without Carter."

"Come on. You're helping with all the decorations. It'll just be friends and it'll cheer you up. We can ask Jack to go with us before someone else asks him first!"

"He probably already has a date."

"I'll call him tonight. It'll be fun."

Sandy turned Josey toward the stables and tugged on the reins, Josey tossed her head and with the addition of Sandy's heels in her side, the horse galloped back to the stables.

Sandy took a deep breath and dialed Jack's number. "I'm calling about the Sadie Hawkins Dance. Are you going?"

He could read the enthusiasm in her tone, but he wasn't crazy about the idea. "Well, uh, I haven't thought much about it," he said.

"I want you to go. With me, that is."

There was an awkward pause. "I'm not sure about this whole Sadie Hawkins thing. Sounds a little corny," said Jack.

"Well, Jessie and I were hoping you would go with us!"

"You and Jessie?" He paused. "Oh. Well, sure. Why not?"

Although Jessie was sure Claire was taking Tom, as expected, she told Claire of the plans for a group date with Jack.

"I'm glad you're going, Jessie. Carter would want you to go. By the way, Missy is coming home from UGA that weekend and will be going with us. She can't wait to tell us all about college. Sounds pretty exciting!"

"Yeah, exciting," Jessie responded.

"Doesn't sound like you're excited to me."

"Oh, I am. I guess there's a lot to think about."

"Like Carter?"

"What about you and Tom? Are you two still thinking you will go in separate directions next year?" She knew that Claire and Tom were serious, but that they also had different college choices on their lists. They would have the same challenges she and Carter were experiencing, except they'd both be away.

"Yeah. I wish things didn't have to be so complicated. Everything in the last year has just been so complicated." Claire was still trying to make sense of her parent's divorce. "My parents. Now college decisions...and Tom." She stopped. "Tom and Carter are so totally different, Jessie. Not in a bad way, but just different."

"What do you mean?" asked Jessie.

"Jessie, you've got to know that everyone wishes they had the kind of relationship you and Carter have. Tom and I will still date when we can next year, but I don't have his ring. It's not that I wouldn't want to be more serious, but we just aren't. We're just right for each other for now. You know, our senior year and all."

Jessie knew she and Carter had more than most of her couple friends. Something special and unique. But something was gnawing at her. When she and Carter had talked lately, he seemed low-key, maybe even a little distant. She appreciated Claire's comments about her relationship with Carter, but couldn't begin to explain to her the impact of their separation. She couldn't explain it to herself.

DURING THE FIRST WEEKS OF SCHOOL and practice at Bradford, Carter managed his time and stayed focused to justify his place on the team. He shared a suite with three other players in the newly-renovated athletic dorm and he was often forced to hear their complaints about their parents.

He looked forward to Jessie's letters and the recent one with Mr. James's quote. He'd written "one day at a time" on a desk note and propped it up where he could see it every day.

He worked hard on the field and in class, but there was something missing. He remembered the words of the school counselor, Miss Clay, about the first year adjustments required of new students.

A new coach had been brought to Bradford by the athletic director. The word on campus was that he was building his staff and team with the assistance of a new funding source. Carter wanted to do everything that would show him worthy of his scholarship.

But, home was where his heart was, and he knew he could call Coach for support to keep everything in perspective. He also knew, too, that the football season at Northwest had just begun. And then, one morning on his way to class, he noticed the campus ROTC office. He'd heard that an Army recruiter was located there, too.

Chapter Twenty-Six

When Jessie got home from Chastain and a horseback ride with
Sandy, her mother told her that Bobby had called and left a
message. She ran upstairs and called him back immediately.

"Marie and I are planning a trip to see Carter for the Bradford
homecoming game," he said. "If your parents would consider it, we'd
love to have you go with us. We'll work out all the trip details and where
we will stay. I know Carter would love to see you and you can assure
them Marie and I will make all the proper arrangements."

Jessie was overjoyed. "Bobby! I would love to go! Thank you so much
for asking me! I'll let you know as soon as I talk to them." The Reynolds
agreed that Jessie could go and that she could miss a day of school to
provide for an early arrival at Bradford.

The week dragged by. Jessie could hardly breathe when Friday
morning finally came and she said her goodbyes.

The day was perfect as they drove further north and the autumn
foliage became more brilliant. With just a few stops for gas and snacks,

they would arrive early enough to have the most time with Carter before his team curfew.

The Homecoming weekend was filled with student and alumnae festivities and the team had commitments until after the game, but Carter moved heaven and earth to arrange for time to be with them. The coaches gave him permission to have dinner with them—he'd been working hard at practice.

Carter sat on the stacked stone wall surrounding the athletic complex, when he thought he recognized Bobby's Chevrolet coming down the street. He stood to be sure and saw Jessie waving from the back seat as they drew closer. Bobby gave a tap to his horn.

The car had barely come to a stop before Jessie was out of the car and into Carter's arms. The waiting was over, and the weekend reunion had begun!

"Hey, Catch," whispered Carter, as he wrapped his arms around her. Some of his teammates passed them heading to the athletic dorm and whistled in approval. He ignored their calls and kissed her.

Bobby and Marie got out of the car. "You've put on some weight. Looking good, brother!" said Bobby. Jessie had noticed it, too in their embrace.

"I hope it's all muscle. The daily workouts are pretty major, but they say my speed is still good. Maybe even better."

Carter looked at Jessie from head to toe. She looked like she belonged on campus with the perfect Bradford blue and white sweater and slacks.

The campus was decorated in the school colors. Floats were parked on the lawns of dormitories and campus clubs as finishing touches were being made for the Saturday morning parade.

The Bradford Conference Center was typically booked well in advance for football weekends but Carter had managed to secure rooms for them. The lobby was abuzz with visitors arriving for the weekend when they checked in. The desk clerk handed Bobby a packet with special guest passes for the campus's homecoming tailgating buffet and other amenities. Marie and Jessie would share a room and Bobby would sleep in the room next door.

Carter helped Bobby with the luggage as Marie and Jessie led the way to the second floor. When Marie unlocked the door, a vase full of red roses was waiting on the table inside. Marie motioned to Bobby and made an excuse to head back to the car for a few more things. Once they were gone, Carter twirled Jessie around the room. "I can't believe you're here," he said.

"I know! Bobby and Marie were so nice to arrange the trip. I know he has really missed you, but no one could miss you as much as I have!" said Jessie. "It's been wonderful getting to know them better on the trip. I heard a lot of Carter stories along the way."

Carter chuckled. "I bet you did."

Jessie reached for a large metal tin. "Here. My mom sent you something, too." The tin was filled with her TLC cookies. "This should last you for weeks!" Carter had told Jessie how many of the players received regular packages from their moms each week.

He opened the lid and took a bite of the cookie on top. "Uh, you haven't met the team. They somehow know where each others' care packages are hidden." Carter was most proud that he would be able to show his suite mates that he too had family ties back home. "These are the best!"

They sat down on the bed. "Bobby and Marie will be back up here soon. I'm going to have to be happy to settle for this!"

Jessie could only have imagined having time to be alone with Carter for the weekend. She smiled and kissed him again. "I still can't believe I'm here."

He looked out the window and a serious expression appeared on his face. "These weeks have taught me a lot, Jess. Sort of like the weeks on the road with the band. My class adviser tells me it is normal and to give it time."

Jessie was puzzled. "Time for what?"

"Time to figure out what I am supposed to do. Where I am supposed to be," he continued. "Your being here makes a big difference. You know, I may just have to kidnap you and keep you here with me!"

Jessie wrapped her arms around him. "No need to bother with the kidnapping. I may just have to stay here with you! How's that for a difference?"

Marie and Bobby returned and the four left for a walking tour of the campus. The grounds were perfectly manicured and the maple and oak autumn trees were magnificent. It was if the grounds crew had scooped up each leaf as it hit the ground. Groups of alums gathered under canopies set with chairs and refreshments preparing for the big game the next day.

Carter led them through various quadrangles and connectors past the library and the administrative building. They passed an Army recruiting tent where a uniformed young man put up his hand to acknowledge Carter. Bobby noticed his interest in Carter and thought it nice that the small campus atmosphere had lent itself to the students being acquainted with each other.

The library was impressive, and they entered the massive glass doors to see endless library stacks and study carrels where Carter spent much of his time. It was also where he could write letters to Jessie uninterrupted.

The librarian recognized Carter when he walked in. "Hey Carter," she whispered.

"Wow! First name basis," said Bobby. "I'm impressed."

"Well, I do spend a lot of time here. The athletic dorm is kind of loud, and it's hard to concentrate. I'm there so much, and it's calm and quiet here."

They returned to the hotel and after changing, Marie and Jessie met Bobby and Carter in the lobby. "Where are we going?" asked Bobby.

"To a really nice restaurant. I have gift certificates for four to a couple of them. The one for tonight is called the Bradford Reserve."

When they arrived at the restaurant, they were escorted to a table with a campus view. "Our very best table for you, Mr. Powell," said the hostess. "You and your guests enjoy your dinner." Carter shrugged his shoulders in surprise that she knew his name.

The dinner and service was excellent and soon the restaurant manager made his way to their table. "I hope everything is to your satisfaction, sir."

"It was very nice," said Carter, confused at the extra attention. "Thank you." He was beginning to feel as if his weekend plans had been mysteriously overtaken by someone other than himself.

The next morning, Jessie, Bobby, and Marie woke early to beat the crowds at the center's breakfast buffet. All decked out in Bradford colors, they spoke of their excitement.

When the elevator door opened, Jessie froze. There standing in front of them were Judge and Mrs. Fields.

"Well, if it isn't our rose girl," said Judge Fields. Marie looked at Jessie, who was speechless. Bobby stepped from the elevator and offered his hand. "Hi. I'm Bobby Powell."

"Powell?" said the judge. "You must be related to Carter."

"I'm his brother," said Bobby.

The judge shook Bobby's hand firmly. "Nathaniel Fields. We're sure glad to have Carter here at Bradford."

Mrs. Fields interrupted her husband. "Look, there's the Hunters," she said and then quickly ushered the Judge away.

Marie turned to Jessie. "What was that all about?" asked Marie.

The blood drained from Jessie's face. "Those are Rick Fields's parents. They bought my rose painting for a lot of money at an auction last year."

Marie looked at Jessie, then Bobby. "The Rick Fields from the Fulton paint incident that Carter was accused of?" She exchanged a glance with Bobby and shook her head.

They continued through the lobby to the buffet breakfast, but Jessie's appetite had disappeared. She sipped her juice and ate half a slice of toast while Bobby tried to make sense of it all. "I never met Rick's parents throughout that whole Fulton ordeal. Carter made me promise to let Dr. Caldwell, Coach and Principal Kelly handle everything."

The game tickets from their guest packet had special fifty-yard-line seats. Carter beamed when he ran onto the field at game time and found them cheering in the stands.

When the game was over, Bradford had won a hard fought game and Carter was proud to have made some special plays. After a team meeting and a shower, he returned to the conference center. When he knocked on Bobby's door, he found Marie and Jessie were there, too. He raised his hand in a high-five to Bobby. "Nothing like winning!" he exclaimed.

Bobby tried to mirror his enthusiasm. "We had great seats, Carter. I'm glad you saw so much playing time."

Carter sensed the somber mood. "What's going on?"

Jessie looked at Bobby and then back at Carter. "We ran into Judge and Mrs. Fields when we came down for breakfast this morning."

Carter frowned. "What? Here?"

"Why don't we find a quiet place to eat and talk?" said Jessie.

"We have another dinner certificate," said Bobby.

"No!" said Carter. "I don't know what's going on, but we're not going to whatever restaurant. I should have trusted the questions in my head when all these special arrangements kept appearing. I know a place out near the lake. It's a bit of a drive, but I'm sure people will be staying closer to town for their dinner tonight. Let's go."

The car ride was quiet. Once they were seated at the restaurant, Carter looked around the table. "You know, when I came here, I knew I had a scholarship, and I thought I would be just like everyone else on scholarship. But I am questioning that right now. I have a lot of questions. I wanted to do something on my own. Make my own way. Not because I didn't have any parents, or because some guy had some vendetta to carry out and his parents had the ability to deal with their conscience with some kind of pay off."

"Carter—" said Bobby.

"No, Bobby. Even you. You gave up so much for me. It wasn't about some big scholarship, but it *was* a sacrifice. You gave up so much for yourself so I could have everything. And I will forever be grateful. I tried to let go of the Fulton issue with Rick and all. But all this is beginning to shed a new light on my being here—why I got a scholarship, everything."

Bobby leaned forward to be sure he had his brother's attention. "Don't sell yourself short, bro. Don't think you haven't earned or deserved everything that has come your way. Sacrifice doesn't have to be a negative. If I did anything for you, it was purely out of love. Papa taught us—no showed us—what real sacrifice is. How to look out for each other. And you never, ever were someone who got down on yourself because you lost your parents or didn't have as much as someone else. That's why your teammates looked up to you and trusted you. You showed them anything was possible."

Carter lowered his head. "I'm going to call Coach. He will know the truth about all this. Maybe the school here too. I just can't accept these things handed to me in this way. It just doesn't feel right."

Jessie's heart ached at Carter's being so upset. She reached for his hand. "Yes, Coach cares about you. He'll find out the truth and help you figure it out, so you can move on and feel good about it. This will all work out. We'll just take one day at a time."

"So, let's order dessert," said Marie.

"Sounds good," said Bobby, nodding.

After dinner, Marie and Bobby dropped Jessie and Carter at the conference center and went to gas up the car in preparation for an early departure the next morning.

"Come on," said Carter, taking Jessie's hand. "I want to show you something." The two strolled through the campus until they approached the small chapel. "I found this place my first night on campus. It's where I come to think," he said. "Next to the Crow's Nest, it has become one of my favorite spots."

He opened the door and they went inside. It was quiet and the lights were dim. A single candle burned on the altar table. Jessie felt as if the building had expected them and was offering solace.

They took a seat on the front pew. Both gazed at the cross in the stained-glass window. "I like it here, too," said Jessie. Carter put his arm around her and pulled her close.

The next morning, Carter stood at the curb as Bobby, Marie and Jessie drove away. He was confused. He'd thought he had let go of his emotions about Rick. His coming to Bradford was supposed to give him a start to a new chapter in his life. But something still nagged at him. *If only Papa were here*, he thought.

He walked around campus for an hour and then returned to the dorm, and looked up Coach O'Connor's phone number.

"I hear your concerns," said the coach after hearing what Carter had to say. "I will call Frank Caldwell and find out if the Fields had anything to do with Bradford's considering you for a scholarship. I'll see Dr. Caldwell tomorrow for golf at Cherokee with Rev. Hamilton and find out about this for sure. My guess is that Frank doesn't know how far the Fields have taken their influence."

Carter was silent for a moment and Coach O'Connor sensed their was something else. "Is there more?" he asked.

"Coach, I keep hearing that I need to give this all time. You know, about my settling in at Bradford and all. But this sheds a whole different light on things here. I mean football is going fine and so are my classes. But I need to find my place."

"You will. I *know* you will. You've got a good head, son, and your heart is in the right place. I know Frank Caldwell has always had the best intentions. And it was up to the Scholarship Committee to make the final decision. Not the Fields."

"I know, Coach, but I don't need someone out there trying to run my life. Not this way," he responded. "Bobby and I had to learn early how to make our own way and that's the way it has got to stay."

The next morning, Carter went to the athletic office and asked about his scholarship. After looking at his file, the assistant confirmed that he had received the Fields Scholarship and that there were several special concessions.

"The Fields family has a lot of influence here," she said. "Judge Fields graduated from here and he's the current chairman of the Bradford Foundation's board."

THE WEEKS THAT FOLLOWED WERE FILLED with highs and lows for Jessie. She tried to remain optimistic in her letters and calls to Carter. She joined Sandy and the others for their trips to the Zesto and occupied her Pep Club spot with Claire, cheering Jack and the other players at the Northwest games. Her days and nights were filled with school and church and activities to busy herself.

Mrs. Reynolds observed her daughter's drive to stay positive. Her mother's wise counsel was ever present as Jessie sorted through her feelings. "Your faith will make you stronger during times like these," she said. "Life can't always be in our control. But love is and family and friends will always be here no matter what."

AFTER THE VISIT TO BRADFORD, BOBBY spent time with Rev. Hamilton seeking his guidance in talking to Carter. "Just keep walking with him, Bobby. Being family for him like you always have," said the minister.

FOR THE FIRST TIME EVER, CARTER missed his church's Veterans' Day service, attempting to let the flags displayed on campus to commemorate the holiday take its place. He wandered to the campus chapel and offered a special prayer.

The coaches put him in the starting lineup for the Bradford's Thanksgiving weekend game against the school's state rival—in practice, he had used his anxiety and, to some extent, his anger to take his game to a different level—and two running plays had helped the team win.

The following week, the Bradford coaches and trainers celebrated his accomplishments and assured him that he would have a place on the team the next year. At a team meeting, they announced they would begin to ask players for a commitment.

Carter asked for more time to make his decision because he had been taught by Papa Ford to be a man of his word and to stand by his commitments.

After finals were over, he packed to head home to Atlanta for the Christmas break, but first he had another stop to make.

Chapter Twenty-Seven

Jessie was enlisted to help plan the senior class holiday display. The junior class's "Ann's Tree" was still the talk of the school. While she counted the days until Carter came home, it felt good to invest her attention to the positive of the "*About Others*" campaign the school had adopted. Coach mentioned a volunteer program at Piedmont Hospital. To add another activity to fill her time, Jessie started training there. The youth volunteers were called "candy stripers," so it was an easy jump for her to make the suggestion that they use candy canes for the class display.

The seniors purchased a tree for the front door and a matching one for the hospital pediatric floor. A candy cane donation program was initiated to decorate both trees. Overflow candy canes and peppermints were gathered in baskets underneath the school tree and were delivered to the hospital to attach to holiday messages for all the hospital patients' trays.

Rev. Hamilton was making his pastoral care rounds on one of the afternoons that Jessie volunteered and when he saw Jessie, he gave her a hug. She felt as if his hug was a touch from Carter, especially when he smiled and said, "Our Carter will be home soon, right?"

She handed the reverend a candy cane. "Yes!" she said. "Very soon."

CARTER ARRIVED HOME, DROPPED HIS SUITCASE and jumped in the Buick waiting for him in the driveway. His first stop would be at Jessie's house.

Jessie's mother welcomed him with open arms. "I know someone who is going to be so happy to see you!"

He returned the much-appreciated hug. "Yes, ma'am. I'm ready to see her too."

"Come in and wait for her. She should be home soon. By the way, I just took some cookies out of the oven."

"Thanks, Mrs. Reynolds. I hope Jessie told you how much I appreciated the ones you sent for Homecoming."

"She did." He sat down at the kitchen table while she removed her TLCs from the cookie sheet. "Mr. Reynolds and I have prayed for you every day."

When Claire's car turned into the driveway, Jessie immediately saw the green Buick parked out front and dashed from the car and into the house.

She dropped her books on the hall table and ran to the kitchen. "You're home!" Carter stood just in time for her to jump into his arms.

"It feels good to be home, Catch," he said.

BEING ON THE NORTHWEST CAMPUS AGAIN and in trusted territory brought good feelings and warm memories to Carter. Coach asked him to help out with the sports program as school was winding down for the holidays. Walking the familiar hallways of the school and seeing friends like Jack, Sandy, Claire and Tom—and meeting Jessie in the lunch room—felt almost like old times.

Bobby asked for his help with some projects at the house. Marie asked Jessie to join them in decorating their tree and the feeling of family began to edge its way back into Carter's heart.

The next morning, Bobby handed Carter his mug of their shared morning coffee. "What are you up to today?"

"Meeting up with Coach first thing at the school and lunch with Jessie. Rev. Hamilton has some time after lunch, so I want to stop in to see him too. You, Coach, the reverend have always helped me feel that I have done all the right things. And then there's Jessie. I must have done something right to have her in my life."

Bobby leaned back against the sink and perused Carter's face. "Yeah, I can tell things are pretty serious with you two and it's all good, I know. But I can tell something else is going on with you."

Carter lowered his head. "Jessie has her whole life ahead with college and all."

"Yeah…" said Bobby, "just like you. You both have so much to look forward to, so much to experience. But, why so serious?"

Carter paused. "Papa did so much for me. For us. I can't lose sight of that," he said. "At Bradford, away from everyone here, I've had a lot of time to think. To sort things out. I just know there are things I want and things I have to do. I know I could never help Jessie understand. I constantly think about us being together. It's all I've ever wanted, but I have to be fair to her."

"Does Jessie know what's going on with you?"

"Not yet," said Carter. "I still have a lot to figure out and I want this to be a happy Christmas for everyone. Let's keep this whole discussion between us for now."

CARTER ARRIVED AT THE REYNOLDS' HOME the night of the Snow Ball. Jessie's father invited him into the living room while her mother helped her with her dress. "Bradford been treating you well?" he asked.

"Yes, sir. Too well," he replied, shaking his head.

Mr. Reynolds searched Carter's eyes. "Jessie told me about the Fields scholarship. I know it's difficult for you. If I can be of any help, you let me know, you hear?" He could see there was something different about Carter since he had returned. "These things will work themselves out in the long run. Just keep your head up and eye on the goal, right?" He laughed when he realized his analogy to football. "You know what I mean."

"Yes sir. About that help, sir. I'm—"

"Here she is!" Mrs. Reynolds appeared from the hallway leading the way for her daughter's entry.

"You like?" Jessie did a twirl to reveal the newly purchased dress for the dance.

"I *always* like," said Carter.

Mrs. Reynolds straightened Jessie's hem. "Get the camera, Ladd," she said.

"I will, but Carter was about to say something about my help." Jessie and her mother paused and looked Carter's way.

"It's nothing," he said. "I'm just glad we won't have to deal with any snow this year," he said. He moved to take his position next to Jessie for a photo.

Jessie couldn't be more happy to have Carter back by her side. They had made it through his fall semester and her thoughts were of the passing of many more semesters in the future. Mike and Missy were both home from college and were at the Ball—as the previous year's recipients—to crown the new king and queen, Tom and Claire. Jack and Sandy came in with Christy, Diane, Robby and Michael. Fran arrived with a date from Fulton High.

Jessie congratulated Claire and they turned to see Carter talking to Mike. "He looks good, Jessie," said Claire. "Why have you been so worried about him?"

"I don't know. He says there's just a lot going on at school and a lot to think about. If only the Fields would have left him alone," she replied.

The band announced that the evening's final dance was about to begin and Carter returned to join Jessie. "Just thinking about what a special night this was a year ago." Jessie nodded without speaking and took his hand. The dance floor lights were lowered and all of their friends joined them.

The Snow Ball also the anniversary of the confessing of their love, Jessie and Carter headed for the Nest after the dance. It was good to stop by and see Crow and Brandi and the others at the hangout. Dissolving the band had turned out to be the best for all of them, but the group couldn't resist doing an impromptu jam session with the instruments still stored in the basement.

Carter and Jessie headed home that evening relishing the time spent with special friends that evening. He stopped in front of Jessie's house and placed his arm around her. He glanced in the backseat at his school blanket. "Didn't have to use my school blanket to keep you warm this time."

"*You* kept me warm, though."

He reached behind him and pulled up the blanket. Hidden beneath it was a box with a dozen red roses. "You didn't think I would forget such a special anniversary, did you?"

"I love you, Carter Powell," said Jessie.

THE CHRISTMAS LIGHTS AROUND ATLANTA WERE spectacular and Jessie and Carter planned an outing to see the displays. First, Carter drove Jessie to Rich's to see the large fir tree atop the bridges. She reminisced, telling him about singing on the bridge in the choir and her family holiday gatherings at home. He thought back to his grandfather's efforts to provide a good Christmas for him and Bobby always with at least one gift that had a military theme.

Special holiday music played on the radio as they drove back down Peachtree past the Rhodes theater toward Brookwood Station. Jessie pointed to the turn at the Sherwood Forest neighborhood.

"Oh look. Our family used to always drive there to see lights and decorated homes." Carter made the turn and Jessie opened her window to hear carolers singing. She turned to Carter. "This should be one of our holiday traditions every year."

"And what other traditions?" asked Carter.

"Well, you know that fireplace you're going to build for me?"

"Sitting by that fire on Christmas Eve after an amazing dinner and having your arms around me. That's all I need!"

They made their way to Coach O'Connor's house who was expecting them. "Come in, you two," said Coach when he opened the door. "What have you got there?"

"We come bearing gifts," said Jessie with a cheerful lilt to her voice. "My mom sent some of her special Christmas cookies and pound cake.

Dad included some of the fruit from the farmer's market—he always buys some for his business clients, neighbors…and special friends, like you!"

The coach walked toward his kitchen and waved for them to follow. "Come see what I have." He showed them garden seedlings in china cups that he would plant in the spring. "Those are Ann's tea cups. The light on these window sills is just right for the seeds."

He chose a special cup painted with roses and handed it to Jessie. "This one is for your mother and tell your parents thanks for the gifts and Merry Christmas!"

On the way back home, Jessie and Carter talked about Coach. "He seems happier now," said Carter.

Jessie laughed. "What a change from that first day in class and you having to run those banks! Jack talks about the team this year and how much they look up to him."

"He does care about his players…and others."

Jessie smiled. "You mean, like us."

The weekend continued and Jessie surprised Carter with the gift of a red rose bush. "I added one more tradition for us," said Jessie. "I was thinking we could plant it together along the driveway and add another one every year."

The tools were close by in the backyard shed. He grabbed a shovel and dug a hole near the carport. Jessie placed the rose bush and scooped the dirt carefully at its base. She sat on her knees and looked up at Carter when they finished. "I bet Papa would have liked this tradition."

He helped her to her feet and kissed her forehead. "Thank you. It's perfect."

On Sunday morning, Jessie joined Carter, Bobby and Marie for an Advent service at their church in Sandy Springs. When the service concluded, Carter excused himself to speak with Rev. Hamilton.

"I don't know what to do about Jessie," said Carter.

"I know you have given it a lot of thought," said the minister.

"But I haven't told Jessie about my decision."

Rev. Hamilton placed his hand on Carter's shoulder. "You are going to have to tell her sometime, Carter. And soon. Jessie needs to know."

THE BRADFORD FOOTBALL TEAM WAS INVITED to a bowl, requiring Carter to head back to school. The day before, Marie planned lunch after church at the Powell home and Jessie and Carter were in the kitchen helping. Jessie leaned close to him and bumped him with her shoulder as they passed in the kitchen. "What's wrong?"

"Nothing," said Carter. "I just wish I didn't have to leave so soon. That's all."

Once lunch was over, Marie started moving the bowls and plates from the table to the sink. "Bobby and I will get the dishes," she said.

"Thanks for the lunch, Marie," said Carter. "Jessie and I are going to go downstairs." He took Jessie's hand and led her to the lower level.

He instinctively locked the door behind him as he and Jessie made their way into its cavernous region. The curtains were drawn and a small portable heater added warmth to the room. The only light was a lamp next to the sofa where a large box wrapped in bright red paper was waiting. Carter had given a lot of thought to a meaningful gift for Jessie as a symbol of his love.

Jessie looked at the box and then at Carter. "Go ahead. Open it!" he said.

Her hands flew through the wrapping paper and the tissue inside and she touched a soft woven object. "I met a woman at Bradford who makes these blankets," said Carter. "She creates each one so that no two are alike."

"Carter. It's beautiful!" She pulled it from the box and ran her hand over the special handmade creation.

"I want it to remind you that our love is like no other. I hope it will keep you warm and secure when I am away." As he had done so many times before, he wrapped the blanket around her. "Bobby and Marie won't be bothering us down here," he said, as he gazed into her eyes. "I just need to have more time with you."

"The way you say that scares me, Carter. What were you and Rev. Hamilton talking about this morning?"

He paused. "You know I've been struggling with school. It's not the classes. I just don't think that is where I need to be. The scholarship and everything with the Fields that has been given for me. But if I don't stay, it will look like I am unappreciative."

"Why couldn't you tell me this before? I thought we shared every single thought and feeling?" He leaned over and kissed her. The warmth of her body made him ache even more, knowing they would be separated again.

Jessie trusted Carter and he knew full well the responsibility of his love for her. She kissed him back even more passionately and they were soon reaching the point of no return. "I love you so much, Jessie," he whispered.

THE AFTERNOON SUN MOVED ACROSS THE basement window and Carter propped himself up on one arm to watch Jessie sleeping beside him. She stretched and turned over and he covered her bare shoulders with the blanket he'd brought from Bradford for her.

He slipped out from beneath their cover and pulled on his shirt. He quietly made his way to the display cases, where he stood, silently looking at the family collection items. *All this sums up my life*, he thought.

Two arms slipped around him and he turned to see Jessie with the blanket draped over her shoulders. Her eyes glowed. The love and intimacy they had shared removed all thoughts of anything else. "I'm sure your parents were expecting you home before now," he said.

She giggled softly and reached up to kiss him. "They *did* think I would be home after lunch."

Carter reached for the blanket and pulled her closer to him. "Remember this, Jessie. There will never be anyone else in my life but you." When she didn't immediately respond, he looked closely at her. "You okay?" he asked.

"Better than okay. Today was beautiful," she said and hugged the new blanket he had given her. "I will never forget it." They shared a bond now that would not be broken.

After taking Jessie home, Carter stopped at the Crow's Nest. No one was there so he turned on the band's practice tapes and began playing along with them on his drums. As he played, he checked off every number on the list in his mind, feeling somehow that it would be the last time he would play them for a long while. He heard a creak on the stairs and looked up to see Mrs. Perkins on the bottom step. "I'm sorry Mrs. Perkins. I hope I wasn't disturbing you."

"Of course not. Stay as long as you like. Can I get you anything?" she said.

He paused and shook his head, thinking again about how nice having a mother would have been about now. "No thanks. Time here is all I need." The Nest was a place for friends to gather, to accept each other, to hang out and get away—the place he'd discovered love in the past. Now it was a place to make decisions for the future.

CARTER WOKE EARLY AND WENT DOWN one last time to the basement before his return to Bradford. He looked once more at the collection of family photographs—Bobby, Papa, Coach and the reverend. He folded the blanket and draped it on the back of the sofa. The faint scent of Jessie's perfume lingered, and he closed his eyes and envisioned her in his arms and the feel of her skin next to his.

He climbed the basement stairs and walked out to the carport. Bobby stood there with a cup of coffee. "You were up early. Downstairs checking on things?"

"Yeah, checking on things. Just looking around," Carter replied. "It's been great being home."

"It's been good to have you home, Bud."

Carter took the cup from Bobby and sipped it. One more time, he treasured their morning routine.

Bobby gave him his brotherly pat on his shoulder. "We better get going," he said. "Your ride over on Druid Hills will be waiting."

Carter set down the mug and put his bags in the trunk of Bobby's Chevrolet. "Thanks for the coffee."

As they climbed in, Bobby glanced at the Buick parked to the side. "Maybe we can get the ol' Buick running good and you can take it back to school soon."

Chapter Twenty-Eight

Northwest was back in session and Jessie was overjoyed when she came home to find her official acceptance to the University of Georgia in the mail. Everything was starting to fall into place—the ending of one chapter and the beginning of a new one! The prom and graduation parties were already being planned, and Jessie couldn't wait for Carter to be back home. She recorded in her journal her thoughts of their last time together and she ached for his return.

Choir rehearsals were beginning soon too. It was good to spend time with Robin again. As with some others, Robin and Mark seemed to be drifting apart. "It's okay," said Robin. "Mark is who he is and I am who I am. We have a good time, but every time we have tried to get serious, it just hasn't worked. I mean, I want it to work, but the romance just isn't happening."

"Maybe he will just always be a good friend. It's sort of like me and Jack," said Jessie. "Remember what you told me your sister said when I was seeing William. You'll know when you know it's right. You'll just know! And all the guys in between will help you figure out what it is and who it is that's right."

"You and Carter sure have it all figured out. You know, knowing he's the one," said Robin.

"The hard part," said Jessie, "is learning how to be apart. That's what we haven't figured out. It changes things." Something her mother had once told her drifted through her mind. *Life is all about changes.*

The sentiment proved to ring true. Tom and Claire would be attending the prom together, but other friends were planning group dates. Jessie was upset when she learned that Carter's final exams were the week after. He was struggling with how to come home and still get in the studying he needed.

When she told her mom about the situation, her mother's observation offered a different viewpoint. "You know we love Carter, Jessie. Maybe you should think about inviting a friend to take you to prom. Just a friend, like Jack."

"I could never do that!"

"It's something to think about. This may be more pressure on Carter than you realize. The trip, the expense and all. Have you thought about that? There is a give and take in life, in relationships, to consider. It will be a part of what you and Carter will continue to see when you're in Athens."

Upset at the thought, Jessie ran upstairs to her room. She lay on her bed and considered what her mother had said. Finally, she rolled over and picked up the phone. Maybe her mom was right.

One of Carter's teammates answered the second-floor phone. "Powell, you got a call!"

Carter welcomed the surprise. "Hey, Catch!"

"My acceptance came from Georgia! "

"That's great, Jess. I knew you would get in. It's what you've always wanted," he said.

"How's it going there?"

"Just studying a lot right now in between spring drills." He cupped the phone in his hand. "How about you? I miss you."

"I miss you too, but I was just thinking. You know about prom and all, " Jessie said. "I haven't been fair to you, expecting you to somehow always be here for me for everything. I just wanted to tell you that."

"What do you mean?"

"Just that I realized I haven't always put your needs first. You know, always expecting you to somehow make the trip home for things here. It must cost you a lot. I wish I could come there again."

"What are you trying to say, Jessie? What's going on?"

"I just think maybe you shouldn't try to come home for prom. It's too much." She worried at his silence. "You've got to know I want you here more than anything, but I know it's a lot for you."

After a few seconds, Carter finally spoke. "I never want to disappoint you, Jessie. But you may be right. I haven't found a ride to Atlanta yet and riding the bus from here is expensive. And that's assuming I can get a waiver from spring practice."

Jessie tried to remain upbeat. "You'll be home for graduation and then you will be home for the summer!"

"Of course I'll be there for graduation. I wouldn't miss it. So, if I don't come, what are you thinking about prom?"

"Well, there's always a group who are going without dates."

Mr. Baker informed the students that all the preparations and funding had been covered for the prom so everyone was free to simply come and enjoy the dance. As she'd told Carter, Jessie joined several friends, including Jack and Sandy, to attend the dance together. Jessie put her disappointment aside and chose one of her sisters' prior dresses for her mother to make the necessary alterations.

Preparations for the evening event began and Jessie stood looking in the mirror, imagining Carter by her side when her mother called up the stairs. "Jessie, you have a package." She bounced down the stairs to see a large flat box wrapped in brown paper and tightly sealed. The return label showed Carter's Bradford address. Inside was the newly-released Beach Boys album *Pet Sounds*. She read the card on top.

Wish I could be there! Listen to the fourth song when you
come home tonight.
Forever, Carter

Jack came to the door for Jessie and walked her to the car. Sandy jumped in the back seat—she knew all too well that if things were different, this would not have been a "friends group date."

Because it was Tom Caldwell's senior year, his parents had secured the Cherokee Club for the prom. As they entered, Jack encircled Jessie's arm and gathered the other single friends to snap a photo together. A half-hour later, Jessie stood off to the side talking with friends and drinking punch, when Jack stepped in front of her. "Dance with me?"

Jessie smiled. "Sure." She followed him out to the floor.

"After all these years, who would have thought we would be dancing together at prom?"

"Or that we'd both go to Georgia," he said.

The two had experienced years of classes together, Northwest football games and pep rallies, and fun times at the Zesto. From the Eight Ball, the first official eighth grade dance, to the Sadie Hawkins and all those dances in between to now, Jessie couldn't remember a time when Jack hadn't been there. They danced for a minute and Jessie giggled. "Remember Mrs. Bruner's dance classes?"

Jack twirled her around and bowed. "Unfortunately, yes."

When the song was over, Mr. Baker walked by and called for everyone to gather at the front of the dance floor. "We want to thank the Caldwells for hosting the prom this year," he said. "We also want to express our appreciation to the Fields family for their donation as well. They made it possible for this evening to be at no cost to the school or any of you!"

Everyone applauded. Most of the students made no connection with the Fields name, but of course, Jessie did. She looked for Coach O'Conner and found him looking back at her from across the room. She had not thought about Rick since the Bradford homecoming weekend. She was suddenly glad that Carter wasn't there.

Jack leaned over and whispered in Jessie's ear. "I guess they are still trying to make up for the trouble Rick caused. You know Rick had a thing for you, don't you?"

"Really?"

"I saw it from the beginning. It was obvious the way he watched you and Carter."

Jessie lowered her head. It had not occurred to her that she might be the reason for Carter's problems with Rick.

"It's okay, though, Jess. He won't cause any more problems here. Coach told me he made sure of that."

"What do you mean?"

"Not sure. I heard Coach had a part in some agreement with Rick's parents, the school, the police, and his doctor. I'm guessing Dr. Caldwell played a part in it, too."

Claire walked up between them and took Jessie's arm in the midst of their conversation. "Hey, y'all. Come back to our table." Jessie turned to smile at Jack as Claire led her away.

Jack stood for a moment, remembering the night he had had a "heart to heart" with the troublemaker Rick. He'd told him that night that there would be a price to pay if he caused any harm to Jessie or anyone she cared about. He'd made certain the boy had taken him at his word.

The friends at their table were raising their glasses and making congratulatory toasts, reminding each other of their times together over the years. Terry stopped and asked Jessie for a hug. She had appreciated his words of friendship throughout the year. He had gotten a football scholarship to UGA, and he called Jack to join them for a photo to celebrate their heading to Athens together.

Jessie stood on the front porch waving to Sandy and Jack as they drove away and after the taillights disappeared, she quickly unlocked the door and ran upstairs. Many times during the dance she had thought about the gift waiting for her at home. She sat on her bed, pulled the vinyl record out of its sleeve and slid it down the spindle of the turntable. She placed the needle at the exact spot Carter had told her and turned the sound low so as not to disturb her parent's sleep. She drifted off to sleep with the sound of the Beach Boys in her mind.

Wouldn't it be nice...

Jessie's white cap and gown hung from her closet door so the wrinkles would fall away by the big day. Graduation invitations had been mailed to family and friends. Senior parties were taking place all over.

Jessie counted the days until graduation. She was excited that Carter would soon be home.

When the day finally came, the Chastain stage was filled with 207 chairs. Before the start of the ceremony, the class members had many opportunities to celebrate, write messages in their yearbooks and say their goodbyes. For some, they knew that the goodbyes might well be their final farewells.

Jessie stood waiting with the other graduates and watched for signs of Carter's arrival at her family's designated row. Her mother was saving him a seat next to her.

The graduates lined up by height first, the girls in their white caps and gowns with the boys doing the same in purple caps and gowns behind them. The principal hushed the students as the Pomp and Circumstance March began. Jessie turned again toward her parents and saw Carter trot down the amphitheater steps and slip into the seat beside her mom. He waved to her across the amphitheater, and then to Coach standing in line with the faculty. He was carrying a bouquet of red roses.

Coach watched Carter shake Mr. Reynolds's hand and thought about the information about Martin Garrett that he still held in confidence. Mrs. Laney, who was standing next to him, leaned over. "Paul." He didn't hear her until she repeated his name.

"Yes? Yes, Laura?"

"I think we can begin now," she said. Coach nodded. Everyone he cared for was in place. The weather was perfect, and all were relieved that their prayers had been answered for the outdoor event. The blue sky above them was an indicator of things to come for the class of 1966!

When the program concluded, the graduates threw their caps high in the air. Tom, Claire, Terry, Sandy, Jack and all of Jessie's friends were all smiling and hugging family and each other. Carter stepped back to be sure Jessie got all the appropriate Reynolds family hugs first and then handed her the roses.

"Congratulations, Catch," he whispered.

After Jessie said goodbye to her friends at Chastain, she and Carter went home for the family dinner celebration. Jessie's sisters, Caroline and Meredith, had made it home for the occasion, and both Granny Reynolds and Grandmother Danby were there. Jessie could not have been more pleased.

After dinner, Jessie missed Carter and found him walking outside with her father. She watched as her father placed his hand on Carter's shoulder and looked to him for confirmation of whatever he had said. Jessie joined them and stuck her arm through Carter's and her dad smiled. "We were just talking about you heading to Athens soon."

"Yes, that's right," Carter said. But Jessie had learned to read him so well that she knew his face was not matching his words.

She looked back at her dad. "Great! Shouldn't I be a part of this awesome conversation?"

"Okay, okay," said her father. "I was just discussing with Carter any ideas he had for the future the two of you might have."

Her mother stepped up beside her husband. "Your dad is only saying that we want what's best for you both."

Jessie raised her eyebrows. "Wow. What timing!"

Carter took a deep breath. "Maybe we could sit down and discuss this tonight, sir. I could come back later."

"No way!" said Jessie. "You just got in town and we have plans, remember?"

Jessie took his arm and the four of them separated. As Jessie and Carter walked back toward the house, he put his arm around her. "You think we could break away for a bit?"

"After *that*, I hope so!"

The party finally came to an end and soon they were walking on the park trail leading to the creek bank. "What about my dad? Can you believe it? That came out of nowhere!" said Jessie.

"No," said Carter, "it didn't, Jessie. He is about to have an empty nest and he's seeing a last opportunity to protect his youngest daughter. I don't blame him or your mom."

They sat down at their spot on the creek bank and Jessie nestled close to Carter. "We're good together, you know?" she said. "I look at other couples and don't see what I see with us. I guess I have discovered there is no set right or wrong with couples. Before you, I thought it all just somehow came together for people. Robin and I were talking earlier about knowing when it's right."

Carter drew her closer. "There was never any doubt, Jess. Never any doubt about you and me. I love you, Jess. You are my best friend. You have trusted me with your heart. With all of you." He paused. "But there is still so much you don't know about me."

"We'll always be learning about each other. Don't you think?" Jessie replied. "My graduation brought us one step closer to our future. My parents are concerned that we are taking things too fast, and you can talk to them again if you like. But just know that nothing can separate us."

She turned to look at him and saw tears in his eyes. "What is it?"

"I'm just grateful for you, Jess. Just so very grateful."

Jessie jumped up. "Come on! We need to celebrate! I have graduated, and we need to celebrate!" Carter welcomed her embrace as she danced toward his car. He ran to catch her and swung her around. For now, he would do as she said—celebrate freely.

After they stopped at the after party at the Caldwells, Carter was true to his word, and returned with Jessie to the Reynolds's to revisit their conversation with Jessie's parents. He would not let his intentions be in doubt. He assured them of his support for Jessie's education and his respect for her teaching dream. It is the only way going forward he knew for their future.

Carter and Jessie spent as much time together as possible during the summer. She took a job at Lenox Square to earn spending money for college while Carter worked with Coach as his summer assistant. July was almost over, and Carter told her he had to take care of some details with the Bradford coaches.

He drove the newly-tuned Buick up the highway, giving himself time to reflect. By the time he reached the Bradford campus he had made a decision that would change everything. He went to an office on the other side of campus; the meeting with the coaching staff was unplanned.

When Carter returned from his morning run, a pot of coffee waited for the brothers to share. Bobby knew something was up—he and Carter had talked many times about forming a partnership and starting a business together once his younger brother finished college and Carter had recently avoided talking about it. He tried again. "Carter, making my own way toward owning a contracting company has always been a goal. A goal for the both of us."

"I know," said Carter. "And I have thought about that a lot. You have always looked out for us...taking care of what we needed." He paused and swallowed. "Papa was there for us too. He helped me see that commitments were an important part of making my own way too."

"You're right. He always used those words, duty and country, over and over again. But we've always talked about the importance of your education coming first."

Side by side at the kitchen counter, the two brothers continued to make their breakfast and stood while eating. Bobby was about to speak when Carter set his plate on the counter.

"Bobby, I made a decision at Bradford yesterday. The school has been great to me, but the connection and influence with the Fields on my time there brought a reality check for me. It brought me closer to knowing the right thing to do for Papa."

Bobby stood in silent disbelief. He watched his brother walk down the hallway toward his bedroom. Carter's decision was final—and there was nothing he could do about it.

Chapter Twenty-Nine

Carter called and asked Jessie to meet him at the park. He pulled into a parking place and reached for his keys, pausing to look at the medallion. He could see Jessie waiting on the creek bank.

When she saw him, she smiled and ran to him. He could feel the hope in her embrace, and he didn't want to let her go. He kissed her and kissed her again, relishing every one, hoping to convey all the love in his heart.

"I was thinking about you this morning just when you called!" said Jessie.

"I was thinking about you too," he said. "I didn't want to wait until our date tonight. I needed to see you now."

Jessie pulled back to look at him, caught off guard by his serious tone. "Are you okay?"

He grasped her hand to walk back toward the creek until they reached their spot near the large shade tree. He sat and took her hand. "Sit with me." He leaned back against the tree with his arms around Jessie in front of him.

She could feel his heart beating when he nestled his head next to her face.

"What?" she asked. She knew him well and sensed the seriousness between them. She placed her hand over his. "What's wrong?"

Carter looked at the creek. "You about to get packed for school?"

"Just about," she said. "Carter, what is it?"

He took a deep breath. "Hey, this is an exciting time for you. Your dream of being a teacher is about to begin."

"I'm waiting to hear about my classes, but the housing office sent me a notice I will be living in Cresswell where Missy lives."

She turned to look at him and tried to read his mood. Ever the optimist, she tried to lighten it. "It's hard to believe I will be on my own soon. But knowing you and I can plan our times together makes it all real."

He ran his hand down her arm and grasped her hand. His procrastination would not ease the pain he would now inflict on the someone who was everything to him. "Jess. You know you are everything to me. No one can ever take that away from us."

"Of course!" She turned and looked at him again, a chill running down her spine. "What's going on, Carter?"

"There has been a lot going on in my head, Jess and I've had a lot to think about. My school, your school, your future, your dreams," he said.

"You mean *our* dreams. *Our* future," she said. "I have thought a lot about it, too, you know."

"I haven't been as truthful with you as you deserve, Jessie. I just couldn't."

"I don't know what you mean. We've always been able to share everything."

"This isn't easy for me to say. I know…how important college is to you."

"Yes…" Jessie's optimism melted and she turned to face him directly.

Carter took another deep breath. "Way before you, Jessie, I made a promise to Papa. He was in the hospital and during one of our last conversations he told me to do something for my country. You have to know I would do anything for him." He paused for a second and searched Jessie's face for a reaction.

"I know you loved him very much and you always said you owed him everything," she answered.

"There's more. I haven't been totally honest with you over the last several months," he said. "The reason I went back up to Bradford wasn't about football. It was to speak again with an Army recruiting officer at school. We talked back in the spring about my return to school this fall."

"A recruiting officer?"

"It has always been important to me to find a way to honor my promise to Papa," he said. "He was responsible for who I am today. He was responsible for me being born. For me being alive."

"What are you saying?" Jessie asked.

"I have enlisted in the Army, Jessie. It's just a matter of time before the draft gets me anyway. The recruiter said that this way, I can go in with more opportunity at a higher level once I finish my training."

Jessie's heart was pounding.

"There have been times when I thought I should tell you about it. About my promise to Papa to serve our country. That time at the Veterans Day picnic at my church. Other times too. I just didn't know then how much you would change my life."

Jessie began to cry. "But we'll have more time together! When you come home or I will come to you. We can't let this separate us! Don't you think your Papa would want you to be happy?"

Carter smiled, tears glistening in his eyes. "Jess, you have made me so happy. So happy. I love you so much and want us to be married. This will bring us closer to that day. The timing of this is important for our future. But this couldn't be *our* decision. It had to be mine."

Jessie began to shake her head. "No. No! I don't believe you. This isn't happening!"

"This will put us one step closer to being together. It will be a good thing and I can do this while you are in school. Please try to understand. It is the only thing that stands in my way of wholeheartedly planning the future with you. It is best that I go ahead and do this now while you are in college." He hesitated. "I just didn't know it meant I'd be going so soon."

"Soon? What does that mean?"

"I've already been ordered to Ft. Benning for basic training."

Several cars had pulled up to the street and parked nearby. Boys were getting out and tossing a football in the park. They both recognized Jack as one of the group and Carter knew they would not have their privacy much longer. "It was the one thing I had to do on my own. I wish I could help you understand."

Tears streamed down Jessie's face. "*How* soon?"

"In a few days. I want us to make the most of our time together before I leave, Jess. Our planning today just needs to look a little different. That's all." Jessie held Carter tight and continued to cry.

They looked up to see Jack walking slowly toward them from across the field. As he came closer, he was concerned when he saw that Jessie was crying. "Y'all okay? What's going on?"

"I'm headed to Ft. Benning in a few days." He looked down at Jessie and back at Jack, his voice shaking. "I'm going to need you to look out for Jessie while I'm gone."

Coach sprinted inside from his garden to the kitchen when he heard the phone ring.

"Hey, Coach," said the voice on the phone.

"Carter. Is that you?"

"You busy?" asked Carter.

"What's going on?"

"I need your help," Carter said. "Okay if I come by in about an hour?"

"Sure, come on by whenever."

Coach wiped his hands and looked around the kitchen to see what he might have to share with Carter when he arrived. He had come to treasure the young man who had given him a new outlook on life.

He didn't know what was on Carter's mind, but it occurred to him that God may just have presented this moment for him to tell the young man about his father and his connection to Carla Peterson. After all, Stephen Hamilton had told him he would know when the time was right. *This might very well be the day*, he thought.

Coach knew immediately when he opened the door and saw the pain on Carter's face that this wasn't going to be just a catch-up conversation. Despite the heat of a hot summer day, Carter stood holding his football jacket.

On previous visits, the two had headed to the kitchen to sit and talk. Rather than heading to the kitchen Coach led Carter into the living room and gestured him toward Ann's chair. Carter placed the jacket on the back of the chair and his hand on the purple shawl on the chair's arm.

Coach sensed the need to say a word of encouragement. "You know," said the coach, "I don't think I ever told you about that purple shawl on the chair. It has one silver thread running straight through it." Carter looked down and ran his hand across the thread.

"Ann always said that was her hope thread. She wore that shawl to all the football games hoping for a victory! She placed it around her shoulders sometimes when she thought I wasn't looking and would gently run her hands over that silver thread, just like you're doing. She told me before she passed away that the thread was her symbol for the child we hoped for."

Carter couldn't bring himself to look at Coach, and he stared at the floor. He began to shake his head, searching for words to begin the conversation. He had held back his emotions when he'd met with Jessie. With Coach it was different. "You and me, we really didn't connect until after she was gone. I wish I could have known her, Coach."

The coach gave a grateful nod. "And she would have loved knowing you. I told her about you when you first started playing on the team back in the ninth grade. She was always interested in all my players, but she knew you were something special." Coach paused. "She brought out the best in me."

Carter touched the shawl again. "You know, Coach, I never loved anyone like I love Jessie. She brings out the best in me, too. I can't tell you how many times when we've been together that she's told me not to give up hope. I know she has always dreamed of being a teacher, like you and Mrs. Laney and Mr. Baker. Her life is precious to me and I want her is to follow her dream."

"Yes, Jessie, is something special for sure. You care about her a lot, I know."

"But for dreams and commitments to come together, certain things have to happen and I had to tell Jessie today."

"What did you have to tell her?" asked Coach.

"Coach, the trip to Bradford was not about the upcoming season. I went back to finalize my talks at the recruiting office. I've enlisted."

"You enlisted?"

Carter took a deep breath and attempted to hold back his tears. "Yes, I have enlisted in the Army. And…I just told Jessie. I am headed to Ft. Benning in a few days. The recruiting officer says I have a good chance by joining up now to have a higher grade with some special training they want me to do."

Coach straightened his back. His face could not disguise his concern. It was early yet, but Vietnam had played such a cruel part in so many lives. He gestured to Carter to continue.

"Jess and I have talked for hours about what it will be like someday, getting married and all. I know it's not in the cards right now. She has to go on to college, and I have to do this now so we can be together when I return. I owe this to Papa. When I told Jessie, she was too upset to talk about it. I just hope she can understand that this is what I have to do."

"You've always talked about him and how much he did for you and Bobby."

Carter nodded. "Coach, I made him a promise before he died and this would make him proud," he said. He paused and looked up again. "You have been like a dad for me, too. Besides Papa, you have always been there for me, and I am grateful for it."

Coach cleared his throat, convinced now was the time. "About your dad, Carter. Your *real* dad."

Carter raised his hand before he could continue. "I decided a long time ago I don't want to go there, Coach. I don't *need* to go there. I have had everything I needed when it comes to a parent. Papa, you, even Bobby in many ways. All of you have made my life complete. There's no need for me to talk about it."

Memories flooded into the coach's mind. He felt helpless, like the way he had the moment the doctor said there was nothing more they could do except make his wife Ann comfortable. Treatment would only be painful and without positive results, the doctor had said, and he had had to face the acceptance of letting her go. "Sometimes loving someone so much also means loving them enough to let them go," he said, stopping short of saying the word *forever*. "You and Jessie are together because you have the same values. She will understand. Give her time and make the most of these days before you leave," said Coach. "I don't think I have ever been more proud of you than I am right now. How can I help?"

"You already have…just being here. But I *do* have a favor to ask." Carter reached for his letter jacket. "This has meant the world to me. When you gave this to me, not only once but then a second time, it told me I was worthy and that you thought I did a good job. I want you to keep it for me." He paused. "And, if there is a reason to someday pass it on to someone else, it would mean a lot to me."

Coach took the jacket and laid it across his lap. "This jacket also came with the respect of your teammates and of mine. They knew they could always count on you. I will keep it here for you when you return."

Then, Carter handed him a white envelope with Jessie's name on the front. "One other thing. This is for her…if I don't make it back." Coach took the envelope, dread filling him at the prospect.

Carter waited and then nodded his head with a sense that he had accomplished his mission. He stood and extended his hand. Coach gripped his hand tightly and then pulled Carter into a hug like none he had ever given before.

"Brave journey, my son," he said. "Godspeed."

Chapter Thirty

Jessie and Carter's friends and families prepared for the days ahead. Jessie's parents were there to console her in her efforts to be brave and to support Carter's decision. Mrs. Reynolds prepared her best family dinner for Carter and invited Bobby, Marie, Coach O'Connor and Rev. Hamilton—as well as Jack, Sandy, Claire, Tom, Mike, Crow, Brandi and the band. Jessie spent every possible moment with Carter before his departure for Ft. Benning. He did his best to fill their conversations with the excitement of her going to college and Jessie focused on the happiness they would share upon his return.

The Reynolds were glad that Jack would also be in Athens. His good nature and friendship would be encouraging knowing the two good friends would be together. He would be living in Payne Hall near the older part of campus, not far from Jessie's Baxter Street dorm.

Uncertain about his own future, Jack packed his suitcases and boxes for the year ahead. Knowing his parents had worked hard to save for his college education to supplement the scholarship he had earned, he was surprised by their unexpected gift of a Volkswagen Beetle. Despite the reality of Jessie and Carter, his first thought was of Jessie sharing the front seat with him.

Carter stood in the middle of his bedroom looking at his army duffle bag. He looked out his window and his eyes fell on the rose bush he and Jessie had planted together. He thought about the fact that while his heart and love was with Jessie just five minutes away, his hope for the future would be several hours away and determined by the people at the Columbus military base. Fulfilling his promise would put them closer to being back together. He was convinced with Jessie pursuing her degree while he was away, the timing would work.

He stopped by to say goodbye to Crow and check on his drums. Brandi assured him that they would be safe and there for his return. Leaving the Nest, he saw Jack driving the new Volkswagen down Howell Mill and raised his hand in recognition. He knew Jack was a good guy and that he would be there for Jessie if she needed him.

Jessie arrived promptly at 10:00 a.m. to pick up Carter and take him to the bus station. Carter removed the medallion Jessie had given him from his key ring and handed his keys to Bobby. The medallion would go with him until his return to Jessie and their cherished happiness.

The brothers had said their farewells early that morning, exchanging an emotional hug. Bobby waved goodbye and stood in the driveway until they were out of sight.

Jessie drove slowly, trying to stretch out the time, and Carter did his best to keep their conversation light and upbeat. When they reached the parking lot at the Greyhound bus station, it was filled with family members sending off other new recruits.

Jessie found an empty space to park and took a deep breath, but before she said anything, Carter shook his head. "Don't get out, Jess," he said. "I want our goodbye to be here."

A lump formed in Jessie's throat. "I love you," she managed. In true Carter fashion, he pulled her close. Not wanting to let him go, she touched his face. He wiped her tears then released his hand and climbed out of the car. The engine of the bus started up and Carter leaned through Jessie's window for one more kiss. "I love you, too, Catch."

His shoulders were straight and proud as he walked toward the bus and handed his duffle to the driver. He looked back at her, placed his hand over his heart, and disappeared onto the bus.

JESSIE MADE HER WAY HOME WIPING her tears as she drove. Going to her room, she sat on her bed and wrapped herself with Carter's blanket. She stared at the journal on her desk and finally pulled notepaper from the drawer and began to write her first letter to him.

> *Dear Carter,*
>
> *You just left the station and my only thought was to come home and begin this letter to you. I have this picture in my mind of you stepping onto the bus that will not let me go. You couldn't see when the door closed that I had my hand over my heart, too. It will be there every time I write to you as a prayer for your safety and return to me.*
>
> *I know that our love will keep us going. You are in my heart every minute of every day. I know you are doing what*

you know is right and that your Papa would be so proud
of you.

I look forward to your letters, so write soon and tell me
everything—your training, what you do every day and the
other soldiers there. Please be careful. I hold tight to the
day when we will be together again. My parents send their
prayers. I love you.

Forever, Jess

THE NEXT WEEK, SANDY STOPPED BY and the two girls went for a final ride on Josey before Sandy left for school in Tennessee. She would be taking Josey with her as her parents had found a stable in Knoxville to board the mare. Jessie had always appreciated Sandy's friendship and optimism during their rides. She spoke that day of her father's military experience and her parents' words about life and service. Jessie was encouraged by their conversation and the pride in the military and hope in life that Sandy had so generously shared with her friends over the years.

Missy heard about Carter's enlistment and called to encourage Jessie. She spoke of the excitement she had already experienced on campus and couldn't wait for Jessie to join her at Creswell dorm. She invited Jessie to go through the sorority rush. Jessie gave it some thought—but, for the moment, she decided to focus on beginning her classes to earn her degree and looking forward to a life with Carter.

Claire asked Jessie to meet her at Springlake for Coke floats and talk before she left for Duke University. Tom had been accepted to Vanderbilt and they'd already made plans to visit each other. Claire was as close to being a sister as any of Jessie's friends and she was grateful for the help she provided in clearing Carter's name. Dr. Ellis visited them at their table and asked about Jessie's "nice young man." When he heard that Carter had enlisted and was in basic training, he added his name to a poster over the fountain recognizing the service of other local Atlanta soldiers.

Choir friends, including William, gathered one last time at the Howell House. William would stay at home and pursue a degree in business at Georgia State while continuing to play his guitar with a local band. Robin and Mark were both going to West Georgia College in Carrollton and they promised to stay in touch. Robin walked Jessie to her car and the agreed to call and write about their experiences.

Within days, Carter's first letter arrived and Jessie's letters to him went out daily. He alerted her to the unknown of the timing of his letters given a hint of the expectation of new orders soon. She tried to let the excitement of being with her friends and talking about college fill the emptiness she was feeling without him. Jack called to check on her and make plans for their time in Athens. Once her parents moved her into Cresswell, he would meet up with her at the Freshman Mixer. With their freshman limitation on having vehicles, he had a friend who would accommodate his car at his fraternity house.

"The gang's meeting at the Zesto one final time," he said.

"I'm not very good company right now, Jack. Maybe you should go on without me. I know Carter asked you to look out for me, but I don't want you to feel obligated or anything."

"Jessie, I'm here. Just like I know you would be here for me. Right?" said Jack. "Come on. You can help me put a new Bulldog sticker on my car." She finally agreed and truly felt a moment of happiness in the ride to the Zesto in Jack's new Volkswagen.

Finally, it was time to pack for school. The Reynolds house was bustling with the activity of preparing for the big day. Besides the shoes, clothes, and accessories Jessie was taking, her mother had gathered all the items she needed for dorm life that sister Meredith had needed her freshman year.

"I'm not sure all this will fit in our car!" exclaimed her mother.

"We'll make it fit," said Jessie.

She made sure she had the perfect stationery and plenty of postage stamps in her suitcase for Carter's letters. Other boxes carried her scrapbook, including Carter's folded "I love you" banner from the Crow's Nest, the many pressed roses, and her journal. She touched his senior ring, still around her neck, and prayed again for his safety as she tied a red ribbon around his letters. The blanket he had given her Christmas, which she had slept with nightly ever since, was placed carefully on top of the last box headed to Athens.

The pink dog from the fair would stay behind on her slipper chair. It would continue to be a reminder of the choices between love and friendship.

Chapter Thirty-One

Northwest classes would begin soon, and Coach O'Connor gathered the files from home to take to his office at school. He passed the living room shelves and stopped to look at the gold box that housed Carter's envelope.

The sunrise painting on the wall always greeted him or sent him on his way with its message of hope. Mr. Kelley had stopped him outside the principal's office after the last summer faculty meeting.

"You're still speaking to the students at the opening assembly, right? Not too long. Something inspirational to start the new year." Coach thought about the painting and planned his speech on his way to school.

Coach O'Connor began to unload his boxes in the faculty parking area when Jack appeared and offered his help with those remaining.

"I didn't really get a chance to talk to you at Carter's dinner that night at Jessie's, but I wanted to say thanks, Coach. I'd like to stay in touch if it's alright with you."

Coach offered his hand and touched Jack's shoulder.

"Of course, and the thanks goes both ways. You have always been someone we all could count on. Keep being you, pass it on and you'll go far." Jack carried a box and followed Coach toward the athletic office. He looked around the Northwest corridors for the last time.

Coach thought about the speech he would give to the Northwest students to begin their new year. Jack was a reminder that there were lives close to him that were beginning new starts in their lives as well.

"Georgia is a great school, Jack. You have your whole life ahead of you, so make the most of every day."

"Yes sir," said Jack.

"Oh, and tell Jessie good luck for me, too. She's a great girl. You two take care in Athens!"

Jack hesitated at the innocent remark. He could still see the look in Carter's eyes when he'd requested he look out for Jessie while he was gone. "Yes, sir. We will. Good luck with the team."

Coach returned home that afternoon and stopped on his way inside to check on his garden. He thought about what Carter had said about his grandfather's adage of how to treat women like flowers. He stooped to remove a few dried day-lily stalks. He made a mental list of other pruning to be done.

When he went inside, he called Rev. Hamilton to make sure he would continue as the Northwest football team chaplain and to invite him to play one more round of golf at Cherokee before school resumed.

Coach had not been a religious man until he'd met Stephen during Ann's hospital stay, and he was grateful for his support, especially with respect to telling Carter what they'd learned about his father. "You'll find the right time, Paul," he had said. "*For everything there is a season and a time for every purpose.*"

WHEN COACH O'CONNOR CALLED, STEPHEN HAMILTON was at the church preparing for his Sunday sermon and laying out his preaching schedule in the months ahead. He saw the Veterans Day weekend coming up in November and placed a call to make sure the preparations had begun for the annual picnic on the grounds. He thought about Carter and how the church would miss him being there if he couldn't come home on leave to attend.

Carter's brother Bobby had called earlier that morning to ask for an appointment for him and Marie to come in. They had recently become engaged and wanted to set a date with him for the wedding, all dependent on Carter's deployment. He stood and walked into the sanctuary, stopping at the Crawford memorial window and bowed his head to say a prayer for Big Jim's beloved grandsons, Bobby and Carter.

When he returned to his office he sat at his desk and closed his eyes. The conversations he'd had with with Jim Crawford still rested on his heart—meeting with Bobby and Carter after Jim died had been one of the most difficult in his ministry. He had seen the face of Big Jim in his mind as he'd counseled Carter when he'd struggled with the decision to leave college and join the Army. He thought of meeting Ann O'Connor at the hospital and then her husband Paul and how all their lives had been intertwined over the past several years with those of Carter and Jessie's families.

PERRY MICHAELS WAS IN HIS OFFICE early preparing for a staff meeting. The Playboys' booking agent had a busy weekend with his many new clients and his assistant had placed his mail on his desk for review. He came across a simple white envelope in the stack and saw the return address from Carter Powell. He remembered the name—the drummer of The Playboys, whose decision to leave the group had led to the group's breakup. He opened the envelope and read:

> *Mr. Michaels – I am leaving for military service soon and I have had these words in me for a long time. I would ask for your assistance to find a musician who could add the music if you agree it could be produced. In the event that something happens to me, all rights, royalties and privileges are assigned to Jessica Elaine Reynolds. The song is for her. Thank you. Sincerely, Carter Powell*

Perry straightened himself in his chair as he read the attachment and quickly reached for his phone and dialed. He met that afternoon with a friend from an up and coming recording label to share the lyrics written on the blue-lined notebook page.

HOPE

Home is sweet with hope inside
Home is welcoming arms open wide
Care for one with hopeless heart
Comes together their worlds apart.

Hope is trust and love for me
Hope is there for orphan free
Hope makes life a gift you see
Hope lifts up my heart to be.

Janice R. Johnson

Today makes hope a possibility
With love and music it will be
Forever knows it day by day
Keep it close I ask and pray.

Tomorrow wishes you next to me
Hope and love that gift to see
Roses for eternity.
Roses for eternity.

Chapter Thirty-Two

The first months of college kept Jessie busy—adjusting to class schedules, dorm life and meeting her new roommate from Savannah. Leigh was kind and outgoing and reminded Jessie of Sandy.

The girls' room looked out over the green-fenced courtyard side of Cressell which was used for the co-eds sunning during the day and not-so-private couple time at night. She could see the car lights on Baxter at night when the dates would park in the middle of the street to run their dates to the dorm doorway to make curfew.

The large communal bathroom with its rows of showers and stalls had its challenges, but the girls quickly became accustomed to carrying their shower buckets to its sinks and curtained shower partitions. Their marked sheets and towels had a weekly assigned drop time at the downstairs laundry and Jessie would identify her numbered brown paper wrapped clean bundle the next day.

She had had to send some of her items back home with her parents when she realized her four small drawers and thirty-six inch closet with overhead storage would not accommodate all the wardrobe she had brought. She saved the bin across her pullout single bed and desk space for the special "Carter items" that would stay close to her.

Her 321A mailbox in the dorm lobby was her favorite destination as she checked frequently for Carter's letters. She would drop her letters to him every morning after writing the night before about her day and her love for him. She was not expecting so soon the letter from him about his platoon being shipped out to Vietnam.

She looked at the date and realized he had already arrived in the war-torn land. Her heart ached when she saw the new address he listed to mail her letters. His letters began to slow in frequency. It made her savor each one even more.

JESSIE SAT STUDYING IN HER ROOM one evening when a new friend in the dorm knocked on her door. "There's a call for you. It's your mom."

She pushed back in her chair and hurried to the payphone at the end of the hall, wondering about the call. They had set a time each week to call home and she'd just talked to them the night before.

She lifted the receiver to her ear. "Hey, Mom," she said.

"What are you doing?" asked Mrs. Reynolds.

"I'm studying for a test tomorrow."

She heard a click and her father got on the line. "Darling, we're afraid we have some bad news."

Jessie's heart jumped to her throat. "What's happened?"

"Bobby Powell called me at my office this afternoon," said her father. "Honey, Carter was…killed…yesterday in an ambush…"

It was the last thing she heard before she crumpled to the floor.

THE SPEAKER CONTINUED TO BUZZ AS the downstairs dorm assistant tried in vain to reach her. Leigh had just run down the hall to get some ice. "Man on the hall" shouts could be heard on the third floor lobby.

"Jess?"

She opened her eyes to find Jack kneeling in front of her. She blinked.

"Jess," he said again. "Your mom called me and told me about Carter. I got here as fast as I could." Leigh returned with the ice and started to pour Tab, Jessie's favorite soft drink over it.

"I'm here, too," said Missy. "I'll stay with you tonight if you want me to." Jessie was numb and surprised to see her there.

And then, it all came crashing down. Carter was dead. She grabbed her blanket and wrapped it as tightly around her as she could. *There must have been a mistake. It can't be true.*

The dorm counselor stood in the doorway and Jack placed his hand on Jessie's. "Your professors are all being notified and Leigh and Missy will help you pack. I'm taking you home tomorrow."

Jessie closed her eyes and in a daze tried to stand. Jack wrapped his arms around her and she began to sob.

Chapter Thirty-Three

The next morning Jessie and Jack drove down the highway from Athens toward home. She stared out the Volkswagen window, watching as raindrops drizzled down the window.

Jack reached over to take her hand. Her hands felt cold and he reached for his jacket to place over her. Jessie glanced at him and offered a weak smile—reminded of the hundreds of times Carter had done the same.

"When he couldn't reach you," said Jack, "Rev. Hamilton called to ask about you, Jess. Crow and Brandi called too. They said they would see you at the church."

When he saw no reaction from Jessie, he continued. "I heard from Coach too. He said to tell you he would see you soon."

They rode for miles and miles in silence until the Atlanta skyline finally came into view. Jessie finally spoke. "I need to see Bobby. I just need to see him." Bobby was as close to Carter as she could get.

Jack nodded and took the highway exit leading them to Northside Drive and onto Moores Mill, hoping against hope that Bobby would be home. They pulled in the driveway and Jessie saw the rose bush she had planted with Carter. It was in full bloom. Carter's green Buick was in the carport and Bobby's Chevrolet was parked behind it. Jack saw a light on in the kitchen and got out of the car to knock on the carport kitchen door. Jessie sat motionless in the car, watching.

Bobby opened the door to speak to Jack and then leaned out to see Jessie. He covered his heart and motioned for her to come in. It was the same thing Carter had done when he'd stepped on the bus to Ft. Benning—one heart covered with compassion and the other covered with the deepest love Jessie had known.

Jack opened the car door and reached for Jessie's hand. Bobby stood beside him and caught her as she fell into his arms. "Jessie," was all he said.

"Something told me to come see you," she said.

"I'm glad," he said.

They walked through the kitchen where she and Carter had made dinners together. In the living room were several arrangements already delivered by the florist. A plant with an American flag sat on the dining room table.

Bobby pointed to the sofa where they could sit and Jack walked out the front door and sat down on the steps outside.

"Why, Bobby? Why did he have to enlist? " said Jessie, tears streaming.

Bobby paused and could see more questions in her eyes. He tried to keep his composure, and then began to explain. "Papa and Carter had a special bond, Jessie. More so than mine or anyone else. Carter felt like he owed him everything. His life." As Jessie listened, she remembered how often Carter made that same reference to owing Papa his life. She had not known what it meant.

"Papa was gone, and Rev. Hamilton had come over to talk one evening some years back. Back before Carter met you, Jessie. The reverend knew we were now on our own, and Papa had asked him to look after us. You know, to make sure we could handle things and take care of ourselves."

Jessie nodded. "Carter told me that, but I knew there was something else that bothered him. He told me a lot about himself, but there was always something else that he never talked about. More and more since finding out about the Fields scholarship, he started to become more distant to me and everybody else, and certain things seemed to upset him more than before."

Bobby looked down at his hands. "Part of it was a pride that Papa instilled in us. Being able to accomplish school or anything else on our own was something Papa wanted for us, knowing someday he wouldn't be around to help us. I know Carter wanted to tell you everything, but he struggled to understand it all himself. Rev. Hamilton helped as much as he could. Before you, Carter always felt he didn't deserve to be loved because of what happened with our parents. The whole story behind it all was what you didn't know."

"What else was there?" asked Jessie, wiping her eyes.

"We learned from Rev. Hamilton after Papa died that he had saved Carter's life." Bobby shook his head with the memory of Carter's reaction after learning the truth.

"What do you mean saved his life?"

"Early on, I was too young to really understand what was happening with our parents. I know there was a lot of hollering and screaming between them. I remember being very afraid most of the time and always glad to see Papa come over. Things would calm down when he was around. The next thing I know our parents are gone, and Papa Ford moved in with us. It was Papa who took care of me and Carter."

"What are you saying?"

"Papa never told us anything about Mama and Daddy's car accident. Rev. Hamilton thought we could handle it that day he came to visit. He told us Papa was at our house because Mama and Daddy had been arguing again. They left us with Papa that night and were driving together when they lost control of their car on Paces Ferry." Bobby shook his head with the thought of the accident.

"How awful, Bobby. I am so sorry."

Bobby paused. "That was bad enough, but what we didn't know was that Papa had learned from Mama that Carter had a different father. I know Carter told you that part already. Mama told Papa before Carter was born, but Daddy didn't know. Mama talked to Papa about not having the baby, but Papa told her not to harm the baby, that he would help her raise us if he had to."

"Oh, I see," said Jessie. Carter's response to Mike when he thought Fran was pregnant now was making much more sense.

"The arguing had gotten really bad and then Mama admitted to Daddy what he already suspected...that he wasn't Carter's father. It was the night of the accident. Papa was here when they left the house that night, and from that moment on, he took care of me and Carter.

"Later, when Carter heard the whole story, he couldn't let go of the fact that Mama considered not having him. *That's* how Papa saved his life. It explained so much about how Papa was always by his side when he younger...before the accident. After that, it was like he couldn't do enough to repay Papa, even after he was gone."

"One of the things I loved about Carter was his loyalty and commitment, to everything. And I loved to hear him talk about his Papa," said Jessie.

"I tried to talk to him about it when he decided to enlist. Rev. Hamilton did, too, but he was convinced the only thing he could do for

Papa was to do this for his country. Papa said that to us all the time when we were growing up—particularly when he told his military stories. He told Papa in the hospital before he died that he promised he would make him proud. Carter believed it was the only way to repay him for saving his life all those years ago."

"But, Bobby, why did he leave me?"

"He was tormented by it, Jessie. One way or another, the time would have come. His bond with Papa was that deep." He paused. "I'm sure Carter never expected to die. He expected to come home, wait for you to graduate from college, and live with you for the rest of his life. He was in misery during the past few months—there was nothing he wanted more than to protect you from any pain and still keep his promise to Papa. The whole thing with Judge and Mrs. Fields somehow triggered a decision that the time was to be now. Neither of us could have changed his thinking about that."

Bobby smiled, tears welling in his eyes. "One thing's for sure, though, Jessie. Carter discovered that he *did* deserve love. And it was because of you. You were his greatest gift."

He opened the end table drawer and pulled out an envelope of photographs. "I got some pictures from Carter not long ago. I think you should have them."

Jessie nodded her head, but she wasn't sure she could look at his face. Her hands were shaking. Yet, she needed a way to be able to touch him again. Just one more time.

Some of the pictures were of the Vietnamese countryside, a helicopter, and Carter standing on top of a tank looking down. The last one was of Carter smiling with some of his buddies.

She looked closely at the last picture—all of the soldiers had writing on their helmets. One soldier had the months of the year written down the side with check marks for each month he had completed. Another had written a girl's name. Across the front of Carter's helmet were the words "One Day at a Time."

"I'd like to think he was trying to tell us something. Something we didn't need to know so much until now. Don't you?"

Jessie nodded in agreement.

"It's yours. Take it," said Bobby.

"No. He sent them to you," Jessie said.

"The funeral will be tough, Jess. Remember the good things and the gift he was to us. I have many pictures of my brother and I will always be proud of him. And I will forever be grateful for the love you gave him. Remember his message."

He placed the pictures in her hand. Seeing the pictures, and now knowing the final piece of Carter's life, would help her through the funeral and bring comfort in the days ahead.

Jack reappeared in the living room. "Jess, I think I need to take you on home."

"One thing," Bobby added. "Marie and I would be honored if you and your parents would sit with the family at the funeral." He looked at Jack. "And Jack, I'd like you to be with us too."

Jessie nodded and stood. Bobby stood with her, reaching to hug her again. As, they all walked out to Jack's car, Jessie stopped at the rose bush and snapped the stem of a flower that was just beginning to open. She heard Coach's voice in her head. *A rose only blossoms once.* This rose would become the memory of her once-in-a-lifetime love.

Chapter Thirty-four

When football practice was over, Coach O'Connor left the stack of papers to be graded on his desk and headed home. All he could think about was the letter he would now have to give to Jessie.

He entered his front door and ran his hand ran over the painting of the sunrise from which he'd drawn his speech for the students at the start of school. The plaque at the bottom—"Gratitude is the heart's memory"— spoke to him once again. He continued to the bookshelf and looked at the picture of him with Carter and Jessie, and smiled, remembering the night they'd all celebrated after Carter's exoneration from responsibility for the Fulton incident.

On the next shelf down was the gold box which held the letter to Jessie. He removed the envelope and turned it over in his hands, then headed down the hallway to his office. When he turned on the light, his eyes fell on Carter's jacket, still folded on the edge of the desk. As he moved to sit down in his chair, he rested his hand on the jacket and felt something in the pocket—another envelope, this one addressed to him.

Coach,

Years ago, Papa asked me to come to the hospital when we knew his time was short. He told me I should know about my real father. His name was Martin Garrett. Papa told me that I would be the man I was raised to be—that true fathers are more than blood. He told me there would be real men in my life who would make a difference in the man I would become.

Papa was my grandfather and loved me like a father, but after I joined the football team, I always looked to you as my dad. Words cannot express my gratitude for what you have given me. You gave me the face to look for after a great play when there was no father's pride to look for in the stands. You were there to give me the pat on the back when there was no else to tell me well done. You gave me your time when I needed to talk. You gave me confidence that I could do anything. You were there to share my celebrations and you were there with your presence and support when times were tough. You helped me to appreciate even the small things like a simple flower and to know that larger things were victories with the contributions of others.

I never needed to know Martin Garrett, but I was honored to know you. Thanks Coach…for everything.

Carter

Tears flowed down the coach's face.

"Come in, Coach," said Mrs. Reynolds, as she opened the door. "Jessie is upstairs. I'll get her." While he waited, Coach O'Connor glanced around the Reynolds' living room. Family pictures were on every bookshelf and table in the room. On a chest near the front door was the picture of Jessie and Carter at the Snow Ball.

When Jessie came into the room, she went straight to hug the man she had come to know so well. As she slid into his arms, she thought of the irony of how she now felt toward the stoic algebra teacher she'd met her junior year.

Neither spoke. Jessie sat on the sofa and Coach in a chair across from her. He leaned forward and rested his arms on his knees. She glanced out the window to see a cardinal land on the front porch railing and Grandmother Denby's words came rushing back to her. "You know Jessie, they say that seeing a red cardinal is like seeing a loved one who has passed. They are here to tell you they will always be with you."

Jessie glanced back at the coach. "Jack brought me home."

Coach lifted his head. "I'm so sorry, Jessie," he said. "You were my first thought when I heard the news. And then students at school, team members, shared stories about Carter that I never knew. Stories about his friendship and how accepting he was of them. Mike…Terry…even the younger players on the team. Rev. Hamilton came over and has made himself available to anyone who needed to talk."

"Did Rev. Hamilton tell you about Carter's parents and Papa Ford?" she asked.

The coach nodded. "Yes. Stephen knew Carter was special to me and shared some of his story. I had no idea. I just knew he was special."

The coach paused and then took a deep breath. "I have something to give you, Jessie. Something from Carter. He gave it to me before he left and told me if something happened to him that I should give it to you."

Jessie sat up when he handed her the letter. She instantly recognized Carter's writing on the outside of the envelope and a tear, then another, streamed down her face. She held it close to her heart.

Coach O'Connor stood to leave and she walked him to the door and hugged him again. Mrs. Reynolds appeared from the kitchen, bearing a tin of cookies. "Paul, I hope you know you are welcome here anytime. Ladd and I will see you at the service. I know Jessie is going to need your support. You knew Carter better than many of us."

Jessie sat on her bed for a long time looking at the envelope. Finally, she opened it—no delaying would change the finality of Carter's death. Careful not to tear even one corner, she slid the letter out and began to read.

> *Hey, Catch,*
>
> *Writing this letter is difficult and compares only to sharing my decision that day in the park. I know because you are reading this and that our dream of being together will never be.*
>
> *I had a promise to fulfill to serve my country and I want you to know that I was proud to have done so. Hopefully, someday you will understand this was something I had to do, and I had to do it alone.*
>
> *I wasn't the best at telling you how I felt during our time together. Please know you always had my heart. You were my inspiration, and you gave me the love I never thought I deserved. I could never forgive myself if I thought I would be the cause of you not following your dream. You will be a wonderful teacher.*
>
> *We opened our hearts and ourselves to each other. Whenever there was trouble or sadness, you always gave me hope. Don't ever let me be the one who causes you not to continue to share that*

hope with the other lives you will touch. The medallion enclosed is for you to remember how to move forward and open your heart again to love. Beside Papa, Coach was the next thing to a father I ever had, and I trusted this letter to be in his care. Look in on him when you can. Papa taught me to open myself to love, and Coach taught me, it also sometimes means having to let go. Make sure he knows he made a difference in my life, just as you did.

Forever,

Carter

A gold medallion similar to the one she had given Carter slid out of the envelope. On it were the engraved words *One Day at a Time*—the same words she had sent in the letter to him at Bradford and the same words written on his helmet in the photograph Bobby had given her.

She opened her journal and reverently placed the letter and picture inside, then made her way down the stairs to the den and her piano. She could not bring herself to sing the words of her father's favorite Irish lullaby, but the melody brought an indescribable peace to her soul.

Chapter Thirty-Four

J essie rose on the morning of the funeral and dressed in the navy-blue
dress she had worn to the Veterans Day service. She had asked Jack
to drive her to the church, and when she saw the Volkswagen pull up in
front, she picked up the medallion Carter had given her and slipped it
in her purse. Her parents stood quietly at the front door as she made her
way down the stairs and out to Jack's car—they knew her faith was strong
and that she would deal with Carter's loss in her own way.

When she and Jack arrived at the church, Jessie stepped from the car
and stood silently watching an honor guard carefully remove the flag-
draped coffin from the hearse in front of the church. Small American
flags waved in the breeze on either side of its fenders.

Many friends had come home from college and were gathered at the
church in tribute to their friend. Missy and Sandy were seated together
with Claire, Tom and his parents, Frank and Tricia Caldwell. Fran walked
in and quietly took a seat next to the Barfield brothers.

Robin and Mark embraced Jessie outside before joining other church friends—including William—inside. The organist played softly as Jessie's parents, Pete, Larry, Crow and Brandi were seated in the family section as requested by Bobby—near the Crawford stained glass window. The church seating full, others took their places along the walls. A reverent hush spread over the crowd.

Jack led Jessie up the steps to where Bobby and Marie waited with Rev. Hamilton. When they reached the top step, she looked to Jack and he pulled her close, and then released her when Bobby reached for her hand. She glanced down the aisle at an enormous bouquet of red roses cascading over the altar. "The flowers from your parents are beautiful," Bobby whispered. The congregation stood to the playing of the hymn *Abide with Me*. Rev. Hamilton slowly walked down the aisle ahead of the honor guard carrying the casket. Behind them were the honorary pallbearers—Mike and Terry and all of the members of the '65 Northwest championship football team.

Jessie felt two hands touch her from behind and turned to face Coach, who placed his wife's purple shawl around her shoulders. Her eyes glistened as she pulled the shawl close around her and took a deep breath. She took the medallion from her purse, closed her hand around it, and stepped forward through the church door.

Carter's fellow soldiers and officers learned from the beginning that he was a man of his word and they could count on him. Killed in action, he gave his life to save others in his platoon. Among his belongings was a medallion engraved "Forever," which was buried with him. In the weeks following the funeral, a shadow box appeared over the doorway into the Northwest High School boys locker room. Inside it was a letterman's jacket—with the number 21.

To this day, Jessie carries the "One Day at a Time" medallion.

Between 1955 and 1975 during the Vietnam Conflict, 58,220 servicemen and women died with over 150,000 wounded and 1,600 missing in action (MIA). *A Heart's Memory* represents one story of unknown thousands of others affecting families and friends who also had to move forward one day at a time.

Never forget.

Special thanks...

In memory of my cherished friend and beloved mentor, Hardy Clemons, who taught me to stretch myself and embrace the confidence within and the knowledge "it is never too late to be what I wanted to be."

To readers Ruth Collins and Paula Overstreet for their investment in my dream and passion.

To Phyllis Flynn for her support on our creative inspiration trips to Boothbay Harbor and Tybee Island.

To trusted friends Paula Wynn, Debbie Paden Mobley, Susan Webb, Freda Lark and Sandy Boozer who cheered my efforts and encouraged me every step of the way.

To Deb Richardson Moore and Beth Templeton for their advice and counsel.

My deepest gratitude to my editor, Vally Sharpe for her patience and gentle guidance in walking me through the process of bringing to life the story that had lived within my soul for years.

The journey continues in the upcoming sequel *After All*.

About the Author

JANICE R. JOHNSON was born and raised in Atlanta, Georgia and graduated with a B.S. in Education from the University of Georgia. She taught business on the community college level until responding to a calling to become a church administrator, a career that would last over thirty years, and for which she would receive national honors, including induction into the Church Management Hall of Fame at the time of her retirement.

In 2004, she co-authored a book with Ruben Swint, *Weaving our Lives Together*. Janice and her husband John have two children and six grandchildren and live in Greenville, S.C.

A Heart's Memory is Janice's first novel.

Made in the USA
Columbia, SC
11 December 2020